THE
DARK
IS
ALWAYS
WAITING

T.J. BREARTON

PROLOGUE

T hat feeling. Being utterly helpless, dwarfed by the massiveness of the universe and its mystery.

Corrine Baines stood beneath a dark, churning sky. The clouds spiraled toward a bright center, lightning pulsed with white veins.

She felt herself pulled upwards, drawn by her chest, lifting her toward the dark, sucking hole.

A bright flash of light preceded a crack of thunder, and in the next instant she awoke, heart thumping.

She took a moment to ground herself.

Calm down. You're okay.

She consciously slowed her breathing, counting to four for each inhalation and exhalation. She sensed the heat of her sleeping husband beside her in bed. Okay. This was home, their big house in Scarsdale, and the earth was not cracking to pieces.

2:48 in the morning. She listened for the children and sensed only the placid hush of sleep, the faintest ticking of brittle snow falling against the windowpane, the growl of a downshifting truck on the nearby freeway.

What a thing, a dream like that. So many dreams were just surreal versions of banal things – being a waitress with never enough time for all her tables; one of her children lost in a giant store as she struggled to find them.

This dream was different. Even now, closing her eyes, she could see it, like an aftereffect: a great gyre of clouds spun like sooty cotton, tunneling up into the sky, twisting faster as they went.

It frightened her.

What was more – she'd seen it before. A long time ago, going all the way back to when she'd first met Alex, during a *Vipassana* meditation retreat. Her first; his fourth or fifth. During a session that went particularly deep for her, that same swirling sky had materialized, a powerfully affecting vision.

But maybe that was a good sign – a reminder of some past experience was not a threat.

She rolled over on her side and looked at her husband's back, just the rough shape of him in the semidarkness.

Back then, she'd confided in the Buddhist nun at the ashram and told her about the vision. The nun said strange thoughts could arise during deep meditation, or *jhana;* a person could penetrate to the substrate consciousness, the source of the subjective experience. When she'd discussed it with Alex, it was three days later, after he'd asked her out for coffee, then dinner, then drinks, and finally to visit his room at the Marigold Guest House. Maybe it had been all the meditation, clearing the mind – the sex had been, frankly, transcendent for a first encounter. Afterward, Alex had disagreed with the nun's take on things. "I don't think it has to be that spooky. People in solitary confinement see things. Hallucinations. Your body can take sensations, deep sensations during meditation, and make a picture out of them. It's not supernatural. It's natural."

"Deep meditation is like solitary *confinement*?"

He'd laughed. "I mean the absence of stimuli. Anyway, you should paint it. It sounds beautiful."

Just like that, she'd been captured by him. His confidence, humor, the kindness in his eyes. He could have been arrogant with all his education and experience, but Alex was down to earth. There was proven science behind the effects and advantages of meditation, things you could observe, data you could repeat. Ways you could breathe – just breathe – and improve your life. Wherever there was experimental evidence, Alex was hooked.

There was no experimental evidence that a dream, re-creating a long-ago meditative experience, was anything more than a neurological burp. A little nighttime indigestion of the brain.

But it *felt* like more. And the longer she lay motionless in the dark bedroom, the more she realized it wasn't going to go away.

When she shut her eyes, the stormy sky was still there. Its smoky clouds churned toward the vacuum suck of the bright-spot eye, everything trailing upward into that celestial funnel.

It wasn't a neurological burp. It may have been beautiful, but it was like looking into the end of time.

1

SATURDAY, DECEMBER 5

Alex paused to adjust his headset microphone. A little audio feedback so far this morning, but not too bad. Good crowd, good acoustics for a small theater like this one. He'd been up since five in the morning, meditated, had breakfast (empanadas Corrine made herself), kissed the kids, and drove four-and-a-half hours into the mountains. Several minutes into his lecture, he was just getting warmed up.

"We are mere hostages to our thoughts," he told the roughly three hundred people. "We witness them like clouds. We don't know how to control our thinking any more than the CEO of Ford Motor Company knows how to assemble cars. The CEO has influence and sets the tone, but he would be pretty useless on the factory floor."

There was a ripple of laughter.

"It's physiology which governs the human experience," Alex said. "Our bodies make white blood cells and synthesize proteins while we make dinner and check email. Childhood experiences shape us, geography is destiny. Life is a series of cause and effect." The mic was wireless, and he was free to roam, pacing to stage left. "That's what we're going to get deeper into here today.

That's what we're going to look at, this question of how much agency we really have as human beings. And here's how we're going to start. Right now, I want you to just get comfortable. I want you to just let your body relax, slow your breathing down – I know this is very exciting, hard to do that…"

A few chuckles. He moved back to center stage. "And then I want you to close your eyes. Take a deep breath; let it out slowly. Do that again. Let whatever is in your mind just arise. Take a look at it as it arises, then let it go."

A few seconds passed.

"Okay," Alex said. "Now, I want you to do something for me. I want you to…"

The lights on him were bright, making it a bit hard to see, but he was pretty sure someone had just stood up. *Right in the middle of this?* In a bigger venue he might not have noticed, but this was intimate.

"What I want you to do is think of a city, any city in the world…"

He shielded his eyes for a better look. There was definitely a lone individual, up on his feet, roughly in the middle section of seats. The figure faced the stage.

Someone screamed.

A loud crack in the air was followed a millisecond later by a thicker sound, a *thump* almost – loud – and Alex felt a tug of air beside his head.

The bullet breaks the sound barrier and then you hear the explosion.

People jumped from their seats and scrambled to get to the aisles; their screams and shouts collecting into a cacophony. After another gunshot, the screaming intensified. Alex froze. He glimpsed the shooter pointing the gun toward an emergency exit. The shooter fired a third time and some people dropped to the ground. The spell broke and Alex headed in that direction, just instinct, then spotted the stagehand off-stage, standing in the wing.

She stepped out, clipboard in hand, and looked into the crowd.

"Back!" Alex yelled. "Get back!" He was moving toward her at the same time he glanced into the seats again and saw the shooter once more direct his aim at the stage. Alex pushed the stagehand into the wing at the same time the gunman fired again.

Is this really happening?

The bullet struck Alex in the leg. He yelled in surprise, jumped away, as if bitten, then fell to the floor, grabbing his thigh.

Shock. Numbness.

The stagehand stared out from the wing, going through her own surge of adrenaline. She dropped the clipboard and reached for him, and he quickly dragged himself in her direction, risking another look at the seats. He couldn't help it: Someone is shooting at you, you look. The shooter stood alone now, everyone cleared out from around him; they surged up the aisles to the main doors now that he'd fired on the side emergency exit. He was still aiming at Alex, but then he turned around.

The stagehand grabbed Alex's shirt to help him along. The wing curtain dangled just above the stage floor and he could see through the gap: Two security guys were pushing their way through the crowd, trying to get down the aisles in order to flank the shooter. This caused more people to turn and run for the stage. The shooter opened fire on a security guard, who dropped. The other one ducked for cover. The screams of the panicked crowd rose and fell again.

Alex scrambled further off stage. His headset mike had gone askew. He yanked it free and kept going.

"Here, here–" The stagehand helped him up. He leaned his weight on her and hopped down the stairs that led to basement dressing rooms below. In the theater, someone shouted "Down! Down on the ground!" It was followed by another gunshot.

Alex flinched, almost fell.

Crack, crack crack crack –

The gunman was having a shootout with the security guards. Alex stumbled again and hit the landing. The stairs hooked right at ninety degrees. With the stagehand's support, he regained his feet and kept going. They reached the basement as people started coming down after them: a stampede, bursts of heavy breaths, people shoving and grunting. The basement door rattled open as someone hit the crash bar and people flowed out into the rear parking lot. Alex was moving slower, pushed aside by the rush of audience members, the stagehand helping as he hobbled along, her breath chopped into bursts: "Okay – almost – there."

"Are you hit?"

"I'm – no."

A man stopped for a moment, jaw working up and down like he was trying to pop his ears, and then he kept going. A woman recognized Alex and neared, then tucked herself under his other arm. Two women now helping him as grown men shambled past, faces pale as clouds. He risked a look back at the trail of blood behind him. A lot of it. Strangely black. If the bullet had hit the femoral artery, he was in deep shit.

The shooting had stopped. Security might have subdued the gunman, or it might be the other way around.

The exit was in front of them, a thick door with a high crescent-shaped window of reinforced glass.

"Hold on, hold on…"

He brought the two women to a stop. By now, the river of escaping people had slowed to a trickle, a few passing by in jerking, uncoordinated movements – someone crashed into Alex from behind and spun around, managed to stay on her feet and move on.

A young man wearing trendy glasses gave them a wider berth,

then stopped and stared at Alex. "Holy shit." He stood with his chest rising and falling, staring at Alex's leg. "Holy *shit*."

"Not sure we want to go out there," Alex said. He needed to think. He listened for screams from the rear parking lot. Heard car doors, engines igniting. When the last panicked audience member tumbled through the exit, the heavy door swung shut, closing off the sounds.

Up the stairs, men were arguing. Then footsteps. Someone coming down – the shooter could have doubled back.

Alex shrugged off the two women, looked at their bewildered faces. "Go – go!"

The woman from the audience ran for the door. The college kid took a few hesitant steps back, his eyes unfocused with shock. The stagehand pulled Alex toward a dressing room. He let her, then pushed her the rest of the way in and slammed the door.

He faced the stairs, his heart beating, leg throbbing, thinking of his kids. Thinking of Corrine.

Feet appeared in the stairwell. Legs. Alex picked up one of the loose chairs beside him in the adjacent actor's lounge – a gaudy throw rug, a small coffee station, the air perfumed by that subtle theater-smell of old clothes and sweaty bodies – such strange observations just before you die…

The security guard called Nyswaner stumbled off the last steps and into the corridor. He saw Alex and his grimace changed to wide-eyed relief, and then his feet went out from under him. He landed on his back, breath exploding from his chest, shoes slick with blood. Alex's blood.

Alex dropped the chair and hopped toward him. His shot leg felt like molten metal, the pain spreading, crawling up his hip and into his stomach. "Where is he? You get him?"

Nyswaner shook his head. His mouth worked, but all that came out was a wheeze; the fall had stolen his air. He pointed back to the theater.

"He's still in there?"

The security guard shook his head. Tried to talk again. "Went out the front. Bernie shot at him. Don't think he got him."

Bernie. Bernie was Bernard Cobb, the other security guy. Guys that Chet pulled in at the last minute. "Is Bernie hit?"

"No. But I am."

Nyswaner pulled his suit coat aside. The white shirt beneath bloomed with dark blood. He'd been shot through the gut.

The dressing room door opened. The stagehand poked her head out.

Alex warned her to remain inside. He sagged against the lounge furniture, going dizzy with the pain. He wanted to help Nyswaner to his feet but couldn't; could only watch him bleed. "You got a phone?"

Nyswaner stretched to unclip the phone from his belt. "Somebody probably already called, but…" He held it up, squinting like his eyesight was bad. He poked the keypad three times and held the phone to his ear.

The college kid with the trendy glasses hung back by the bathroom, just past the dressing rooms. He held onto his own phone, staring at the screen, like he was recording. How long had it been since the gunman fired his first shot? It felt like five minutes, but that wasn't right. A minute, minute and a half, tops. The brain didn't actually slow things down, but processed more, distorting time. If the shooter didn't approach from backstage, he might have circled around the building…

Someone screamed outside.

The college kid swung his phone toward the exit. The door was solid, but for the small half-circle window near the top.

The security guard spoke to 911, where they were, what was happening, that there'd been a shooting.

"Active shooter," Alex whispered, and heard another scream as the top of someone's head appeared in the door window.

2

There was victory in having the two children occupied, the house (mostly) clean, and the dishes done with half the day still in front of you. Corrine felt triumphantly domestic. She set down the laundry beside the dinner table and opened her laptop while she folded.

Facebook was weird. It not only preserved the dead (Alex's departed mother remained on her friend list), but past acquaintances, people you'd ordinarily never hear from again. She'd decided that friendships meant to endure did so with or without social media. Texts, emails, even phone calls – phone calls, imagine that!

She navigated to Alex's page and looked at photos emerging from today's engagement while creasing his pants into neat piles. Then she stopped. Someone had posted a picture from outside the theater with people panicked and running. The caption beside the photo blared: *Happening now! Live shooter at #AlexBaines #AtheistThoughtLeader! Send help!!*

Corrine pulled the laptop closer, feeling the blood drain from her face.

Hang on a second, though – Alex had trolls on social media –

maybe this was fake news. Or just some terrible attempt at a joke. She opened a new window and went to his Twitter page. Nothing, just the announcement from that morning that he was lecturing at a small theater in the mountains. She did a quick Google search for the theater and compared it with the Facebook picture. Same structure, lots of windows, mansard-style roof.

The phone rang – her cell phone, vibrating from somewhere in proximity. She got up so fast that her chair fell over.

"Mom?" Freda, in the other room.

"Mommy's okay…" Corrine heard the low panic in her own voice. Found the phone hidden beneath the local newspaper. The incoming call was from Alex's assistant. "Hello?"

"Mrs. Baines…"

"Did something – Drew – did something happen?"

A brief pause, a noisy background. "We've got an issue. It's pretty bad."

"Where is Alex? Where are you?"

"I'm outside the Arts Center in Lake Placid. We just had this –"

"Alex is with you? Where is he?"

"He's – we don't know, Mrs. Baines. He's inside the building still, he's – there's a guy, somebody shooting. He – Corrine – we think Alex got hit. That…that he's been shot."

She felt weakness in her knees, the joints turned gummy, and leaned against the kitchen island as Freda came wandering into the room. "Mom? Can I have a snack?"

"Where is he?" Her voice was an urgent whisper.

"The police are coming. I just didn't want you to find out some other way. He's gonna…they're coming."

"I did find out another way – I saw the – oh God…"

"Mommy?" Freda pulled on Corrine's pant leg. Worry now twisted her round face.

"You found out?" Drew was saying. "What – someone called

you? Okay, here come the police, that's them coming now, hang on…"

Corrine heard the sirens over the phone, playing their high-pitched notes of panic and authority. It was more than she could take. She slid down the island to sit on the floor.

Freda climbed into her lap. "What's the matter?"

Corrine looked into her daughter's hazel eyes and pulled her close, smelled the fruity shampoo of her hair. "I don't know, honey. I don't know."

"Is it Daddy?"

"It's okay. It's okay."

Freda looked at the laptop, looked at the phone, figuring it out. "Something happened to Daddy," she said.

3

The person's head hovered in the window, like they were about to come in.

Alex applied pressure to Nyswaner's wound. The guy was going to bleed out if they didn't get him to a hospital. The blood spread out beneath him and oozed around the cell phone on the floor.

The emergency operator at 911 was already aware of the situation. Multiple civilians had called and police were on the way. Sirens wailed in the distance. Alex didn't know if they'd get there in time to deal with the man on the other side of the door.

The stagehand had emerged from the dressing room to stand beside the college kid filming with his cell phone, his expression somewhere between shock and awe as he recorded Alex remove his shirt and wad it up, use it to staunch the flow of Nyswaner's blood.

Alex glanced at the door window again, his thinking now remarkably clear: Diving into one of the dressing rooms to hide was pointless. More people could get hurt. Beyond mayhem and terror, the gunman's purpose was unclear – he'd both fired on

Alex and into the crowd – but he wasn't finished. The certainty of that felt like a magnetic charge.

You knew this was coming eventually, didn't you? On some level, you knew this was inevitable.

His gaze fell to the holstered gun on Nyswaner's belt. He'd never fired a gun, hadn't handled one in years. Even if he thought he could figure it out, there were people in the rear parking lot, still getting into their cars, probably stuck as everyone tried to leave at once – if he fired on the shooter, he could hit someone back there.

The bullet breaks the sound barrier and then you hear the explosion...

The door jiggled but didn't open; it was locked from the outside. Any second now, the shooter might blow apart the lock, or somehow force his way in.

Alex decided what to do – it had all taken just a few seconds. He got to his feet and moved toward the door by pulling his thick, heavy leg behind him. For forty-five years old, he was in good shape – kept up his treadmill and free weights, ate healthy...but now, he felt like he'd been through a month of fasting with regular beatings thrown in.

He held up a hand, warning the stagehand and college kid back. The doorknob rattled again. Then the silhouette of the head in the half-moon window dipped out of sight.

Alex picked up speed, lurching forward.

"Hey," Nyswaner croaked. "Don't, don't – he's got a gun – don't –"

Too late. He couldn't let anyone else get hurt. He hit the door with his shoulder and shoved with everything he had. It swung out and impacted the figure on the other side. Alex almost tumbled to the ground but managed to stay upright when the door ricocheted back against him.

This is it.

He heard the person grunt and sensed him stumble back, and then he shoved the door the rest of the way open.

This has always been the way.

The guy standing there on his back heel with a bewildered expression was Bernard Cobb, the other security guard. Not the shooter. Cobb kept his balance, put a hand to his cheek where he'd been struck and said, "Ah, shit…"

In the parking lot, people trying to flee in their vehicles were all snarled up. Horns blared, people shouted behind the glass, someone in a car close by, a woman's face, looking out – she was crying. The air smelled like it was just about to snow.

Cobb's expression changed from pained to worried. "Mr. Baines…"

"Where is he?" Alex's leg was a block of ice tied to his waist. The cold worked its way through the rest of his body, invading his bones, making him shiver.

"He's gone," Cobb said. "Disappeared with the crowd – lot of people left on foot."

The world grew fuzzy, the evergreen trees edging the lot gone smeary, like paint diluted with turpentine. The sirens seemed to swirl in his hearing.

"Disappeared?"

"Lot of people left – in their cars, on foot – over to the gas station, across the street – a lot of people got out."

"Are you hit?"

He'd never asked such a question in his life, but today it was a regular greeting. *You shot? You hit?* The whole thing was insane. Like a dream.

"We exchanged fire. Hey…hey, you need to sit…Mr. Baines, you don't look so hot."

He sensed someone coming up behind him and turned, tensed and ready, but the momentum took him down. The fall to the asphalt felt instantaneous: one second on his feet, then the world had tipped on its side. People approached at a horizontal angle. He rolled onto his back but the vertigo spun him, as if in a barrel, with the image of the college kid and his phone rolling past, rolling past – like a picture on a slot machine.

His death was going to be recorded.

4

He came to in a white room, machines whirring and beeping. Not dead.

People surrounded him in a blur. One drifted closer. She wore a winter parka with law enforcement patches on the shoulders.

"Mr. Baines," the policewoman said. "Can you think of anyone who would do this?"

He could only whisper. "Where's my wife…?"

Another figure wearing a white smock mumbled to her, and the cop stepped aside, and Alex was moving, wheeled down a hallway, people saying things about a helicopter.

Corrine, he thought as he trucked along.

She was driving faster than she should've been, and now snow was coming down, sticking to the road north of the Cuomo / Tappan Zee Bridge. She'd had the presence of mind to use GPS, but it was a pretty straight route up the interstate and into the mountains. To this small town where someone had shot up the theater and almost killed her husband.

Shot in the leg, Alex's assistant had specified in a text.

And later: *What are you going to do with the kids?*

Leave them with her sister. Mara lived in Croton, a stop along the way. Corrine had barely managed to convince the kids of a white lie – Daddy had gotten sick and Mommy needed to bring him home. Freda had accepted the story at face value, but Kenneth was older and probed her with questions while she threw things in a bag and hustled the kids into the car.

"What do you mean, sick?" Kenneth had asked.

The texts had kept coming from Drew, updating her:

Lost a lot of blood.

Air-lifted to Burlington.

Going into surgery now.

"He just isn't feeling well. We'll talk about it later."

"Why can't we come with you? Is he infectious or something?"

"Kenneth…"

Freda, in her rear car seat: "Did Daddy throw up?"

"Is he quarantined? Are you going to have to wear one of those hazmat suits?" Kenneth's brown bangs hung in his eyes – the snowboarder look. He had his father's nose and lips. When he grabbed her phone and started poking at the screen, she snatched it back.

"Stop."

Twelve years old; too smart for his own good. They had a policy not to lie to the kids. If you want the truth *from* them, you had to give the truth *to* them. A lofty position when no one was bleeding profusely from a gunshot wound. And the real problem was, it was already all over the internet.

"Dad hurt his leg," she admitted.

"How?" Freda asked.

Corrine looked at her daughter in the rearview mirror. Maybe she had to come clean with Kenneth, but Freda could be spared.

"Hey, honey? You want to watch something on my tablet? I've got a couple of shows downloaded."

Kenneth helped arrange it. When Freda had the earbuds in and her face aglow with *Wild Kratts*, he looked at Corrine and waited for an explanation.

"He was shot." The words were alien.

"In the leg?"

"In the leg."

Kenneth stared outside and thought about it. "At his lecture or whatever?"

"During his talk, yeah. That's all I know. I don't want Freda to…we'll tell her later, but not while I'm gone, okay?"

"Okay."

He surprised her by putting his hand on her arm. Tears stung the backs of her eyes and she let out a shuddering breath.

The children knew their father was a public personality. Kenneth understood it better, of course, that Alex was a scientist, but also an author and public intellectual. Mostly, though, Alex flew under the radar. His type of work wasn't exactly mainstream. He talked about the benefits of meditation and made philosophical and physiological arguments – not exactly a movie star or social media influencer. They'd never really had to deal with anything like this; for the most part, they led normal lives.

In Croton, she gave the children big hugs and smiled and nodded at Kenneth before he went inside Mara's house. Mara just shook her head and put her arms around Corrine. "Who was it? Do they know?"

"They haven't said yet," Corrine said, thinking *terrorism*. She could smell Mara's perfume, always the same, since college, light but musky. "Thank you so much for taking the kids." She sniffed back tears and pulled away, but Mara caught her arm and held it.

"It's going to be okay."

"Yeah."

"Mark my words, this is some violent asshole who can't get laid." Her eyes flitted away and she said, "It's some mental health case. Or a neo-Nazi. Both. Like that."

Despite being marginally younger, there were times – like now – Mara seemed like the one who had it together. She'd gotten the jump on parenthood – Layla was already seventeen – and even through rough times, she seemed to come out on top. Standing in the driveway, Corrine gazed at her giant, remodeled farm house. "Is Stephen here?"

"He's in the city. Working the weekend. I'll see if he can come home, if you think…"

Corrine shook her head. "No…I mean…do *you* think?"

"We'll be fine."

The snow had just started at this point, a few fluffy flakes. Corrine decided not to make any more of Stephen's absence. This was not the time or place. She was grateful enough her sister was here.

"You better go." Mara gave her hand a squeeze and let go. "Be careful."

"Okay. Love you."

Be careful. Just something a person said. Or, not really. People said, *Keep your chin up. Take care. Keep me posted.* If worried about bad weather: *Drive safe.*

Be careful meant something else. That there were snares ahead, unseen trip wires. Blind alleys. *Be on your guard* – that was how their mother put it. Their father had left her to raise two girls alone and she'd adopted it as her principal admonishment – *Be on your guard* – as if to say, *You never know. Men up and leave. Anything can happen in this life. You have to be ready.* Mara had shortened it to a simple *Be careful.* Like "God be with you" had been shortened to "good bye." A world of hidden meanings, there for the unpacking…but who had time for that when everything was a rush of progress and expansion?

A four-hour drive into the middle of nowhere. No matter how you tried to slow life down, it hustled on. No matter how much you tried to protect yourself, it found an open window, a crack in the wall. It fired a gun at your husband.

She gripped the steering wheel as the emotion hardened to anger. Why had Alex let Chet book such a tiny gig? While not a celebrity pop star, her husband could fill much larger venues. Why give a talk in some rural town almost in Canada? He'd been to places big and small, but...

It was because Alex said every person mattered – that was why. It was because Alex was one of those "I fucking love science" people, one of those grown men who acted like little boys at the prospect of new discovery. He just wanted to help people.

The car swerved and Corrine felt a bright bolt of panic light up her spine – *ease down!* The roads had become slick, the temperature verging on freezing. She saw the cyclone from her dream in the sky for just a moment, just a flash of it in her mind, twisting the clouds upwards into oblivion. Then it was gone.

5

He'd made it through surgery. That much he knew. And a blood transfusion. Couldn't recall where he was – maybe Albany? He wondered if anyone had told Corrine. How was she getting here? She'd probably left the kids with Mara and Stephen and was driving up. He attempted to talk, but he was so dry and thirsty. His eyes were shut. Tried to open them, but the lids felt like concrete. Just a minute…just a minute…

He finally opened them with the vague sense that he'd dropped out of consciousness for a while. It took a moment, squinting in the bright light, to find and focus on the clock in the room. Almost seven at night. His talk had been scheduled for noon.

Crack-thump!

He jolted further alert, his heart pounding. The man stood amid the scattering crowd, aiming the gun at him. The screams, the terrified people seeking escape, trampling one another in the progress. When the chips were down, we were animals. That was just how it was – you couldn't judge a person's morality when it came to survival.

His mind jumped forward through time: The stagehand had

helped him down the stairs, a young woman. Where was she? Was she okay? And Nyswaner had been shot through the gut. Who else was hurt?

He probed the edge of the bed with his fingertips – beds like this one had a call button somewhere. He lifted his head to look, but it weighed a ton. When he found something that might be a remote trigger, he closed his hand around it, felt for the button, pressed it, and slumped back.

So thirsty.

Someone came into the room dressed in white, a nurse with a pleasant smile. "Hello there – how we doing?"

Alex wheezed, pointed to his mouth as the nurse checked him over. His tongue felt like a rag sitting on his lower deck of teeth.

"Here, you can suck on these. We'll get you something to drink in a little bit."

She tipped a plastic cup to his mouth, let a couple of ice chips tumble in. Amazing. Outstanding. Compliments to the chef. He tried to say these things and felt water trickle down the side of his mouth, slurped it up.

A man with gray hair and a thick black mustache entered next. There was an absurdity to it, like actors walking onto the set of a sitcom, everything surreal and hyperreal at the same time. Here was the burly cop character, moving toward the bed. "Mr. Baines? Sergeant Tandy. How you feeling?"

Alex tried to speak, produced a gurgle, cleared his throat, tried again. He remembered a woman cop. "Where's the...other one? Was there someone else?"

Tandy furrowed his brow, glancing at the nurse. Then the expression cleared. "Oh, yeah, yeah. Roth, from New York." He leaned in and spoke like Alex was mentally impaired. "You've been moved. You're in Vermont now, Mr. Baines." Like he was slightly deaf, too. "This is Fletcher Allen Hospital in Burlington. You were brought here for surgery."

Sur—ger—ee. You know? Chop chop? Slice slice?

"My wife – what's the –?"

"I believe she's on her way. Investigator Roth called your home, then relatives, spoke to a…" He looked down at something out of view, probably a notebook. "Spoke to Mara Mayhew. That's your sister?"

"In-law, yes."

"Sorry? Oh – sister-in-law."

Alex nodded, feeling like there were rocks in his head, packed loosely and grating together. His giddiness faded.

"Mrs. Mayhew has your children," Tandy said. "She gave Investigator Roth your wife's cell phone number, and she's been contacted. She – ah – she knows where you are."

"Thank you." His voice was still a whisper.

"So." Tandy glanced around.

The nurse was still doing something, reading machines, writing on the chart at the foot of the bed. Like nurses were supposed to. Like an actor would do who was portraying a nurse. The sense of surrealism persisted.

"So, Mr. Baines. Investigator Roth sent everything over to us, and we're going to help. Do you remember what happened?"

"Shooter…"

"That's right. What can you tell me?"

"Anybody else hur –?" Something caught in his throat and he coughed. The nurse watched, then offered some more ice chips.

Tandy seemed to know the question Alex was trying to ask. "Peter Nyswaner was shot. That was one of your security guards. Maybe you knew that. Did you know his name?"

Alex nodded. He made it a point to learn the names of everyone on his security team, wherever he went. Most places had their own people, often just a single guard and a can of pepper spray. Once, before a talk at an atheist convention in Sydney, someone had called him up and threatened him. Alex's manager had taken extra precautions after that. Usually just for big venues, though.

"We hired local," Alex croaked. "Two retired policemen. My manager got them through an agency. Sort of last minute."

"Any reason for the concern?"

"Not that I'm aware of. We usually have security. Just sometimes we…don't."

Tandy seemed to think about it. Then: "Nyswaner was airlifted down to Albany. There's a good internist there. He should pull through, but – several other people were injured, mostly in the crush of getting out of the theater. One woman is still unconscious. Brain is swelling."

Alex closed his eyes. A tug of despair threatened to pull him under. "No one else shot, though?"

"No. No one else shot. There were a couple of fender benders, which slowed up the people trying to get away. Not everyone tried to run, though. Some people went into the art gallery that attaches to the theater and, I guess, hunkered down there. And they're okay – everybody there is okay. But someone else got hit by a car, suffered a concussion, a broken arm…"

The longer Tandy spoke, the worse it felt. It wasn't his livelihood that concerned him. Hell, if he never gave a public talk again, if people were too afraid to come, so what? All the travel and the time away had been driving a wedge in his marriage anyway. But just the idea of it – that he was the cause, and this was the effect – who was this son of a bitch? Some random person who'd come across a gathering?

No. He remembered feeling sure about it then, and that insight hadn't diminished with time: This was someone who had sought him out, someone acting with intention. You didn't do a shooting on a whim. You lay in the dark and thought about it, built up the nerve. Maybe something set you off, though – that too. But what?

Alex waited until Tandy was done listing the people who'd

been injured. Maybe his sense of proportion was off, but he detected a hint of perverse pleasure in the sergeant. Like this was all just what Tandy expected from the world of big-shot intellectuals who made their living talking about brain chemistry. Someone who dismissed religion as outdated.

"Who –?" Alex cleared his throat. "Who did this?"

"We're looking at everything. This place where you were doing your…where you were giving this talk, there's one single camera. It's not great. A lot of people were lined up this morning for the show, but we're checking through it. There's a massive manhunt going on over there. But, you ask me…" Tandy clapped his hands and rubbed them. "You ask me, this guy parked a block away or something, ran out of there, cutting through the crowd, you know, everyone leaving. He jumped in his vehicle and crawled back into whatever hole he came from. Probably turned the gun on himself. That's how these things – you know – how they tend to go. Roth and her people are checking all cameras around the area, too, but over there it's…security cameras aren't a big thing." He scratched his jaw and looked away.

"What about the taping?"

Tandy's gaze slid back. "The taping?"

"My talk was being recorded. There was an audiovisual technician up in the lighting booth with a camera."

"Oh. Okay, right. The taping, yeah, the recording. New York State Police have got it, but from what Roth said, the image was framed on the stage, on you, and when the shooting started, the cameraman ducked for cover. So it just stayed there on the stage." Tandy's eyes crawled over Alex. "Can you think of someone who'd want to come in and do something like this? Anyone been threatening you? Threatening action?"

"Not really."

The sergeant dipped his head to the side. "Does that mean something? 'Not really'?"

"Sorry. I mean I've been threatened in the past."

Tandy pulled a notebook from his breast pocket, clicked a pen. "Okay. Let's talk about that. Who?" He started writing before Alex answered.

"We don't really know. Someone called my mobile phone about an hour before I went on during a conference in Sydney, Australia. I was the keynote speaker."

Keeping his eyes down as he wrote notes, Tandy asked, "Paid speech?"

"Yes."

"On?"

"It was an atheism conference."

"Atheism. How much you get for something like that?"

Alex paused, thinking it wasn't relevant. But he might as well get all the information out in the open. "That one was twenty-five thousand."

"Huh. Okay. So we're not talking Obama money."

"I'm not sure what that means."

"So you notified local law enforcement in Sydney. What did they do? They track the number?"

"No."

"No?"

"No."

"What was the nature of the threat?"

"It was a guy with an Australian accent. He said if I went on and gave my talk, I would regret it. That God would take his revenge. I asked the caller if that meant he was going to do something, and he hung up. The caller, not God."

Tandy stared at Alex. "Uh-huh. This guy, at the theater in Lake Placid, he seem Australian to you?"

"There's no way I could say. But I really doubt one has to do with the other."

"You doubt it."

"I don't think this…it's unlikely this person followed me from Australia. And that was two years ago."

"Could be people working together. A group, a coalition, something. Any other threats since? Because you said your, uh, manager pulled in these security guys last minute…"

"No other calls like that. But I get plenty of emails. My assistant, Drew Horvath, flags anything suspicious, and if there's anyone who is particularly aggressive, he turns it over to my manager, Chet Warman. On very rare occasions, Chet might then talk to a private detective."

"Lot of people working for you."

"There're a few, yeah."

Tandy lowered the notepad and fixed Alex with a bemused expression. "And so what exactly is it you do? You give these talks on…atheism."

"Not really. I'm a neuroscientist."

Tandy blinked. "I thought you had a radio show?"

"It's a podcast, yeah. Called *Here and Now*."

The doctor came in before Alex could elaborate – not that he wanted to. "Mind if I interrupt?"

"Not at all, Doctor." Sergeant Tandy faded back, slapping his notepad against his palm and looking thoughtful.

The doctor picked up the chart, smiled at Alex. "How are you feeling?"

"Should I answer honestly?"

"Please."

"Like I really have to fart, but can't."

"That's some of the medication. It will pass."

"I hope so. One way or the other. Besides that, I feel like I got shot in the leg."

"The bullet nicked your femoral artery."

"A .38 caliber," Tandy said from further away.

The doctor resumed: "It lodged in your femur, and we were

able to remove the fragments. You've had a blood transfusion – you'd lost a pint of blood – and we've got you on a strong course of antibiotics. Recovery is going to take some time, Dr. Baines. Your muscle and nerves have been damaged, so it may be hard to fully extend your leg. I'd like to start you on PT in a couple of days, see how things go…"

Alex listened, watched the door, waiting for his wife, and the tears, at last, brimmed in his eyes. He was going to be okay. He was going to be around for his wife and kids.

You lost, you son of a bitch. You took a shot at me, yet here I am. I'm here, and this is now. With your host, Alex Baines.

You lost.

It didn't feel like a victory, though. It felt like his life was changed forever. He just didn't know exactly how yet.

6

The ferry bucked in the water on its way to Vermont. Corrine left the car and enclosed herself in the bulkhead, sat on the toilet, breathed through the swell of emotion.

Drew had called back three times while she rode the gas pedal north. He'd been on the phone with the police. The more he'd told her, the more it overwhelmed her. They thought that the man, the shooter, had first stood, taken aim at Alex, and missed. Then he'd fired into the crowd. This was mostly coming from a witness named Amy Cross, Drew said, the stagehand Alex had shoved out of the way, getting shot in the process.

But Drew said Alex was going to be okay – his vital signs were good; he was even making jokes.

Drew also said the police were checking ticket sales. People could buy them online, or over the phone, or in person at the box office – unless a show was sold out, like Alex's was. Regardless of the method, people gave their name and phone numbers.

"Even if this guy refused his personal info, or if he gave a fake name and number – that'll be a red flag," Drew said. "They're going to get him and put him away in no time."

"So how does that work?" She'd paid the fare and had been

sitting in the car, watching the inbound ferry plow the water, still a few minutes out. Feeling restless, she'd gotten out to pace around the parked cars. A gray-haired man keeping warm in his truck seemed to watch Corrine as she moved around in the cold, talking to Drew. "With Alex in Vermont – I'm just catching the ferry now – with Alex over there, what now? Do the FBI get involved or something?"

"No. No, I don't think so. I haven't heard anything like that."

"I thought the FBI responded to shootings."

"Um, well, no one was killed; that's the thing, I guess. Lots of injuries, but no deaths. And it's over. Anyway, rather than sending someone over with Alex to the hospital – I mean, because he was going into surgery anyway – I think the state police just called over and asked local law enforcement in Burlington to talk to him when he came to. Something like that. How are you doing? You still holding up?"

"God, Drew. My God…"

"I know."

Drew had been with Alex for almost three years, but she hadn't wanted to lose it over the phone with him. She hadn't cried in front of the kids, choking it back when Kenneth had touched her arm, and kept the valve closed when she'd turned them over to her sister. Her chest had burned, eyes felt wrapped in nettles, but she'd focused on the driving, getting information from Drew as she went. So far, Alex's manager, Chet, had been MIA – according to Drew, he was in the air, coming back from some conference in LA. He'd touch down at Kennedy or LaGuardia and would get the news on his voicemail, probably jump right into another plane and head up to Burlington.

She was sort of racing against time, racing against Chet, racing to beat the media, too. The word had surely spread, but unless someone had followed the damn ambulance, the newspapers and TV people would be scrambling to pin down where Alex had been taken. She'd kept it all together until she'd hung up with Drew, boarded the ferry, found the bathroom, and now, with the hollow clanging and the stink of urine, she held her head and cried through a blend of feelings – the fear of losing Alex, the kids growing up without a father, the fact that he was still alive, what it said about the world that he almost wasn't…

When it was over, she splashed some water on her face from a tiny sink near a sign that warned *NOT for drinking!* She pushed out of the heavy door and walked back to the car. The air felt thin and smelled metallic; a few motes of snow danced above the ferry deck.

Her phone was buzzing again on the passenger seat – she hadn't even realized she'd left it in the car. The incoming number was unfamiliar. She enclosed herself in the vehicle. "Hello?"

"Mrs. Baines?" The feminine voice sounded like a cop's.

"Yes?"

"Raquel Roth, New York State Police. How are you?"

"I'm, ah – I'm on my way to Vermont."

"Good. I'm heading up the investigation into the shooting. I just wanted to assure you we're working hard on this. Is there anything you can tell me about your husband that might help? Any difficulties lately, anyone he's been having trouble with?"

"No. No one."

"No strange phone calls, anything like that?"

"No."

"Any tensions with family? Friends?"

"I don't…no."

"How about social media? Maybe someone trolling him, posting on Facebook or Twitter, something along those lines?" Roth had a pleasant voice, her tone soft but no-nonsense.

"Alex has close to a million Twitter followers," Corrine told her. "He has people who read his books, listen to his – I don't know – maybe two hundred thousand listeners for his podcast?

And his Facebook page and Twitter. Honestly, he can't keep up with it. He hasn't really been tweeting or posting lately, just work-ing." She felt like she was babbling and stopped.

"I understand. You think he would have told you if anything had been going on?"

"Would he have told me?"

"I mean, in your lives. Life is hectic, you have two children – he's very busy. I'm just wondering."

"I'm sorry. This has been a lot."

"It's okay. I'd much rather sit down with you in a comfortable setting, but this is a critical time, when everything is fresh. So…"

Corrine opened her mouth to ask about the ticket stubs, the ease of capturing the gunman Drew predicted, but it zipped out of her mind. So much had happened in the past few hours. Had she been making lunch? The dinner table came to mind, her open laptop resting on its polished surface – that was it. She thought about Alex's research into the neurobiology of traumatic events, how easily details were lost as the mind entered survival mode. And then how, in many cases, those forgotten details later became the metric to prove credibility that the trauma ever occurred in the first place.

She wondered how Kenneth and Freda would remember it in the coming years – Kenneth, really. Would it create fear of an unpredictable, violent world? Maybe it *was* that kind of world.

"So can you think of anyone?" Roth sounded patient, consid-erate, but she had a job to do.

"I can't."

"Do you…well, let me just ask you – what did you think when you first heard this happened?"

"At first I thought it was a, ah, a mass shooting. There's been a lot of…but then I…"

It felt like a knot untangled in the back of her mind. Folding laundry, that was it. Thinking about Facebook. "There was a post on Alex's page, I think someone – right, I remember – someone uploaded a picture with the message 'Get Help,' or 'Send Help,' or something."

"Do you know who that was?"

"I can look. Or, I mean, his Facebook profile is public."

"Okay, thank you for that. We also have a –" Roth cut off, voices burbling in the background, then a high squawk, like police radio chatter. "Sorry. Yes, so, listen, Mrs. Baines, we can talk more once you've seen your husband. But again, nothing you can think of at this time? Other than the post? Phone calls or texts? Anything at all."

"No. I'm sorry."

But there was something. She just couldn't recall the precise memory. And she knew she could be confabulating. What Alex did – promoting neuroscience, meditation – was a kind of mixed bag. It was what made him unique among the so-called modern moral philosophers. It was also what made him some enemies. But they were intellectual enemies. She'd never thought anyone would elevate things to real physical violence.

Maybe the religion thing, though. Maybe that.

"Mrs. Baines?"

The ferry had clunked softly against the pilings of the Vermont-side port.

"Yes, sorry. I'll keep thinking on it."

"All right. Stay in touch. We're doing everything we can here. We'll get this guy."

7

R oth disconnected the call and tossed the cell phone onto the passenger seat of the car, her last words to Corrine Baines leaving a bad taste in her mouth. *We'll get this guy.* They'd already been through Alex Baines's Facebook page – the man who'd posted the alarming video of the Arts Center under siege was named Eric Leifson, an area college student. They'd spoken to Leifson, gotten a statement, went through his phone. As happy as he'd been to record an active shooting, there wasn't one digital frame which revealed the gunman.

Two hundred and ninety-eight people had bought tickets to see Baines speak, making it a sold-out show. The Arts Center accepted cash payments and did not assign seats. The shooter had been somewhere in the middle section, slightly closer to the stage than to what they called the back-of-house. Only one person sitting close to him had come forward so far. That person, another half a dozen eye witnesses, and the woman Baines saved were all taking turns with a forensic artist. But word had already reached Roth: So far, the artist had been given too many interpretations to come up with a viable composite sketch.

She rubbed a hand over her face and picked up the radio as a call came through. "Dispatch, this is Roth. I'm sitting in the parking lot of the Arts Center, over."

"Copy that. Officer Hertz responded to the possible 417. It was someone with a big stick, over."

"A big stick?"

"Yeah. Two kids in the Rite Aid parking lot. One of them had a stick."

"Copy, dispatch. Over and out."

So much for that – three hours after the shooting and no one had seen the gunman. Plenty of calls mistaking joggers and teenagers goofing around, but that was it. She hung up the radio and watched the activity around the Arts Center; the crime scene unit was still combing through the building and grounds. Roth tallied the damage: Traffic collisions involving six automobiles in total, most of it just nicks and scratches, but one pick-up truck had a crumpled rear end after being smashed into by a van. Roughly half the people with vehicles had frantically fled the scene.

Seventeen wounded, ranging from GSWs to broken bones, one concussion, one woman still out cold, and plenty of mental shock.

Two projectiles had lodged in the back wall of the stage, two more in the east wall of the seating area, one in the proscenium, one that had passed through Peter Nyswaner's gut and burrowed into a plastic seat. And one in Alex Baines's leg – well, taken out by now, the fragments being brought back to New York for analysis at the forensics lab in Albany.

Roth had been a state trooper for seven years before applying to the state's Bureau of Criminal Investigation, and she'd been with BCI for three years since. Originally from Jersey, she'd been in the North Country long enough to know that things like this didn't happen up here. Didn't happen most places, honestly. She had a sister in the FBI and both her father and grandfather had been in law enforcement. Mass shootings got a lot of media coverage, but thankfully, they were still the rarer kind of gun violence.

Which was a really good thing.

Chain of custody for all the evidence was a monster on this one. Not to mention the two-hundred-plus eyewitnesses. Only a few of them were local. Of the people from out of town, some had left the Arts Center but stayed in the area. Some had left and just kept driving, putting miles between themselves and their afternoon of terror. Just about every one of them had a cell phone with a camera, but according to Baines's assistant, he had a pretty tight policy on no pictures and no videos. The Arts Center staff recorded shows, but she'd already seen that video, and it wasn't helpful in identifying the shooter. The recording started with ten minutes of Baines warming up the crowd, launching into his spiel, then there was the sound of a gunshot, followed by several more, and Baines was running for the wing, pushed the Cross woman out of the way, took the bullet, and went down. After he crawled out of view, more gunshots spiked the audio, a panicked audience member scrambled up onto the stage, another ran across it, left to right, and then there was forty minutes of nothing, screams fading to background; nothing until the technician at last returned to shut down the camera.

Ten minutes.

Roth sat up straighter in the vehicle. It hadn't occurred to her until now: The shooter had been seated there for ten minutes, letting Baines ease into his routine, before standing up and opening fire.

Maybe it meant something, maybe not, but it felt good to focus on when everything was so huge and sprawling. Cops flooded the parking lot, the media surged against the crime scene tape spanning the entrance. A police helicopter chopped the air high overhead. Too much to think about all at once. She needed to keep doing what she'd been doing since she'd caught the call four hours ago – break it down into bite-sized pieces, put one foot in front of the other.

Roth opened the door and got out of her car.

8

"... And forget these small-town gigs." It sounded like Chet's voice. Somehow he'd beaten her there. Corrine pushed the door open the rest of the way. Her husband instantly turned his face to her, like he'd been waiting.

Chet, oblivious, continued talking from the foot of Alex's bed. "I mean, this is a whole new level of security, and this time you're going to listen to – oh, Corrine. Look at you….How are you?"

She flashed Chet a quick smile as she crossed the room and practically dove for her husband. He smelled like antiseptic and bad breath and coppery traces of blood, and she'd never felt anything so wonderful. She crushed him with her hug, lips on his neck, fingers in his hair.

He stroked her face, a tube flowing from his wrist. "I'm okay. I'm all right."

They stayed like that for half a minute – she was afraid to break the moment, to let him go, to ever let her guard down again.

"But I've got a whole list of bioethics violations I've suffered," he said. "I'm super gassy and I want to start suing *right now*."

Her laugh was a burst of exhalation, the release of a breath held probably since entering the room. She pulled back to see his face – the big brown eyes, the slight hook to his nose, his smooth, thin lips, the stubble around his chin and jaw – he'd decided he was going to get with the times and grow a beard. Thinking that made her laugh again, though it came out more as a sob, and he reached up and wiped her eyes. He was crying too, the way he occasionally did, where he mashed his lips together and scrunched his face like he was going to either sneeze or pass a stone, and that made her laugh harder. He started chuckling too, showing teeth, the tip of his nose turning red. She buried her face into his neck again.

"There's a cop outside the door," she said against Alex's skin.

Chet, overhearing, gloated, "There's more downstairs."

"They're just being careful," Alex said in Corrine's ear.

"You see the news people downstairs, too?" Chet asked.

Emotions subsiding, Corrine pulled her head back and hunted for any deception in her husband's eyes.

"There hasn't been anything else," he said, staring back. "They're just being careful. Really."

At last she untangled herself from him, wiped her eyes some more, and then looked sideways at his personal manager. "I did see the news people. I came in through the emergency entrance; they were over by the –"

"There are, like, three vans down there." Chet took a step toward her and opened his arms for a hug. He looked like typical Chet, maybe a little grayer around the ears since she'd seen him last. He wore the same calf-length camel-hair coat, a scarf around his neck, his thinning hair done up in a gelled, messy look and his potbelly stretched against a too-tight button down shirt. Today, the fug of his cologne was overpowering, but it was good to hug him anyway.

Alex had really cultivated quite a group of people to surround himself with and make his life go. Chet was a typical money-driven LA type, but in seven years, he never got flirty or touchy with her. Maybe there was a reason for that – but whether he was gay or not, he'd never said. He was a fixture in their lives, a near-constant presence, even if she knew little about him. What she knew was that he scored big gigs for Alex, all over the world.

And some little ones, too, where people opened fire.

She let go – he seemed more relaxed now that he'd gotten some attention – but kept her gaze fixed on him. "How did you get here so fast?"

He strode to the window and pushed aside the curtain. "I was in New York."

"I thought Drew said you –"

"I was able to catch a flight. It was a half hour after hearing what happened. Look – I can see one of the news vans from here. They're aiming a camera up at the room."

He let the curtain drop when she didn't join him. "For one thing," he said, "your husband is a hero."

She looked at Alex. "Hero, huh?"

"He dove in front of a bullet to save this stagehand girl."

Alex frowned. "I didn't dive anywhere…"

"Well, that's what she told the cops, my man." Chet sat down in the corner chair, took out his giant, brand-new iPhone, prob-ably checking the buzz on the whole thing. Good. He'd be preoc-cupied now.

She moved close to Alex again and took his hand. "How are you feeling?"

"I'm all right. How are the kids? Mara was able to take them?"

She nodded and bit her lip. "I made a quick call, you know? I thought you'd –"

"No, you made the right choice, honey. This is better. They don't need to be involved in all of this. I'll call them – maybe in just a few minutes, I'll call them."

Another tear slipped down her cheek. "They'd like that. I'm sure they really would, yeah."

He looked like he knew what she was going to say next.

"Alex, I had to tell them. Well, I had to tell Kenneth. He already suspected. And it was all over the place. He was gonna see something. Sooner or later."

"I know."

"But he's okay." Her chest jumped with a post-crying breath. "He's okay and – ah, can I get you anything? Water? Have you eaten anything? When did you get out of surgery?"

"No, I haven't eaten."

"I'm getting you some water. Your lips feel like a mummy's." She started for the bathroom.

"I have some right here." He held up a plastic cup, gave it a little shake, then tipped it to his mouth, made a big show of drinking and smacking his lips afterward, trying to put her at ease.

Corrine returned to his bed and took the cup. "Just give me a second."

"Honey…take your time with this. You're here. That's what matters."

She turned from his smile and shut herself in the bathroom. She set the cup on the sink where it tumbled off. When she picked it up, she was shaking.

Relax.

Breathe.

Everything is okay. Everything is fine.

Clutching the sink, she lowered her head.

It's over now.

The bathroom smelled like rubbing alcohol. Her face was there in the mirror as she looked, but so was her vision, those dark clouds, as if superimposed on her reflection. It happened that way sometimes – her dark-cloud vision appearing in real life – not remembered, not drawn up in her mind's eye, but seen. That knotted sky, spiraling toward the center glow. Pulses of light in the dark clouds. She could shut her eyes, make it go away, but she couldn't always control when it would appear, and just now, her chest tightened at the image.

"Holy shit," Chet said, his voice making her jump. He sounded excited.

Corrine flushed the toilet for effect and risked a look in the mirror again – this time, just her own paleness shone back, gummy circles beneath her blue eyes – and opened the door. "What?"

Chet slowly rose from his chair in the corner, staring at his phone with big eyes, mouth hanging open. "Un-frikking real," he exclaimed.

She met eyes with Alex, who then looked at Chet. "What, man?"

"This…" He took slow steps. "This, oh, man." Tinny sounds emanated from his phone, like shouts in an echoing room. She wanted to know what Chet was talking about, but feared it, too.

"Chet," Alex said, "you're freaking us out…"

Chet poked at his screen, then held it so they could see. "Watch this. Oh my God, Alex, you fucking guy…"

He hit the play button on a YouTube video. It was posted by *E-Leifson* that same day and had almost ten thousand views. She didn't recognize the moving image at first – the person recording descended a stairway, people in front of him moving fast. They rounded a corner and stepped into a wide, low-ceilinged room, like a basement…

And there was Alex. He was being helped along by a young woman – probably Cross. He trailed blood, his face twisted in pain and determination. Another woman stepped in to help.

Corrine glanced at the real Alex beside her, his expression hard to read.

"Watch," Chet whispered.

She dragged her eyes from her husband and watched. On-screen Alex pushed Amy Cross into a room. This had to be downstairs at the theater. Lighted mirrors and dressing rooms. There were screams and voices in the distance. Alex picked up a chair and faced a set of stairs.

Corrine put a hand over her mouth as she sat down beside real-life Alex in the bed. "What are you doing?"

"Watch, watch." Chet was breathless.

Alex held the chair like a lion tamer. So this was after he'd taken the bullet, obviously. He'd come down stairs with Cross assisting him and then pushed her into the dressing room and now was wielding a chair for some reason. Drew hadn't said anything about this.

She gave Alex's hand a squeeze, as if to verify for herself – and for him – that this was over, that he was safe – and watched as a man in a black-and-white security uniform came bounding down the stairs, then slipped in some blood. Alex dropped the chair and hobbled forward, got down and put pressure on the security guard's wound, blood seeping through his fingers. Then Alex took off his shirt, popping buttons like a superhero, used it as a blood-stopper.

Corrine watched, breathless, and wondered who *E-Leifson* was. She knew people did this sort of thing – they recorded police action and car wrecks and natural calamity, often with little regard to the victims they were documenting – or themselves. Disaster porn. Maybe it was the guy who'd posted on Facebook.

Everything felt extra tense, and she wanted to ask more questions but became transfixed again when on-screen Alex shakily gained his feet and limped toward a door. The security guard said, "Don't, don't – he's got a gun – don't –" But Alex had his arms out, as if to protect the people in the room as he built speed.

"Ho-lee-*shit*," Chet whispered.

There was a shape in the window, just the head of a man, and

Alex suddenly lunged for it. The person recording the video rushed forward, and Corrine held her breath. The thrall of the video was so powerful that for a split second she worried for his life. Then the Alex on screen crashed into the door and went sprawling outside, tangling with another man in a security guard uniform.

Clearly Alex had thought it was the shooter. Now, as they recovered from the collision, the security guard got an arm around Alex. The person recording the video turned and aimed at the stagehand still inside, who was walking toward the open door with her hands covering her cheeks.

The video ended with Alex being held up in the arms of the security guard and one other person, having at last succumbed to shock and blood loss. The final image of Alex, his head lolling forward, arms out, being held up by these other people, was both haunting and electrifying.

Chet swiped the screen, and the image of her splayed-out husband disappeared. He scrolled through the comments. "Look. Look at these. Look at these! These people. This is incredible. This is huge."

Alex seemed at a loss for words, staring into space. Corrine bent over him, lay her head on his chest, listened to his beating heart. It was another wash of mixed feelings – love, fear, anger, pride. He had a wife and children, and instead of protecting himself, he'd been brandishing chairs and bull-ramming doors. Dangerous. Unforgiveable. Heroic.

"Listen to this!" Chet sounded like a kid with a new toy. "'This is what it's all about,' one of these commenters says, 'this is why I love this guy. Doesn't need God, just needs a set of brass balls.' Ha! Shit – the video has jumped to twelve thousand hits since we started watching! People get it, people get it. First you save that girl's life, then you're ready to go toe-to-toe with this fucking deranged lunatic – listen to this: 'Why I've been a fan of this guy for years. Nothing stops *Baines the Beast*.' Oh and this is my favorite – 'Baines brings the Pain.'"

Chet continued quoting, but at least he was wandering away from the bed. Corrine tuned him out, looking instead at her husband's face, seeing their son in his features, their daughter through his eyes, remembering a life with this man that had begun so many years ago. They'd had their ups and downs, and lately it felt like they were hanging on by a thread. But it was all back now, it was all right here, in this room.

Fragile, precious, like it could be torn asunder at any moment.

Chet read another comment: "'Another reason why religion is bullshit. Some priest or pastor would have been running for the hills.'"

Chet laughed, and she felt her heart sink. The way Alex was looking at her, something was wrong.

9

They had him boxed in.

Roth walked slowly up the dark street, the Kevlar vest snug around her chest, radio in one hand, gun in the other. The temperature had dropped with the sun, but she was hot with adrenaline.

Someone called for her and she squeezed the transmit button twice, which meant she was all set, radio silence from this point on unless critical – Gary Sheffield was in the motel just fifty yards away.

He was their shooter. Roth and her team of state, county, and local police had been interviewing every witness left in town and chasing down those who'd left. Eight more had been able to add to the visual account, including one with a fuzzy cell phone video taken as the gunman battled it out with the two security guards. But when the forensic artist completed his composite and they ran the image, it came back without a hit. The case had briefly nosedived.

The brass casings left behind at the scene were from a .38, specifically a .38 Super. Projectiles recovered from the scene confirmed this, and the witness cell phone video was sufficient to show a point-and-shoot semi-automatic pistol. Quite common, and a relatively fruitless lead on its own, unless there were good fingerprints or enough touch DNA on the casings.

She and the team had focused on questioning witnesses seated in the middle section, rows six through eight. Whether he'd switched seats or not didn't matter – he'd started shooting from there – and no one admitted to a switch anyway. The questioning cleared twenty-eight people, leaving five. One was found at a rest area heading south who was then cleared. Two were located in the next town, huddled over soup and coffee, trying to get their shit back together. One was a woman from Montreal who'd likely already slipped back over the border, and the last was a man named Gary Sheffield. They knew because he'd paid by credit card.

Crazier things had happened. Criminal cases were full of lawbreakers pulling off elaborate schemes only to get tripped up by some simple mistake. But then there was another jaw-dropper: cross-checking Gary Sheffield had turned up quite the result – he'd applied for his pistol permit about two years before.

The guy had bought a ticket, in his name, walked into the theater, took out a gun that was on the books, and opened fire.

He's either insane, he just doesn't care, or he expects suicide by cop. Maybe all three.

She'd told her team as much, as well as the SWAT guys – moving like Special Forces on a raid, they presently approached Sheffield's motel room from both sides, their hunched shapes silent and dark. Roth watched from the far edge of the parking lot, from where she could see the 2004 Ford Escort registered in Sheffield's name. Yet another interesting thing: he had no priors. He was unmarried, childless. He worked as a UPS driver. If Sheffield was connected to any terrorist groups, they didn't know.

And it didn't much matter right now, not as the first two SWAT members struck the door with the small battering ram and took the room.

10

Jan Abendroth was a mentor to Alex and considered by many to be the godfather of the mindfulness meditation movement in the West. A seventy-eight-year-old throat-cancer survivor, his voice was barely discernible: grit blown against weathered wood. "How is our patient?"

Corrine had Alex's phone to one ear, her finger in the other so she might better hear. "He's good."

"He in any condition to talk?"

"I'm sure he'd love it."

Alex watched her with an expectant expression and she handed the phone over with a smile, still feeling off in the pit of her stomach. For the past hour or so, her husband was present but distracted, fixed on something remote. Maybe he was thinking along similar lines to her – this event was likely to raise more ruckus on at least two major social issues: gun control and religion. And that he and his family would be stuck in the middle of it. But she thought there was more, something subsurface, a piece to this whole thing she wasn't clear on yet. Or he wasn't saying.

A fresh snow fell outside. Flakes caught light from the window, the sky deep and black.

Chet was gone, likely pacing the hospital on his own phone, camel hair coat flapping around his waist. Among his duties, Alex's manager functioned like a PR man. He was seeing the angles here, a mother lode of free marketing. Regardless, Alex called all the shots – *he* controlled the narrative of his public persona, carefully constructed from years of study and experience. Maybe the distance she sensed was nothing more than Alex getting a handle on how to proceed. How to navigate potential disagreements with his intrepid promoter, He of the Colored Scarves. Neither she nor Alex were watching the news; they were avoiding social media while Chet acted like a kid at Christmas, giving them the blow-by-blow when he was around.

While the talking heads mused over the potentially religious, or at least anti-science, nature of the shooting, the police had given a press conference and declared no known motive. They'd only listed the injured, provided a hotline number, and suggested people lock their doors while the massive manhunt was underway.

While Alex was on with Abendroth, a call came in on her own phone. "Cor," Alex's father said in his baritone, opposite of Abendroth's. "My God. I've been trying to – how is he? How are you?"

"He's okay; we're fine." She gave Howard the damage report and let him absorb it. "My God," he said again. "Lucky that maniac didn't have better aim."

Lucky, she thought. No one in her husband's orbit was going to suggest anything at work beyond random chance or physical correlates – narrow gunsights on a pistol, a nearsighted shooter. Especially not Howard Baines. She watched Alex, propped up on pillows as he talked quietly to Abendroth, and she felt it again: He wasn't telling her something.

It weighed in her gut, gripped her bones, the way a person

knows bad weather is coming during a flight – the subtle drop when the stomach floats for a second.

"What are the police saying?"

She'd almost forgotten Howard was on the line. "Um, as far as I know they've been looking at everything. He was there with three hundred people. Someone saw him up close or took a video. He'll show up."

"They'll get a net around him," Howard said confidently. "This day and age. It's only a matter of time."

She thought of something from the Buddha: *The thing is, we think we have time.*

Time was a living thing – no better metaphor than sand running through the glass, through your fingers.

Howard said, "And how are you? How are the *kids*? Oh, Cor. This thing. What can I do for you?"

She could hear it in his voice that he wasn't coming. Not that he ought to, not that he was needed, but it was there in the space between his words – Howard Baines was always indisposed, always busy. As a surgeon, that was often verifiable. As a person, it was a feature, not a bug.

"We're fine," she said. "Alex is going to be here for a few days. I'll return to Croton at some point, bring the kids up, and –"

"Let me send a car."

"Howard, that's not –"

"Corrine – I wish I could rush out right now. Wish I could drop everything. I just – it's not in the cards. But let me help. Will you let me help? Let me send someone, put the kids in a car, put them on a plane?"

She cleared her throat and stepped away from Alex, who'd caught her tone and was watching her.

"Howard, they're twelve and six."

A pause. "I went to New York to visit my grandparents when I was ten. Parents put me on a bus. That was that."

"I appreciate it, Howard. But, ah, you know? I'm sure we've got it. We got it."

Finished with Abendroth, Alex set his phone down beside him on the bed. "Is that him?"

She smiled and nodded, held up a finger. "Alex is asking for you. Here." She handed off her phone before either man could object. As soon as Alex started talking – he had a stiff, quiet way with his father – she picked up his phone and stepped into the hallway. The phone vibrated in her hand as soon as she was out the door. His literary agent.

And this is how it would go, she thought. Howard hadn't called her personal phone because Alex was talking on his. Smartphones were perfectly equipped to handle multiple calls. Howard had used her to size up the situation before speaking to Alex directly. It was about men being uncomfortable talking about feelings with other men, making bellwethers of wives and daughters.

Alex's colleagues and business relations, on the other hand, would ring his personal phone, the one she was holding.

"Hi, Angie."

"Corrine? Oh my gosh. I debated whether or not to call…"

"Not at all. I'm glad you did. Alex is just on the other line with his father."

"This is *insane*. What the hell, huh? How is Alex? How are *you*?"

She went through it all again, finding it easier now to stay calm and unemotional as other people broke themselves against the news, although in Angela Gifford's case, while she was well-meaning and a genuinely nice person, this had to be a bit of reconnaissance, too. There was a new book deal with Penguin Random House in the offing, and Angie was partly probing.

After a minute of trading in reassurances, Corrine ended the call and stuffed Alex's phone into the pocket of her jeans. He was still on with Howard, so she caught his eye, jerked her head toward the door. He nodded and winked before she wandered to a coffee station a few doors down, got herself a Styrofoam cup, and poured some ink-black coffee into it, drank it straight.

There her thoughts swung to the mystery shooter, the cops, and if they were going to get him.

11

"On the floor! On the floor, now!"

As soon as Roth heard their shouts, she sprang up, sprinted across the parking lot, two hands on her weapon.

She breached the room: cheap-looking, paneled in fake wood, old shag carpeting on the floor. Sheffield sat on the edge of a twin bed, a dozen men and women in black tactical gear surrounding him, guns drawn. He wore jeans and a faded T-shirt that said *Daytona Beach*. A doughy, smooth-shaven youthfulness belied his age: late forties, dishwater blond hair going gray.

"Down!" the SWAT leader shouted. "*Now.*"

He did as asked, slid off the bed to his knees, then lay down on his chest.

"Arms in front! Keep them out in front! Now put them behind you, one at a time. Slow, let me see 'em…"

As Sheffield obeyed, Roth put her weapon away. She straddled him and bent down, locking his wrists together with her handcuffs.

Heart going hard, she said, "Gary Sheffield, I'm placing you under arrest for attempted murder, aggravated assault, and public endangerment." She read him his rights as SWAT got him back on his feet.

Investigator Harlan Banger stepped into the room wearing a bulletproof vest like she was, flakes of snow gathered in the horseshoe shape of his hair. After giving everything a quick look, he took Sheffield by one upper arm; Roth had the other. They went sideways through the door and walked Sheffield outside to Harlan's car.

She dared a look at the suspect's face, his serene expression. He wasn't bad-looking, for an attempted murderer, just maybe a little baby-faced with that small nose and dimpled chin. You thought about these things, not for any trivial reason, but because you wondered about people, what their story was, what brought them to the edge.

Roth and her supervisor pushed him into the backseat. SWAT was giving her looks, like they didn't trust it, but she'd been clear that if the suspect cooperated, she'd be the one to bring him in. She and Harlan. She'd expected aggression from Sheffield, even wild abandon, but then again, he hadn't tried to hide himself. He'd checked into a motel ten minutes out of town using the same credit card. What could have taken days, even weeks, had lasted six hours.

They put him in a room at the state police barracks in Ray Brook and let him sit. Roth watched him on the monitor, feeling a cold in her bones that wouldn't go away. Harlan stood beside her. "All right. You ready?"

"Ready."

They went into the room. Roth sat across from Sheffield and Harlan hung back in a corner. No one knew they had him yet: not the media, not the public. It was like their own little pocket of time.

"Gary Sheffield," Harlan said from the corner. "From Portland, Maine. What are you doing here, Mr. Sheffield?"

The suspect made no response. He looked from Harlan to Roth – his eyes were flat blue – that baby-soft skin paled by the overhead fluorescent. The graying hair was cropped tight around the ears, but not military-style, just neat. Your neighbor's haircut.

"Can I get you anything?" Roth asked. "Coffee? Soda? Some water maybe?"

Nothing.

Harlan said, "Maybe you'd like to tell us the point of all of this. I'd like to hear it." He added, "And I'm sure the world would like to know. Like to know what you're thinking. Why you did this."

Sheffield glanced at the camera in the ceiling, then continued to watch the cops in a benign, almost disinterested way.

Roth: "You used a credit card to attend the Baines talk, Mr. Sheffield. From there, we ran you through the DMV to learn what you drove. A state trooper spotted your 2004 Ford Escort with matching plates at the Black Bear Motel. I had contacted the motel owner and verified you were staying there." She raised her hands, then let them drop. "Why didn't you run, Mr. Sheffield? You wanted us to find you?"

He sniffed, about the most expressive he'd been so far.

"You just felt like that was it? You'd accomplished what you'd set out to do? What? Make an example?" She leaned in a little. "Look, we've all been there. Pent up, frustrated, pissed off. It's either too many people, or its too loud, or they're just too stupid for their own good. You know what I mean?"

He showed her a pleasant smile. At least that was something.

She eased back into her seat again and glanced at Harlan, who walked over and leaned on the table, knuckles down. "All right, here's what happens now," Harlan said. "You're going to go to Essex County Jail. Following that you'll be arraigned, possibly as soon as tonight. What we're going to do now is write up our report. We'll turn that over to the prosecutor. Once we write that report, once you go to County, the machinery is moving." Harlan stood straight and cycled his fingers, indicating said machinery. "Anything you want to say on your behalf, you might want to do that right now. Otherwise, it will be too late."

Sheffield kept his eyes on Harlan a moment, then turned his face and rubbed his chin on his shoulder, scratching an itch. Then his eyes came back to Roth, and she could see the secret crouched there. Sheffield was withholding information with pleasure.

Harlan touched her shoulder and nodded toward the door. Roth stood up and moved in that direction. Harlan followed her, and before he closed the door on the shooter, said, "Okay, Mr. Sheffield. Enjoy your stay."

12

C het found Corrine at the coffee station. "This is unreal." He tore open three cream cups and four packets of sugar, dumped it all in. "Who knew your husband was such a daredevil? I mean, this guy never ceases to surprise. But I guess you knew that."

"He put himself in danger," Corrine said, hearing impatience in her voice.

"He did what he thought he had to." Chet swirled his coffee with a red stick, tapped it on the edge of the cup, and threw it in the trash. "Your husband just went from a semi-known intellectual to a national hero."

Normally, Chet's sensationalizing wasn't an issue for her. But the bluntness with which he was spoiling to turn a family crisis into a marketing opportunity, right in front of her, had gotten to be a bit much. She spoke in a low voice. "I don't know if we need any more of this. Any more...I don't know. Any more putting Alex into this role. The 'atheist hero.'"

Chet looked dumbfounded. "That's how you –?" He shook his head. "I think you're missing it. No, I do. No offense – you're amazing. You know I love you guys. But there's a bigger picture here. Listen to this, the cops have *another video*. The one the in-house people shot from up in the lighting booth, per my request. So I called around, finally tracked down the guy who runs the venue, Doug, but the police have it in evidence." Chet leaned in, wafting aftershave and a tinge of perspiration. His eyes had gotten big. "It shows the *whole thing*, Cor. Alex and this girl, him saving her *life*."

"Woman, Chet – she's twenty-eight."

He arched an eyebrow as he pulled back. "I thought you weren't looking at any of this stuff?"

"I peeked."

He smiled broadly. "Well, this *woman*, she called me, crying, told me to thank him."

"She called you?"

He nodded, took a sip of his coffee. "Yeah. She's beside herself. Saw her life flash before her eyes and everything."

Corrine rubbed the back of her neck, trying to get out the tension. "I can't help it, but I see a down side. That this happened during one of *his talks*. People got hurt *because of him*. People who are religious, maybe, or more traditional – they think Alex is already against them, and they're only going to turn this into an example of why he's dangerous."

"No. No way."

"I'm not saying that's what I think; you know that. I'm saying someone is going to spin it that way."

"The optics on this are too good."

But he wasn't saying something. Just like Alex, Chet had that look – some canary in his belly.

She glanced in the hallway at a nurse walking past and lowered her voice a notch. "Was this guy…did he just shoot randomly? Or does anyone think this an attempted…" She couldn't get the word out. *Assassination*? It felt too grandiose, too JFK. Alex was a public figure, but he wasn't a president. And it felt too calculated. *Lone nut,* and you imagined someone who'd just finally cracked. *Assassination* was darker, scarier. Something that might not be a standalone event. Something that might keep coming.

Chet opened his mouth, but she beat him to it.

"You know what? It doesn't matter. At this moment, it doesn't matter. What matters is that he's okay. And I want him to stay that way. Which means he doesn't need people clamoring for him right now – TV and reporters, spinning this into a case of secular morality. That's all I'm saying."

Chet shook his head some more, and looked into his coffee, took a drink as he backed toward the wall and leaned against it. "Come on. This is how the world works. People don't engage with nuance and complexity."

"It's the last thing anyone needs," Corrine said. "The last thing *he* needs. He's a scientist, Chet. He's not a 'new atheist' poster boy, or whatever else you and the rest of them say in order to sell books."

Chet acquired a look in his eyes she'd seen only once or twice, hard and direct; she realized she was backing him into a corner. "Well, Corrine, he *is* an atheist. We're not leading with that – of course not, we never have – but it's pretty hard to hide when your husband talks about the dangers of Islam and says Christians worship an Iron Age god."

She'd kept it together for the kids, then for Alex's family, but by now she was frazzled. Before saying anything to Chet she might regret, she squeezed past him and left the cramped break room, headed back to her husband.

Chet caught up with her in the hallway seconds later. "Corrine…hey. Look, I'm sorry."

She stopped walking, head down, and took a breath. "Me too."

"I'm gonna let you two have some time while I deal with this.

Okay?"

She nodded, raising her eyes to him. "That would be nice, Chet."

He got ahead of her and stopped in front of Alex's room, effectively blocking her way in. "But those reporters down there – they're not going away empty-handed."

A sigh escaped her. "I'm not going downstairs."

"No, I'm saying I'll handle it. Cor – you know I'll handle it."

"Okay." She patted his arm, started past him again, but stopped and looked him in the eye. "Is there something else?"

"What?" He pulled a guileless face. Chet had a million faces. Alex said he'd once been an actor.

She lowered her volume even more, with Alex just inside the room. She could hear him, still on the phone to Howard – it had to be a record for them. "Is there anything I need to know about?"

"Like what?"

"I don't know. Anything. Business is good?"

"Business is good, but it could always be better. You know how it is. Whether you....All I'm saying is that this is a tragedy. But what Alex did, this video that's out – it's going to sell us a million more books. And when we get the in-house video released from the police, a million more. And there's nothing wrong with that. Nothing immoral or unethical."

She hadn't told him yet about Angie, his agent, calling. One thing at a time. "Chet, he's been going, essentially, for eight straight weeks. Promoting the latest book, giving these talks, having his debates…"

"Yeah?"

"In all that time, nothing has come up? He hasn't said anything but – I don't know, I can't keep track of it all. Has anyone threatened him?"

"Absolutely not. I would know. It's just the usual stuff. Nothing substantive."

"Who did you talk to in law enforcement?"

"The one, ah – Roth."

"You've spoken to her?"

"Sure." Chet sipped his coffee, looking proud. "She called me right away. Asked me about booking this gig, the security – I told her everything I could. This was some Podunk town. I didn't even care if Alex did it or not. But you know how he is – no mission too small."

She chose to ignore the subtle way Chet was shifting blame, like somehow Alex was responsible for what happened – the exact response she feared from the public. And it wasn't that Chet would suddenly name a likely culprit if he hadn't already; if there was a ready-made villain, Chet would know it before anyone. It was something else that bothered her. "How has he been doing, though? I've hardly seen him. He's barely home. And when he *is* home, he's like a…"

Chet got his voice down as low as Chet was capable. "You asking me if he's sleeping around?"

"No, Chet. Of course not." She cast her gaze down, getting an eyeful of his expensive boots. What was she asking? "I know Alex would try to protect people. I'm not saying that's out of character. It's just…seeing him like that – I don't know."

"Alex is great. He's a champ. And that was pure adrenaline. I mean, the guy is shot in the leg and he's playing commando, bum-rushing that door. God knows what's going through his –"

"You guys talking about me?"

The door was ajar; Chet pushed it the rest of the way, leaned in with a grin. "You're the man of the hour. We're going to have to give you a superhero name or something. 'Baines the Beast.'"

Alex stared across the room at her while Chet kept the door open. When she walked in, Chet said, "I'm gonna leave you two. Be back soon." He hurried off for the elevators, slopping his coffee in eagerness to talk to the reporters downstairs.

Before she reached the bed, Alex's phone vibrated in her pocket. She chose to ignore it this time. She sat beside him and took his hand, searching his eyes – not exactly guilt there, not quite sorrow, but something. "You look tired," she said. "You should rest."

"Who else called?"

She told him about Angie and he shifted in the bed, trying to get more comfortable.

"You okay?" She helped with his pillow.

Grimacing, he clenched his teeth and arched his back. "My butt is getting numb."

"What have they got you on? I haven't even asked anyone." She looked at the door, as if a doctor or nurse would appear.

"Hydrocodone." He tapped his wrist where the IV was going in. "Barely touches it."

"You're in a lot of pain. Let me get someone."

He held her arm. "I'm okay."

After that they fell into a silence, both watching the snow stick to the window, the distant lights of Burlington, amber and cool white. A traffic light swung in the wind a half a mile away. This was uncharted territory. Someone had gone on a shooting spree at one of Alex's talks. Chet's reaction to it, and to the video capturing it, was predictable. But she had trouble anticipating how she was going to feel from one minute to the next. There was an idea, a rough map – be gracious, be humble, concerned for the people whose lives had also been affected – but that was the thing. Whose lives had been affected, beyond the actual witnesses and victims?

"I don't want this guy to turn out to be a fanatic," she admitted, feeling that same sense of altitude-drop in her stomach.

"Me neither. Better he's a garden-variety psychopath. No religious or political affiliations." He paused. "But if he's an extremist, I'm not about to make this an issue of religious

65

reform, and I'm certainly not going to tell anybody 'I told you so.'"

The quiet returned, just the beeping of his heart monitor, the murmur of voices outside the room, a squeaky wheel as someone rolled past with a cleaning cart.

"The lights were in my eyes."

She'd barely heard him. "What's that, honey?"

Alex stared into the night outside. "I would've gotten a look at him, but the lights were, you know, on the stage. They turn those lights up so bright. Someone screamed. I didn't even have time to – at first I just – I stood there."

At last, he looked at her. "I felt the bullet. It went right by my head, right there. I felt it...*pull* the air. Just a couple of inches. Maybe not even that much. If I had just been standing a little – just a *little* bit more to the left..."

She tucked into him and hugged him. He touched her head, lightly this time, and she felt his heart beating, sensed his body relaxing. "It's all right," she said. "We're getting through this. One week and you can come home."

"Sir," someone said, out in the hallway. "Sir, visiting hours are –"

"I'm his personal manager." Chet strode into the room, his eyes wide all over again, a vein in his temple bulging and purple. He left wet footprints and breathed heavily as he stopped and looked at Alex. "They got him."

Alex sat up straighter. "They got him?"

Chet stuck out his phone, swallowed like he'd lost his spit, nodded. "Just heard from Drew. They rolled up on the guy at a motel about fifteen miles from the Arts Center. Fucking A."

He walked to the chair in the corner and sat down. After he lowered his head and caught his breath, he looked up. "Fifteen miles from town. Rolled up on him and took him down. It's over," he said.

13

He wanted to get caught.

No one was saying it, but everyone was thinking it.

They celebrated anyway, tucked in a corner of the local bar. Harlan Banger approached the table with a round of drinks, and the group of cops was jovial, clapping Roth on the back and giving her the job-well-done.

Harlan offloaded the drinks, pushed a pint of beer at Roth. She held up her hand – *No thanks* – and a local cop, Brian Stearns, made a face. "What? Come on, man. You got the report in; he's arraigned tonight. The rest of it can wait."

Roth sipped from a bottle of water and smiled at Harlan, who winked and took the pint for himself. Everyone else – two state troopers, two more local cops, a county deputy, and a correctional officer, like the beginning of a joke – grabbed their drinks and made merry.

"He say anything?" It was Carla Gladd, the only other woman.

Roth just looked at Harlan, who shook his head. "Didn't say a word during the interview," Harlan answered. "Didn't even ask for a lawyer."

"What about on the ride? He say anything then?"

"Stared out the window, like he was on a bus."

Everybody settled, drank, and contemplated it. There was music playing, but that was the nice thing about The Alibi – it was a cop bar. Cops liked to talk, and the owner kept the country-twang-tunes to a reasonable decibel. Being that it was a cop bar didn't mean other people couldn't come in, and Roth glanced around at the handful of barflies belly-up to the bar or occupying the booths. Her table was the entertainment, though, everyone sneaking looks and obviously eavesdropping.

"Probably he's got some bone to pick with the speaker guy," Stearns said. "He's kind of a celebrity. The shooter is probably hot for him or something."

It was still an open case, discretion required. "Let's just keep it tamped down, okay?" Roth said.

Stearns looked irritated. "Okay, okay. Touchy. I'll keep it down, boss." He drained his beer and stood up with a ruckus. "I gotta piss." He shot her a hard look as he staggered to the bathroom.

Great. Would she need to smooth his feelings over? She didn't want to play into the stereotype, the woman rushing to assuage the male ego.

"He's a good guy," Carla Gladd mused, when Stearns was gone. "Just gets a little devolved when he drinks."

"Yeah," Roth said.

BCI had a separate chain of command within the state police. Roth spent time with the troopers, like Gladd, but even then, they called BCI the "back room" for a reason; you didn't much mingle with the cops out on road patrol, much less the local PD.

But what really separated her from the cops around the table was that most of them had grown up together or knew each other from back when. Roth didn't. And her seven years as a trooper had been in another part of the state. She was still on the outside looking in.

Gladd kept her voice more measured, leaned in to the table. "If this Baines guy is a celebrity, I've never heard of him. What's his deal?"

"He draws a crowd, though," another Lake Placid cop said.

"He's a neuroscientist?" Gladd asked. "I saw the poster – just his face, looking intense, little half smile going on. He is kind of cute, though. He's got a couple books, I guess."

"People still read those?" The other Lake Placid cop was trying to be cute.

"I heard men read more nonfiction," Gladd said.

"He's an elitist," the corrections guy said. "Know what I mean? Talks down to you. Bet you this Sheffield guy is fed up with it or something. Like Brian said."

Roth looked at her bottle of water "Well, he's not talking until his PD shows up, so we don't know."

"I'm not justifying it or anything," the corrections guy said. She thought his name was Travis or Trevor. His eyes were glassy from drinking. "I'm just saying, you got people who say what they mean – maybe it's crude or whatever – and maybe other people don't like it, but oh well – it's real. Then you got these guys like Barnes, who talk in circles. I YouTubed him and it was like, what the fuck?"

"Baines, not Barnes," Harlan corrected.

"All I'm saying is, whether the shooter's a Christian, an everyday guy, whatever – he did the wrong thing – you know, of course – but there's too many people in this world talking down to you."

Roth started to get up, all eyes on her. "I'm pretty tired, guys. Think I'm gonna, ah..." She caught Harlan's gaze before she could finish her goodbye.

Harlan jerked his head at an empty booth. "Give me just five, all right?"

She relaxed a little. "Sure."

Expressions were somber, but Gladd tried to smile politely, and the local cop nodded and said "G'night." The correctional officer looked into a corner and finished his pint.

She followed Harlan to the booth. He was older than her by twenty years, plenty experienced, easygoing. He was lanky, with a bony face, a bump in his long nose. Even if he treated her as an equal and they both answered to the same captain, he was still above her in the chain; he was her supervisor and had been since day one.

They sat down opposite each other. "You did good today," Harlan said.

"Thanks."

He raised a wiry eyebrow. "Something's bothering you."

"I'm just tired."

"You don't get tired. I've been working with you for three years. Did you know that? They dropped you in the gap three years ago this week, I think. So, happy anniversary to us."

She unscrewed her water bottle and took a swig. It was true; she didn't feel physically tired. She was sore a bit from being on her feet all day, doing a bit of running, and all the tension toward the end. It all took its toll – but she was mentally fatigued. Something. Cloudy. Like she needed a hot shower and six hours of solid sleep, a gift she rarely got.

"Maybe too easy," she said. "Maybe that's it."

"Guys like this don't care if they get caught. Or they check out. This is their big swan dive. They're at the end of whatever messed-up mental carnival they've got going on, and this is the final act."

"You mixed about three metaphors, there, I think. Hang on, let me count."

"How is this guy any different? Okay, maybe he was docile, went out like a lamb – that's another metaphor – but so what? Maybe he's just not crazy enough to want to live."

"Or it's the other way around. Maybe people who've got some shred of conscience left, they *want* to die because they can't handle what they've done." She put the cap back on the bottle. "Sheffield didn't want to die, or he would have picked up the gun in his motel room and turned it on himself. Or on us."

"Well, then he's just flat insane."

"Didn't seem it to me."

"Yeah, me neither, but you know how this goes. Can't always know." Harlan took a sip of his beer. "Isn't your sister into all this behavioral analysis? Talk to her. See what she says. She'll agree with me, I bet."

"She just caught her first case for the Bureau. Worked a serial killing in Syracuse."

"The Park Killer?"

"Yeah."

"No shit. Your old neck of the woods, even. That why they called her in?"

"I guess so. I haven't talked to her."

Harlan studied Roth, decided to leave it be. "Anyway, he's done. There were multiple people injured. Just because nobody died, he'll take a plea deal and get twenty years. Mark my words. And believe me when I tell you he isn't the first guy who played mute in the box. I've interviewed ones like him before. Think it's cute to not say anything, like it's going to help."

She let him talk, part of her just happy to be comforted by the gravelly ramble of his voice. As far as cops went, Harlan was one of the nicest she'd met. And that was saying something, since most cops she'd met were good people trying to do right.

As if to counterpoint her thought, Stearns came back from the bathroom like a herd of elephants, his boots tromping across the wooden floor, laughing about something he'd just said to the bartender. Stearns gave her a look, his smile vanished – a bit dramatically, she thought – and he sat back down at the table with the other officers. Now he was making a big show of not looking at her.

"All I know is what I see," she said, mentally back-burnering Stearns. "Sheffield has no record, a couple parking tickets. He's not – from what we know – he's not a part of anything. No affiliation with known hate groups."

"We don't know his church."

"You really think this is about that?"

"Could be. I'd say, not that it matters. If you're the type to shoot people in a crowd, you'll pick whatever excuse you can find." He waved a hand, finished his beer. "But this, you know, this is becoming a thing, too. These guys used to have a simple motive. When I was coming up, guy shot someone, there was a reason. He went crazy at the post office, it was because his wife was cheating or because he got laid off. Now, you get a guy who holes up in a hotel room with an arsenal and lays siege to a crowd, we don't know why. We say maybe he had mental health issues."

She tapped the table with her two fingers, jittering them rapidly back and forth. "Sure. But people with mental health issues are usually victims, not perpetrators."

"Yes, but I'm saying it's interesting that – well, if it *does* turn out he's got something going on, he's bipolar or majorly depressive – it's interesting that he goes after this guy who's a brain guy. A guy who talks about how the mind works. You see what I'm saying?"

"I see what you're saying. He could be making a statement. The mental health system failed him or something."

"Exactly. Like, *Hey, this shit is not working*. But even if it's not that, he's got some ideology driving him, something to prove, religious beliefs or otherwise. It was like...the way he was quiet, it was more like a vow of silence than legal strategy. You know?"

After a moment of contemplation, Roth said, "Well, he's locked up. Can't do anything else." She slid out from the booth. "Thanks, Harl. I gotta get home to Matt and the kids, though."

"Hey – you know? Get some rest." He looked at the table full of cops. "And forget Stearns. Don't let him get to you."

She smiled and nodded. "I'll see you in the morning."

She started for the door, then stopped. After a second, she picked her way back to the table with the officers, thinking that despite what Harlan said, she shouldn't leave the place with tension in the air. The cops stopped talking as she neared and came up behind Stearns. She leaned over him and ran her hands down the front of his chest, feeling him tense, then moved her mouth close to his ear. Using her best Marilyn Monroe voice, she whispered loud enough for the group to hear: "Good job out there today, big boy."

The table busted up with laughs and wide eyes and cries of "Ohhhh!" Stearns blushed with a crooked smile. He patted her hand as she withdrew. "Nicely done, Investigator Roth. Another day, another bad guy."

She dropped a twenty-dollar bill on the table. "Next round is on me."

There were cheers, but Stearns looked at the twenty and said, "Something cheap, anyway," and Carla Gladd punched him in the arm.

Roth said, "Cheap is good for your last drink. You need to get your asses home and into bed. You've got wives and husbands and families – and in Stearns's case, you've got to spend that ten minutes looking at yourself in the mirror."

Carla Gladd whooped with delight, and Harlan gave her a big grin as Roth strode out of the bar, flung the door open, and stepped into the cold and snowy night.

14

Two new critical patients were admitted to the ICU. With Alex continuing to recover without incident, the hospital relocated him to another wing. After delivering the news of the shooter's arrest, Chet had returned downstairs to talk to the press. He was back now, taking up residence in the corner chair, talking nonstop about the two "outstanding" events which preoccupied him – the video of Alex's heroics (now up to a hundred thousand views) – and Gary Sheffield, the gunman who had gone quickly and quietly into the fold of law enforcement.

The name, Corrine thought – Gary Sheffield. Something about having a name for the man who'd shot her husband changed something, but it was late, and she was too tired to figure out what.

Alex had to be exhausted. Up since five that morning, the talk at noon, the shooting; he'd been airlifted to Fletcher Allen by one thirty and right into surgery. Four hours or so after that, and Corrine had arrived and then Alex was fielding phone calls. His hair stuck up in the back, fatigue shadowed his eyes. Aside from a few catnaps, he hadn't slept. Said every time he closed his eyes, he saw the shooter and relived it.

"Is this guy just stupid?" Chet uncrossed his legs and stood. "I know you're looking at me like a spin doctor, but it's not that. This is about your safety. Because maybe this guy is some one-off, maybe he's not. We have to know if he acted alone. We have to be thinking about that. We gotta, you know, really…"

Chet trailed off because Alex put up his hand. If there was one person on Earth who could shut him up, it was Alex. "I appreciate it, Chet. And I appreciate you. You're right – and I want to look into it, but…" He conveyed the rest with his eyes.

Chet, being Chet, then decided it was all his idea. "Listen to me – you guys have had a day like you've never had, and I'm sitting here….We should put a pin in this for now. You're in a safe place – still two cops downstairs – I'll handle everything else." He swiped up his coat, wound his scarf, and grabbed the bed rail – Chet didn't touch too many people for fear of germs. "You get better, my man. Rest up, heal up. This is the start of a whole new level. We just gotta keep an eye on our blind spots. That's all I'm saying."

"I know. We'll see you in the morning."

Corrine leaned against the wall beside the windows. Chet gave her a hug, then bussed each cheek, something he'd adopted from trips abroad.

"Good night, Chet," she said.

He leaned back and looked deep into her eyes like he was cooking up some final words. Instead, he left silently, closing the door behind him.

They listened a while to the machines.

"I have to tell you something," Corrine said eventually. "Well, something I'd like to talk about, I guess."

He waited, but she found it hard to bring herself to it.

"What is it?"

"I'm just – I'm scared. About this. About all of it. I think we need to be very careful."

"That's why I'm not letting Chet run things."

"That's not all I mean." She felt her courage draining and decided to be quick getting it out. "This is more than luck, Alex."

She waited for his reaction, but he just watched her with that slight look of concern.

She said, "I'm not normally an 'everything happens for a reason' person. You know that. But this is something...this is..." She started to shake, and rushed to beat the oncoming emotion, but it was impossible. Tears fell as she raised a wavering hand to the side of her head. "You said you felt it. You said it went right by you. Just an inch to the left....That we were so close, so close, Alex..."

He reached for her and she took his hands, but braced herself instead of folding into him again. "We were so close, Alex, to the end of this. The end of you, us, everything. But...it didn't happen. It didn't happen, and now maybe we..."

"What?"

She wiped the tears with her palm and gave him a quick peck on the cheek. "Listen. Let's talk to the kids. And then we'll get you cleaned up and ready for bed. You're due for ablutions." She wiggled her eyebrows to be funny.

"We can talk about this. You don't have to stop."

"No. It's good. Maybe later." Even the slightest chance of a disagreement, philosophical or otherwise – no. She couldn't handle that. Not now.

He sighed. "Okay. Yeah. Do you still have my phone? Your battery is dead."

"I've got it, yeah." She glanced at the clock. Almost ten. But the kids would be up, they were waiting – it had just been one thing after another. She'd texted Mara that the call was imminent.

"I miss them," he said.

"I know." She also knew he wasn't talking only about the last eighteen hours. She scrolled through his contacts searching for

Mara, saw a couple of names she didn't recognize. She put that out of her mind for now – Alex was bound to be in touch with people she didn't know – and dialed Mara when she found it.

He spoke briefly to Mara when Corrine gave him the phone, making light of his situation (the president of the Shot-in-the-Leg Club had already offered him a keynote speaker position, he told her), and then Kenneth. Corrine could tell he was holding back with their son, afraid to become emotional. When he spoke to Freda next, tears brimmed in his eyes. He assured her he was okay, and told her he loved her half a dozen times. "Hey, Freed," he said, "Why did the meditation teacher not give any change when the student paid for a meditation cushion?" He paused with a grin. "Because change has to come from within."

Corrine rolled her eyes, then talked to both kids, made sure they were behaving. She got Mara back on the line.

"Freda has a rash," Mara said.

"Where?"

"It's just a little one – it's on her chest – and her arms and legs a bit. Her face is flushed. I didn't know if I should tell you."

"No – of course, tell me."

Alex must have detected her tone, because he tilted his head and frowned. Corrine asked Mara if Freda had a sore throat.

"Yeah, she's complained about that. So…"

It could be strep. It was that time of year. While Corrine was thinking, Mara said, "I'd take her to the doctor in the morning, but it's going to be Sunday. So that's out, or it's the emergency room."

"All right, let me talk to Alex – I'll call you right back?"

"Sure. I'll be here. How are you guys?"

"We're good. It's like we're on a very weird date."

They said goodbye and Corrine relayed it to Alex.

"You should go," he said.

"Honey…"

"No question. I'm fine. I'm just going to be lying here. Maybe I'll finally watch *Breaking Bad.*"

She looked at the dark window, snowflakes still accumulating against the glass. Her maternal instincts had already kicked in – her baby was sick and needed her mother. The Land Rover had good tires. She'd only slipped on the way up because the weather had just turned, the roads oily. It would be plowed and salted now. She'd just needed that concession from Alex.

"All right," she said, resigned.

"I didn't mean now, though. Wait until the morning."

"Well, if I'm going to wait until the morning, I might as well let Mara take her to the emergency room. Otherwise…"

They went around like this, trying to figure it out, and in the midst of debate, his phone vibrated on the table. She picked it up, thinking Mara had forgotten to say something.

"I don't know this number." She showed him the screen. "You know it?"

He looked, shook his head. "Probably someone for Chet, called my number by mistake. Ignore it."

She set it back down, unable to drag her thoughts away until the thing stopped spinning with the vibrations. And she remembered her own phone had a dead battery. She plugged it in while they continued discussing what to do.

"I don't know, hon," Alex said. "It's late. I really think you should wait. Yeah, let Mara take her, and if –"

"Then she has to miss work."

"She's working on a Sunday? What about Stephen?"

"He's in the city. She is, was going to leave the kids with Layla."

He arched an eyebrow – a signature Alex expression. "*Layla?*"

Layla was Mara's teen daughter. She'd gone through a wild phase that had lasted from around age twelve to at least sixteen, getting kicked out of prep schools, a pregnancy scare followed by a suicide attempt at fifteen. Well, to hear it from Mara, it wasn't a suicide attempt – Layla had only taken enough pills to knock her out for a few hours – but it was a cry for help.

"It would've only been for a short time," Corrine said. "Mara has a photo shoot tomorrow, and she was going to…forget it – I'm going."

She started gathering her things, aware she was feeling irritated, defensive, but unable to direct it at anyone. She'd had her own wild period, too, and sometimes felt that rebelliousness streaking her emotions, like a crack of lightning.

But then it was gone and, holding her bag in one hand and coat in the other, she sagged against the wall, looked at the floor. Feeling torn was a regular part of family life. And when it rained, it poured.

"Honey. Listen." His voice was soft, rational. Sometimes his imperturbable calm irritated her, but at the moment, it was comforting. "I'm sorry I reacted about Layla. I know she's…let Mara leave Kenneth with Layla, let her take Freda to the –"

The phone buzzed again, interrupting. Corrine dropped her stuff and crossed the room to it.

"Cor," Alex said, "Honey, just –"

"It's the same 949 number."

Alex started to say something, but she hit the green button and put the phone to her ear. "Hello?" She waited. When there was nothing, she held it out and looked. Still connected. "Hello? Who is this?"

Nothing. Quiet breathing. The snuffle of traffic in the distance.

"Hello? Come on…"

Now she canceled the call and immediately dialed it back.

"What are you –?" Alex was trying to sit up. He stretched out a hand. "Give it to me. Let me see."

She walked away, the line ringing. After just three, a computerized voice broke in. *"The cellular customer you're trying to reach has not activated their voice m –"*

She hung up again, dropped the phone beside Alex. Feeling keyed up, feeling those jags of wild energy from days gone by, she plunged her fingers into her hair, shook it out, took a deep breath, paced to the window, let the breath out.

Easy, kid. Go easy.

She closed her eyes, focused on her breathing some more.

In, out.

Stay with the out-breath. Let it go.

It started to work, but then the image formed – the familiar funnel of ashen clouds, pulling everything up into oblivion. A sky for the end of the world. Last night, she'd dreamt it. And today, it kept reappearing. Like a warning.

People didn't see visions…unless, perhaps, in deep meditation or an altered state. Otherwise, it signaled some sort of neurological issue. Maybe what happened to Alex was more disruptive than she understood. Maybe she was in shock, parts of her mind on the fritz.

"Cory? You okay?"

But her dream had occurred *before* the shooting. She could question it, she could question herself and her sanity, or she could try to understand what it meant – which wasn't necessarily any easier. Something was wrong; that was the baseline. Beyond that, the sense that if they didn't now hew to a narrow path, things would get worse.

Decided at last, she returned to the bedside. "You know how it is with Freda."

He nodded.

"She's always been prone to fevers," Corrine said. "If it's strep, that means out of school for a few days, antibiotics. So when I go, it's going to be hard to come back."

He was silent, watching her.

"I'll stay tonight. We'll keep in touch with Mara. And then I'll go in the morning."

"Maybe we'll get lucky, though, and it's just heat rash from a fever. I mean, she's a healthy kid with all kinds of energy."

"But she always seems to get the worst of what's going around. That's just how it is with her."

"I know."

"And we're getting Kenneth a cell phone. I don't care if it's nine months until he turns thirteen. I want to have a direct line to my children. I'm reversing my position."

He smiled. "If memory serves, I was the one who put my foot down on phones."

"Whatever. I'm serious." Her gaze fell to the phone on the bed. The odd call had been forgotten while making the decision to stay the night. She backed away from the bed and turned for the door.

"Where are you going?"

"To get the necessaries for your sponge bath, Mr. Baines."

She winked at him, trying to overcome it all, to forget that dark sky and the fear in the pit of her stomach. "Don't go anywhere."

15

SUNDAY, DECEMBER 6

R oth couldn't sleep. Big surprise. She kept turning it over in her mind as she rolled around beneath the covers. Gary Sheffield: In like a lion, out like a lamb.

In the rush of the investigation, there'd only been so much time to learn about Sheffield. Interviewing him hadn't revealed much but his stoicism – if it *was* that. Harlan had hit him with the standard stuff all cops did with someone in the box – tried to get him comfortable, get him talking. Most people, you let them lead the conversation, talk long enough, and they hung themselves.

His silence hounded her.

She threw back the covers and shivered in the cold. Matt had let the fire go out. She found her fuzzy slippers, pulled the quilt from the bed, wrapped it around herself. She picked up her phone, found her earbuds on the dresser, and took them into the kitchen.

She loved their big house. That was one of the benefits of living in the boondocks – if she'd been stationed closer to head-quarters, they probably couldn't have swung a place this size, with this much land. Working as an investigator for the state paid pretty well, and as a trooper for five years prior, she'd been able to sock away some savings, enough that she and Matt had had the means to put down forty thousand on the house they'd fallen in love with. It was cozy and remote, but not too remote. She'd been on scene at the Arts Center in less than twenty minutes after getting paged, which was pretty good.

Local PD had first responded to the 911 call – shots fired. A state trooper had arrived next, assessed the scene, and immediately called the back room. Harlan had been working a shift and she'd been on-call. Once Sheffield had been located, they'd brought in SWAT, surrounded and took him down. But anyone who watched *Law and Order* knew that a cop's role didn't end with an arrest report. It was up to the DA to formally issue the criminal complaint or seek a grand jury to return an indictment, but the police often continued to compile evidence and take statements from any corroborating witnesses to strengthen the state's case. While there were no outstanding factors keeping the DA from filing, complacency was not an option. Anything could happen. She had to stay vigilant.

First, she ran some water in the kitchen and put the kettle on the gas stove. Then she went to the living room couch, wrapped the blanket tighter, and opened the browser on her phone.

What they knew from tolls and the motel registry: Sheffield had driven up the night before the event, checked into the motel at six p.m. But who was he? Sometimes you could learn more about a person from everyday sources than criminal databases or even FBI data. Just a basic search: start with Google, enter his name and known address from Portland, Maine. Not much there but a "G. Sheffield" who'd completed a 10k race a couple of years before. He'd come in second for his age group, the 40-50 cohort.

So he was a runner. He hadn't done any running as the net closed around him at the Black Bear Motel. He'd been sitting on the bed with the television off. Just waiting.

She replayed the moment, scrutinizing every aspect. He'd laid on the floor when commanded. She'd held his arm on the way to the cruiser, and while she hadn't exactly taken his pulse, she could sense that he was calm. Which was interesting.

As a trooper, Roth had pulled over innumerable speeders. When caught, a person typically showed some nerves. Sure, there were people who acted righteous, some tried to throw out the devil-may-care vibe, but there was always something. Even during a drunk stop, a civilian too blitzed to care about consequences still displayed emotion. Once she'd jumped to BCI, she'd participated in all sorts of busts. Whether a Medicare fraud bust, a hydrocodone drug network, or myriad domestic violence cases, everybody showed something, even if it was their poker face. With Sheffield there was nothing; he'd sat there like it was his break room at work.

Sometimes a hardened criminal had those steely nerves – getting busted was business as usual. But Sheffield had a clean record. Just a man with an incredibly adaptive temperament, then? Or did he have some kind of mental health issue, like Harlan suggested?

The intake procedure and piss-test would reveal if he'd been stoned. Blood work would show if he was on something other than marijuana. He'd be evaluated, his primary care physician consulted – maybe he was on Xanax or Klonopin – it might come out that he suffered some condition after all. But what? And why Baines's talk, unless the attack was ideologically motivated? Why make no effort to get away; why say nothing once caught? When John Hinckley Jr. attempted to assassinate President Ronald Reagan, he'd done it to impress actress Jodie Foster. Hinckley wound up found not guilty by reason of insanity and went into a psychiatric institution.

Was Sheffield angling for an insanity plea? Was that it?

Or was he simply fearless?

She realized the water was probably boiling on the stove. She paused the video at the start, poured steaming water over a bag of chamomile tea, and let it steep while she went back to the couch.

Baines's talk had been about mindfulness meditation. No, it wasn't three hundred people sitting around on yoga mats, it was more intellectual than that, but it was nevertheless about calm and tranquility, letting your thoughts go, things of that nature. These were people who could get their resting heart rate down to something like a few beats per minute through meditation. People who could sit for hours in extreme cold in just their yoga pants.

Maybe Sheffield was some kind of practiced meditator. He might've had a strong sense of purpose, too, relaxing him. If you felt like you were doing God's good work, for instance, it might keep you sober and steady.

Because Baines's talk wasn't just about meditation, but about free will. According to the pamphlet from his show, Baines was promoting advances in neuroscience, using them to "inspect the notion of real choice."

Few things were as upsetting to people as the idea they had no choice. And free will was sort of the linchpin for major world religions: God gave us free will so we could choose to love Him. Something like that.

But this was all speculation.

She ran through Facebook without finding a match; the top "Gary Sheffield" hits were for an African-American baseball player, an actor who'd been in nothing much, and a guitar shop owner from Oklahoma. No Instagram account, either, and if he was on Twitter, she couldn't find him. At least, he wasn't using his real name.

She searched for Baines on Twitter and reviewed the copious tweets about the shooting, many of them hashtagged #Atheist-ThoughtLeader, others #MindfulnessMovement, and then the expected gun violence and gun control tags.

One tweet – *This is what happens when you go against God* – had ignited a firestorm of rebukes and support.

How dare you

How horrible

What a thing to say

It's sad but the Lord will find another way

Oh stuff it you pompous Jesus-wanking twat

Roth clicked on a link to Baines's website, a springboard to his podcast, best-selling books, YouTube videos of various debates and talks. A brief biography said he'd studied religion in college, but dropped out, spent the next several years traveling back and forth from the Middle and Far East. After discovering *Vipassana,* he'd returned to school and obtained his doctorate in neuroscience, intent on researching the practical effects mindfulness meditation had on the brain, even "changing its physical structure." But he'd first come to prominence lending himself to a sexual assault case. A woman had accused a powerful man of a past rape but was fuzzy on certain details. Baines spoke out on her behalf, explaining how the brain often preserved core memories in a "mental safe room" while discarding what it deemed irrelevant details to a sort of neural wasteland.

All of his work seemed tethered to this central principle: Life was better with an understanding of the brain and by learning to control it. Religion, he thought, clouded the issue unnecessarily. He even shied away from any mystical tendencies within Buddhism, where meditation basically came from. If he couldn't demonstrate it through experiments and cognitive behavioral studies and MRI scans, it wasn't there. "Meditation is like turning down the voltage of the brain," he said in *Jhana Magazine.*

He and his wife and two kids lived in Scarsdale, just north of New York City.

She performed a more localized search using his address and found an opinion piece in *The Journal,* a newspaper serving

Westchester County, critiquing Baines's work as "self-indulgent intellectual totalitarianism." The writer was a man named Paul Halloran. Roth clicked a video link, popped in her ear buds, and watched some of a debate between Baines and Halloran, with Halloran citing evolutionary biology to claim that chimpanzees exhibited proto-religious behavior, whatever that meant. She had a quick look at Halloran: He ran a religious charity that had gotten into some trouble with the IRS, had a radio talk show, wrote editorials for *The Journal*, and generally seemed preoccupied with a "potentially godless" society. So, Baines had at least one detractor.

He also had legions of followers. Apparent fans even assembled videos of "best moments" across his many talks and debates. She found one that began with Baines seated on stage with several others. He looked years younger, fewer facial lines, no detectable gray in his auburn hair.

"Some people claim that God is synonymous with consciousness or the laws of nature," he said, "but if we talk about consciousness or the laws of nature, we're not talking about the god our neighbors believe in, which is essentially an invisible person, a deity who created the universe to have a relationship with one particular species of primate. Lucky us."

The audience laughed, and then they applauded. She clicked on another video. After Baines was introduced by a moderator, he looked over the crowd and said, "Let's try something. A little experiment. All right? First, close your eyes. Get comfortable."

Roth kept her eyes open; her gaze flicked to the sign behind Baines declaring, "The Atheist Foundation of Australia."

"Just breathe. Breathe in through your nose, breathe out." His voice was calm, not quite the cadence of a hypnotherapist but close. "Try to let your thoughts go. Think of them like people leaving a room, and there's only you left. Just get to a nice place where you're open. Good. Come back to the baseline....What we know is that we're conscious. That something is happening. Sensations, thoughts, these are the contents of consciousness. Let these things go – your senses, your concerns and distractions. Just relax, eyes closed, breathe in; breathe out….Okay. Now, I want you to think of a movie. It can be any movie ever made. Take a moment. Got it?"

One came to Roth's mind – she'd watched it with Matt a few nights ago. Something he'd picked out. She was also thinking that this was similar to the way Baines had begun the talk at the Arts Center. Even if he wasn't an entertainer, per se, he had a kind of script he followed. One would have to, she figured.

"Okay," he said. "So, free will would tell us that you could pick pretty much any movie in the world. It's totally arbitrary – it's purely your decision in that moment to select one movie out of many thousands. Right? But, really, that's not the case. First, we have to eliminate from that pool all the movies that you've never heard of. All the foreign films you're unaware of, all the little indie films that never got a wide release – you can't pick those. And you probably didn't pick a movie like *Any Which Way but Loose*, with Clint Eastwood. Chances are you've heard of that movie – you know the one, where he's friends with a chimpanzee – you've heard of it, maybe you even saw it years ago, but you didn't pick it. Your choice was probably *Forrest Gump*, or maybe *Casablanca*, or *Star Wars*."

Roth thought, *Nope.* She got up and retrieved her tea, taking her phone with her. What was this guy? Some sort of mentalist?

"Now, let's say you picked *Forrest Gump*. Why did you pick that? Was it truly random? Is it because you just recently saw it? Maybe it's a movie you've seen a number of times – it has those memorable lines. The one about a box of chocolates. Or maybe you thought about a big popular movie like that, but then you thought, 'Nah, I'm going to go with a little something more obscure.' And so then you came up with *Miller's Crossing*….Why that movie? There are thousands of obscure movies. Tens of thousands....It's because somewhere along the way, the image of that DVD, or that movie poster – the black hat sitting there in the middle of the forest – that got stuck in your mind."

She sat back down, focusing on his face, his calm. Did he have a condescending manner, like Travis (or Trevor) had suggested? She didn't think so. He seemed playful, quick to joke around. Carla Gladd said he was cute. Roth could see that, but Matt was more her type, even with his dirty white socks and oil-stained work pants he wore in the house. Baines was dapper, and his features were more angular, exuding an easy confidence.

"But I'll tell you this – okay – I know what you *didn't* do. When I said, pick a movie, you didn't – with your eyes closed – envision some vast library of movies, some virtual shelving where you were able to see every title of every movie ever made, and then you truly, freely, arbitrarily chose any one of those. You couldn't see that; you didn't have the information. So your decision was first influenced by the limits of your life experience, the limits of information. You can't pick a movie you'd never heard of, right? After that, your culture, what's been popular lately, what your wife or your husband might have picked. All these elements conspiring to choose a movie *for* you, at the same time you have the sense *you* are the one doing the selecting."

Okay, so he had her there. Matt had chosen the movie they watched.

Baines said, "I'm not making a claim that some laws of the universe are fundamentally different from anything you've been taught to believe. I'm saying, we go around with this story we tell ourselves that we're making everything happen, we're in control. But all evidence is to the contrary." Baines got a certain gleam in his eye. "If I'd asked you to come up with a random city in the world instead of a movie, the same thing applies – influence. It applies to any decision we think we make. Because we are each an open system. We're constantly susceptible to influence. In fact, that's all it is. Track back to your childhood and you'll find a cascade of causation. *This* caused *that* and so on. The story of our lives, of our *selves* – it's shaped from the time we're born. Really, even before that, because our parents were similarly shaped. And we can go back before that, one event causing an –"

She hit pause and sipped her tea. A moment later, she typed in the name of the video posted by Eric Leifson. She'd seen it several times already, but went through it again, watching Baines drag his leg around. This guy poised at the lectern in Australia, two years ago, where he ran thought experiments on free will...then dragging his leg behind him as he rushed toward the exit, as if he thought he was going to single-handedly stop the assailant.

Maybe Sheffield didn't like him talking like this. Didn't like how it made him feel. Trevor (or Travis) could be partly right.

The house creaked a little in the wind, the joists contracting as more cold weather came sweeping in. She heard her daughter mumble something, decided she was talking in her sleep. Roth gripped the warm mug of tea in both hands as her gaze wandered to the calendar on the wall. Christmas was just a few weeks away. It was time to let the prosecutors do their work; she'd be called on to give her deposition and go to the preliminary hearing. Maybe to trial, if the lawyers didn't cut a deal. Her job was to keep finding evidence and feeding it to the DA's office, but they already had more than they needed for a conviction, with or without a confession.

When they arrested Sheffield, the semi-automatic pistol had been right there in the motel room with him, unloaded, cartridges nearby in a box. Everyone knew that ballistics would match the gun to the bullet fragments removed from the walls and chairs and Alex Baines's leg, and that it was part of an orgy of evidence implicating Sheffield, and that he would be going to prison, crazy or not. That was the sense of it.

Satisfied, at least for the time being, she switched to a little Christmas shopping on Amazon and finished her tea. The tea was regrettable, because now she had to pee, and probably would again before morning.

We make choices, she thought at an imaginary Baines. *We make choices and live with the consequences.*

16

Alex's assistant, Drew, showed up in the morning while Corrine was preparing to leave. Alex slept while they stepped out into the hallway.

"Let me walk you down," Drew said. "I'll carry your things."

"It's just this." She lifted her small duffel bag. "I wasn't even thinking when I packed it – forgot my toothbrush, but I brought a bathing suit."

He smiled. "I insist."

She handed the bag over and started toward the elevator. Drew remained by the door, frowning and not understanding, so she turned back. "He has to rest," she explained. "He was up, three or four times in the night – I kept waking up with him. We talked for a while around six, seven – as the sun started to come up. He said he'd dreamed about his mother."

"So you're all set."

"Yeah, I said goodbye to him already."

They moved together down the hall. She raised a hand to a nurse she recognized, and smiled, but didn't feel it. Her thoughts were scattered, everything fuzzy from lack of sleep, that kind of paradoxical heightened-awareness-and-absentmindedness combination. She worried about leaving Alex but was anxious to tend to Freda.

Drew hit the button to summon the elevator and swung the duffel over his shoulder. "He talk about the dream?"

"Just that Muriel was alive. She was sitting in the audience of the theater. He said it made him feel good."

"That's good."

"Then the shooter was there, and it was Howard."

"Oh. Not so good."

The doors opened and they stepped into the car and Drew hit the button for the lobby. She liked Drew – he was smart and soft-spoken. For twenty-eight years old, well-built and handsome, he was disarmingly humble. She and Alex sometimes joked and called him "man-servant" when he wasn't around, but it was clear Alex respected him and trusted him. Drew helped her out, too, keeping her regularly informed of events. Rarely a week passed without emails between them; sometimes they were communicating for days in a row. She'd learned to read him a little bit, and right now, something was on his mind.

"You okay?"

He watched the floor lights as the elevator descended. "Well, first we need to get around the media. Unless you want to –"

"No."

He nodded like he'd expected it. "I talked to the staff. We can go out a side door that's not rigged to an alarm."

She felt a chill at that, and when they landed on the main floor, they moved away from the entrance. Drew led her down a long corridor, through a door marked *Staff Only*, into a large kitchen that smelled like burned eggs. They picked their way around stainless steel prep tables with the kitchen staff giving them looks. It was a bit like being in a spy movie.

A back door opened on an alleyway rank with garbage. They

passed two teeming dumpsters and emerged in one of several parking lots.

"I'm all the way back," she said. "That far lot."

"Yeah." He already knew.

They moved quickly, kicking through slushy snow, breath puffing in small clouds. The fresh air was welcome after the sterile environment of the hospital and she felt a pang of guilt, knowing Alex was still trapped inside. When Drew looked over his shoulder, so did she. So far so good – the hospital was immense, and wherever the press were camped, she couldn't see them, and they couldn't see her.

Her car had a couple inches of snow on it. Drew started to clear it off with his jacket sleeve. "We need to talk," he said.

She was apprehensive. "Okay…something wrong?"

"Let's just get you going here."

She unlocked the doors and started the engine, found the snow brush and helped him with the rest of it. She shivered in the cold. "How about we get in while it warms up."

"Yeah."

She slid behind the wheel, Drew in the passenger seat, filling the small space with more vapors of their breathing. Drew stared out the windshield, avoiding eye contact, which wasn't like him.

"You're freaking me out a little bit," she said.

"Sorry." He blew on his hands, reddened from handling the snow. "I just – I don't know if this is my place. I work for Mr. Baines. I mean, I work for you, too."

She put her hand on his arm, trying to soothe her own nerves as much as encourage him. "Whatever you – you know – whatever it is…"

"But this is, ah – I know this is a new thing for everybody. We've had it pretty good. No major upsets."

She nodded, only half understanding him, and shivered again.

She went to dial up the heat, but the vents were already at full blast.

He noticed. "I should have started your car for you earlier. Sorry."

"Ah, come on. I'm not royalty; I'm just a girl from Mt. Vernon. And you've been with us for a while."

"Not as long as Chet."

She sighed, crossed her arms and glanced out the window. "Yeah, Chet…"

"Chet and I talked."

"Okay – about?"

"Well, I mean – you know there's this thing with the video. And people are…I mean, it's already crazy. Have you been online at all?"

"I've been mostly avoiding it. Alex, too."

"That video has half a million hits. A few hundred comments. And there are papers interested. Chet's lining all of that up. Some are so anxious they're coming today.…Has anyone called you?"

"The phone was ringing all night. I left it on because of the kids, in case my sister called. But we let everything else go to voicemail."

"Good." He nodded. "I'll go through all of that. I'll deal with it."

She steeled herself. "Have there been threats?"

"Not overtly."

"What exactly does that mean?"

"You know, there's what you'd expect – more traffic than usual, emails – mostly supportive, I mean, ninety-eight percent, most of the comments, too, but then you have these outliers, people saying things like, 'This is what you get.' We had one that said 'Sheffield should have finished the job.' I gave that one to the police."

Sensing he was finished, she asked, "Do you know anyone with a 949 number?"

His brow dimpled in thought. "I don't think so. Shit, that sounds like California. I'll check. Might even be movie stuff. But it's a bit soon for that."

"I just heard breathing."

"Like, heavy breathing? Then that's definitely Hollywood."

She flashed him a smile, feeling the tension break.

"I will," he said, serious. "I'll look into it." He paused. "Did Angie call you?"

"She did, actually. Well, she called Alex's phone, but I talked to her. Why?"

"I'm sure it's fine. I talked to her too. I think there's…well, they want to adjust expectations for his latest book. But it's like, how do you frame that? You know? 'Hey, um, how long are you going to need to recover from this gunshot wound?'"

She chuckled without feeling the humor. "Yeah. Angie seemed a little…tentative." She faced him. "Was that it? You wanted to tell me the publisher's worried he won't complete a book on schedule?"

"No. That's not it."

A pause. "Well, here we are. Out with it, young man."

He pulled a tight breath. "Okay, so with all this stuff happening – so here it is – Howard wants to put a security detail with you. You and the kids."

"He – what?"

Drew slowly nodded. "Yeah, it's um – well you know how Howard is. He's got people, friends who do that sort of thing, work private security, ex-military guys. He said it was a phone call and done."

"He said this to who – you? To do what? Be our bodyguards?"

"Right. Sort of like that."

"Did he talk to Alex about it? What did Alex say? He didn't

mention anything to me..." She thought back to their conversation about heightened security at any future speaking engagements. Alex had been bothered by that, and now maybe she understood why. It was uncomfortable on multiple levels to think you needed people keeping you safe from gunfire. She didn't think she could get used to it.

"Howard didn't talk to Alex," Drew said. "He talked to Chet."

She let it sink in a minute, trying to pick out the most obvious reason: because they thought this shooter was connected to other people? Or because they worried all the praise for Alex's so-called heroics would set off more violence?

But before she could respond, Drew said, "I talked to Chet about it. I thought maybe we would discuss it with Alex, too, this morning, but like you said – he needs rest. We're all in agreement there."

"What did Chet say to you?"

"Well, I told him I didn't think Alex would like it, Howard getting involved..."

She shook her head. "He would absolutely not like it. And for that matter, I'm not sure I like it." Picturing men in black SUVs with earpieces following her everywhere, it felt scarier than being on her own. It also made her defensive. "I mean, everybody gets together, thinks I can't be alone for a week?"

"Chet said maybe I should go."

She leaned back in the seat, calming. "You?"

"Mostly to help out. Look, no one thinks you're in real danger. I think it's Chet, talking to Howard, getting him paranoid, and then it's Howard needing to control things for his own peace of mind."

"That's exactly what it is. You hit it."

Drew lowered his head, seeming at a loss for words, or embarrassed by her praise.

She shook her head. "They talked for twenty minutes last

night, Alex and Howard. And the whole time, Howard never...? Ah, these men. Did you bring this up with Howard? You coming instead?"

"I did. He thought me going wasn't as ideal, of course, but I kind of know you guys, know the kids."

She said, "Good. At least if you come with me, then maybe Howard stays off Alex's back. It's the last thing Alex needs."

"So you definitely don't want Howard's security guys?"

"No. I don't want Howard Baines's ex-military security guys following me around, sitting outside the house. Unless there's some other concern that..."

"There isn't."

They both faced forward, neither speaking for a while.

"I got here in a rental, but I'm good to drive it down," he said. "Or they can pick it up and we can go together. If you want the company. My bag is in the rental. I didn't want to presume anything."

The car had warmed up and the windows were clear. She carefully reversed out of the spot. Drew told her where he'd parked his rental and they cruised the vast hospital parking lots in silence.

She tried to find the normalcy: Howard was being a protective father; like she said, he wanted peace of mind. That's what happened when there was a tragedy or a crisis. People banded together; friends and family stepped in to help out.

But it highlighted the distance between her and Alex, which was a shame, since she had just started to feel close with him again. He'd already been away from home so much – on the road or doing his research at the lab. Now people were making decisions for him while he recovered from major surgery, from a terrible trauma. People were deciding what he represented, who he was, what this all meant. And none of it, really, had to do with her marriage to him, or their family. Instead, it was like some great big vacuum of media and public opinion, ready to pull them into oblivion.

"Grab your bag," she said to Drew once they'd arrived at his rental car. She finally met his gaze again. "Might as well keep each other entertained through this thing."

He seemed relieved, smiled and got out. But she was left wondering what he hadn't told her. Because it had been right there in his eyes. Just like with Alex.

17

From her desk, Roth called the Portland Police Department in Maine and asked to speak to an investigator.

A moment later: "This is Detective John Libby."

"Detective Libby, this is Raquel Roth, investigator with New York State BCI."

"How you doing?"

"Good. So we've had a shooting up here in Lake Placid. Suspect is Gary Sheffield, lives in your city."

"Oh no, not *my* city," Libby joked. He spoke in a Maine accent, the kind that elongated vowels. He probably dropped his R's, too. She thought they called the accent "downeast."

She said, "Yeah – Sheffield is in custody at Essex County Jail. He's been assigned a public defender and things are moving quickly."

"He taking a deal?"

"It doesn't look that way. This is a funny one – he didn't do anything right. We've got a weapon in his name, credit card purchases, you name it. But I want to be thorough and search his residence. I was hoping I could send everything over to you before the DA makes a disposition."

"I can do that. Hang on, let me get a pen."

Roth felt relieved. Usually cops in different jurisdictions worked well together, but there was always the chance of friction. Libby would get everything to the judge, who'd issue a warrant, then they could have a look at Sheffield's house, poke around on his computer.

"Okay," Libby said. "Just making a note to myself. You said this guy is named Shepherd?" *Shep-ahd,* he pronounced it.

"Sheffield." She spelled it.

"You got anything in particular you're looking for?"

"We want to make sure he's alone, for one thing, no co-conspirators. We get something from his house or his computer that jumps out, we pick them up on a warrant. If they're in Maine, the judge will hold the extradition hearing to see if he or she should be brought back to New York. Local court can handle the big stuff."

"Sure. They do it all the time. Okay – you want to be part of the search?"

"I'm not sure I can make it down there in time, but I will if I can. If it's not a problem."

"Not at all. Always good to have the investigating officer on hand. You reach out to the feds on this?"

"They're monitoring. But Sheffield was caught in six hours. Didn't try to run or hide, stayed at a local motel. I was a little worried something might jump off, you know, escalate, but he came right in, didn't seem bothered by any of it."

"Sounds like a sociopath."

"I'm hoping for any background on him. Neighbors, family, whatever you can find. I'm going to talk to UPS myself – his employer."

Libby didn't say anything for a moment. Roth wondered if she'd lost connection. "Hello?"

"Yeah, sorry – just had someone looking over my shoulder –

this is the Alex Baines thing? Another officer here just pointed it out to me – he's the atheist meditation guy or something?"

"That's the one."

Libby seemed excited. "Wow, yeah, okay. Pretty high-profile. I saw him on Facebook once. It was like a greatest hits of his – like – his religious takedowns. My kid posted it."

Roth didn't have any comment. "Thanks, Libby."

"No problem. Wow. Okay, yeah, I'll be in touch."

She hung up, musing how people changed when any sort of celebrity was involved. She wondered why that was.

Half a minute later, her desk phone rang again. The DA's office. Shit, they were moving fast.

"Investigator Roth?"

"Yes."

"I'm here with your supervisor, Investigator Banger. We have – ah – well, we have a situation."

"Everything okay?"

"I don't know. Sheffield is talking."

18

This would be the height of his power, so Chet said.

Maybe he was right. Two hours after Corrine left, a journalist from *The New York Times* sat in the room, going over Alex's story. *VICE News* arrived ten minutes after the *Times* left. The YouTube video was up to a million hits. According to Chet, Drew had intercepted several hundred emails since the shooting. Twitter and Facebook were blowing up, and Alex's phone rang nonstop, Chet now handling the calls.

Then there was Amy Cross. She came to Alex's room just before noon, looking like a Number One Fan about to meet her music idol. She was pretty in designer jeans and a puffy coat with a fur-lined hood, which she removed and set down on a chair while her eyes darted to him, shy, star-struck. The flesh-toned V-neck under her coat was, Alex intuited, her best sweater. Her blonde hair was pulled back in a ponytail, her blue eyes shone, and she wore understated makeup. He consider all of this because of the camera crew that followed her in; Chet had made a call to New York, and a buddy at CNN had sent up a producer and cameraman and sound guy. They crowded around in the corner of the room while Cross made her way to his bedside.

"Hi," she said.

"Hi." Alex smiled at her then glanced at Chet, grinning behind the CNN crew, eyebrows up on his forehead, like an expectant parent at the ballet recital, hoping all goes well. Then Alex tuned it all out, focused on Cross. "How you doing?"

Their eyes stayed connected, then she looked him over and her brow dented with concern. "I'm good. Because of you."

"Why don't you have a seat?"

"Okay." She pulled a chair closer to the bed and sat down, putting them at eye level. He could see she was trembling a little, loose strands of hair jittering. "What about you?" she asked. "You look like you're coming along."

"I'm okay. This is giving me a chance to catch up on Netflix." It was a similar line to one he'd used on Corrine, but it worked; she smiled.

Then the smile faded and the emotion took shape, eyes filling with tears. "You really might have saved my life, you know. I'm sure of it, really."

"I wasn't even thinking. I saw you, and…"

The blank eye of the camera loomed close. The room held its breath.

She saved him from having to say more. "That's just it. That's what happens. You just don't think. You do what's right, what's in your heart to do."

"Like anyone would."

A tear formed and rolled down her cheek. She brushed it away with a knuckle. Then she took his hand. Her grip was warm and a little sweaty, flesh faintly quivering. He could smell her, a light and subtle scent like jasmine. "I don't know that anyone would have," she said, eyes shining. "I think who you are – what you do….Not everyone would have done that." She lowered her gaze and shook her head. "No. It's very special what you did, and I want you to know how grateful I am."

Alex almost glanced at Chet again – but he didn't need to see Chet to know he looked like a kid at Christmas. Instead, he stayed in the moment. "I'm grateful to you, too. You helped me out of there. Downstairs, backstage."

Her eyes came up, and she said, "You rushed over to me when I stupidly stepped out like that. I was so confused – I thought there was something happening out there, like pipes exploding. I never thought about a shooter. But you saw me and you came running over, and because of what you did…" Another tear fell and she pursed her lips; her mouth was shaking. "He was aiming at me; I saw him. He was going to shoot me. And I saw the white flash. But you were right there, and you got me out of the way, and you took the…you took the…"

Tears running freely now, she couldn't finish.

"It could have been worse," Alex said. "No one was killed. We were lucky."

She nodded slowly at first, then with more force. "We were very lucky. *I* was very lucky. Lucky that it was you and not someone else."

Getting uncomfortable with the praise, he patted her hand and changed the subject. "So do you live over there in Lake Placid? How did you end up working for that theater?"

She told him her story and they talked for another ten minutes. She was local to that region, from Saranac Lake, and had done some college, returned home when her father became sick with gallstones, then never left. She acted in some of the Arts Center shows, worked lighting a bit, and functioned as a stagehand for other productions. Meditation was an important part of her life, she said, even though, truth be told, sometimes she felt like she was crawling out of her skin with boredom.

At least it made him laugh. And he told her a joke: "What did the Hallmark card say that one Buddhist monk gave to another?"

She lit up. "I don't know. What?"

"'Not thinking of you.'"

When it was over, Chet went out with the CNN crew, giving Alex a thumbs-up before closing the door. Alex put his head back and closed his eyes, thinking that he'd never minded the spotlight before – at least, he'd built up a tolerance for it over the years – but he was going to press Pause for now, tell Chet to back off.

Five minutes later, Chet re-entered the room. He was talking on the phone, pacing, his back straight, like he got when he was onto something big.

"Uh-huh," he said, eyeing Alex. "Absolutely. No, I understand. Yes, he's right here." He looked away from Alex and walked to the window. "Okay. We'll get right back with you." Then he hung up and said, "You are never going to believe what that was just about."

Alex waited.

"You are never," Chet repeated slowly, turning, "never, never…"

"Come on –"

"…Never going to believe." Chet rubbed his chest like he was making sure it was still there, or afraid of a heart attack. "Apparently, our guy – the shooter, Sheffield – he had his lawyer reach out to the district attorney over there. They've been going back and forth on it for a little bit I guess, but they decided to play it forward."

"Chet, please just tell me what you're talking about."

"He wants to meet with you."

"He wants to what?"

Chet paced again. "Yeah – Sheffield wants to sit down with you, face to face."

"Why?" Alex blinked a few times, emotions jumbled. Confusion, skepticism, fear. "No district attorney is going to facilitate something like that without a very good reason."

"Sheffield says he has information."

"About what?"

"About other crimes."

Chet stopped walking, a pause for effect, letting it sink in – women murdered in dark alleys, dead bodies stowed in crawl spaces.

"*His* other crimes?" A man who'd shot up a public venue could easily have committed other heinous acts, maybe as a run-up to the big one that'd just landed him in jail. Then again, Sheffield could know criminals. Fellow travelers he'd met in dark corners of the internet, who'd confessed – or bragged – to him.

"He hasn't said what," Chet explained. "That's the whole thing – he's only willing to talk to you about them. You, and only you. We're guessing he's killed people, but we don't know. The cop, Banger, he's going to call you in a minute. But, Alex, what do you think, man?"

The pressure was intense and sudden. He picked out one piece of the bomb Chet had just set off in the room. "You said 'we.' 'We're guessing he killed people.'"

Chet shook the phone. "That was a cop I spoke to, one of the arresting investigators. His name is Harlan Banger. Sounds like a bad porn name. Anyway, he's going to call back, talk to you – see what you want to do. The DA is kinda concerned with PR. I get that. You know how politicians are; she's worried about the optics. But imagine if she said no to this, and it turns out someone is locked away in a basement somewhere? Right?"

"Is there any evidence of anything?"

"They've had local Portland police go to the house – they're in the process of searching it now, logging everything in or whatever they do, and checking deep into his life. Banger didn't mention anything standing out. Just that Sheffield lives alone, like a recluse. The DA is willing to come here and talk to you about it, if there's any chance you'll go for it..." His eyes got wide at the thought. "I mean, Alex. Holy shit, man. If you end up finding out that he's got bodies stashed? I mean, this guy sounds like a real – what're you doing?"

The room felt too small, the bed too constrictive. Alex started to get up, using his elbows and grunting with the effort. Once seated, he picked up his leg and swung it over the edge of the bed.

Chet stared at it. "Hey, man. Take it easy. I didn't mean 'Get out of bed.'"

Alex got to his feet, hopped there for a second and pointed. "Can you hand me those?"

Chet retrieved the crutches from the corner by the window. "I don't know, man. Maybe this isn't such a good idea. The whole thing. Look at you. You know how I can get worked up. Maybe this is no good, bro – when they call back, we'll just say no way."

"Oh, please."

"Or we can do it over the phone or something. Do it by Face-Time. You're supposed to be here, like, five more days. They said this could happen in as little as two or three."

Alex seated the crutches under his armpits and risked a step. First time on crutches since a football accident in the sixth grade. He'd only had one PT session so far, but he felt strong. Standing, the sense of pressure seemed to slip away. It had been a lack of control, he realized. Now he was back in charge.

"Two days?" he asked Chet.

"They've got this guy at some county lock-up over there. He's been arraigned, but he's there until he's sentenced. He's got a public defender, and the public defender says Sheffield either wants to do it right away or not at all. But two days, three at the most, is what they said it would take...well, depending on *you*, in part. Getting the DA over here, and those cops to talk to you about it."

The phone rang – some hip-hop song Chet liked. "This is them. Shit, this is them, calling back. You want to sit down?"

Alex, balancing on the crutches, held out his hand. "Give it to me."

19

C orrine stopped at a rest area off the interstate. Drew pumped gas while she went inside and bought some over-priced sandwiches. They were only an hour from Croton, but she didn't want to arrive on an empty stomach. Mara would want to talk and get details, and the kids would be pawing at her...if she didn't eat, she'd start to get that low-blood-sugar thing, woozy on her feet, irritable. She dropped the food and drinks in the back of her car and said to Drew, "Go ahead and drive, if you want."

"Sure. Okay."

Once they were on their way, she picked up on his vibe. It was that same sense she'd got back in the parking lot – he'd disclosed the thing about Howard wanting to hire security, but she'd suspected more Drew wasn't saying. Something about Alex.

Or maybe she was just paranoid now and would be unable to ever let down her guard again.

"Drew? You okay?"

"Yeah. Good."

"If there's something else you want to tell me..."

"Well, yeah, I...shit." Drew squirmed like he couldn't get the words out.

"We're friends, Drew."

"I just don't know if it's my place to say anything."

Her heart rate started to pick up as she waited for it – the reve-lation she'd been expecting: Alex was having an affair, after all. It was in the way he sometimes looked at the undergrads who thought he was a modern Aristotle; the fans at book signings, blushing as he scribbled his name and smiled up at them. He was on the road or away from home twenty-five, thirty weeks of the year. All that time alone in nice hotels. Big, soft beds...

"Drew, we already went through this," she said. "You work for us, but you're also a friend. I trust your judgment." *Please just tell me. I can't handle any more.*

He took a deep breath, glanced at her, and then watched the road. Finally, he said, "Alex has been microdosing."

She blinked at him. For a moment, her emotions seem to hang suspended, as if waiting for her to pick which one. "Sorry – 'microdosing'? You mean – are you saying Alex has been *drop-ping acid*?"

Drew kept his hands at ten and two on the wheel, a boy scout. "Okay, well, it's not 'dropping acid.' It's LSD and it's psilocybin, but –"

She couldn't help it. The worry, the tension, the fear of losing him, the kids, the sense that Alex had been hiding something – it all had to go somewhere, and it came out in a geyser of laughter, involuntary and from the gut.

Through her bout, Drew kept a straight face, and each time she glanced at him, she laughed harder.

He finally cracked a smile. "Mrs. Baines..."

The formality made her laugh some more. It finally tapered off and she had to wipe her eyes. "Alex has been *tripping?*"

"No, see, no – it's not like that at all. These are micro-doses. They're sub-perceptive. It's like one percent of a full dose – you don't even consciously realize it."

Still finding the humor, she fixed him with her best stern look and pointed her finger. "Young man, are *you* tripping, too?"

"No. I'm not doing it. And…" he laughed, just once, but it was a sympathetic gesture. "And Mrs. Baines, it's really not tripping. This is science-based –"

Her mood shifted abruptly. "Ah, 'science-based.' You all say that like it's some kind of get-out-of-jail-free card. Shooting at people is 'science-based,' too. I know what microdosing is. I know it's controversial, and it's illegal."

"These guys in Silicon Valley, they've been doing it for years. This is phase three of –"

"Silicon Valley? Is that a 949 area code?"

"I don't think so. No. That's 650. Or 415." He paused to think. "You know, 949 could be Irvine. Irvine, California. Because that's where –"

"Wait – was this some microdosing *pusher* who called Alex last night?"

Drew's affable demeanor finally gave in to a little agitation. "No. That's not who it was, I'm sure. It doesn't work like that. It's all set up. There's a regimen. It's part of a study."

"Is there a doctor overseeing it?"

"There are several professionals involved."

"Abendroth?"

He nodded. Reluctantly, it seemed. "That's one."

"How about you? Have you been helping Alex with this?"

"Yes. I help him. I help him keep track. But there are people who – look, this is all part of a study. A legit study. But it's totally confidential. And, yeah, this stuff is controversial. So when it comes out –"

"It's – wait – why is it going to come out?"

"Because it might show up in the blood work. Well, it *definitely* will show up in the blood work."

"At the hospital? Doctors have to keep his records confidential."

"Right. But it's a gunshot wound. Everything is part of the investigation. The police will find out. If not from the hospital, it could turn up in the forensics from the scene. Alex was bleeding everywhere. They send all that to a lab, see whose blood is whose. It's procedure."

"Ah, my God…"

He held up one hand, a pacifying gesture. "Mrs. Baines, I just thought you'd want to know. This isn't me being worried about Alex from a legal standpoint. Or from a health standpoint…"

"How does it affect him?" She thought of Alex doing everything he did, from brandishing chairs to ramming into doors, seeming almost invincible. Chet had said, *adrenaline.* "Is that why he acted like that, during the shooting? Almost fearless?"

Drew hesitated. "I don't think so. No."

"Then what?"

Drew paused, derailed. New emotions lit his eyes. "That's just it. This has been really effective for Alex. I mean, he's on top of his game. He's always been on top of his game, but this is a whole new level. You know about the new book he's writing? *Flow State?*"

"I don't know about his book," she said, feeling sour. "We don't talk about things like that anymore. We talk schedules and kids, if we talk at all." The anger was back, just below the surface, pushing upward. The idea of him on some drug – it carried the strange weight of finding out he had a mistress anyway. "Alex may be at the top of his game professionally," she said, "but it hasn't been exactly a wonderful trip on the home front. Okay?"

She stopped herself from unloading. But if she had to pinpoint where it had started, it was just after his mother's death. After she'd battled it out with cancer for several years, Muriel had succumbed, and Alex poured himself deeper into work. He'd missed school plays, dance recitals, sports games. Chet kept him running all over the globe, and when he wasn't on the road, he was holed up in the lab.

Or out in California. At Irvine. The university there.

She breathed. She gave herself a moment to assess, to sort through the feelings.

"I guess since it's a study, he had to keep it quiet. Keep the results pure or something," she said.

"Exactly," Drew began, "and I'm not just defending him, I promise – but I think he planned to tell you, and then things just got going, and then all of this happened." Suddenly Drew's eyes widened and he snapped his fingers. "You know who the 949 caller might've been – that could be the private investigator Chet hired. Do you have the number?"

"He called Alex's phone."

"I'll check it."

"Why would he be calling?"

"When he heard your voice...you've never met this guy, right?"

"No, never."

"Well, maybe this guy just hung up because he doesn't want you to know who he is or something."

"That would be weird."

They fell silent. Drew turned on the wipers to sluice away a mix of rain and snow.

"Thank you for telling me this."

He stayed quiet.

"Do you think this is going to be a problem?"

"It could be. If it comes out – *when* it comes out – there's likely to be some blowback."

"Why?"

"Well, one thing, some people might use it to discredit his

work. 'Here's a guy on drugs,' they'll say – tripping, like you said – and he's been involved in some high-profile work…"

It leapt to mind before Drew said it. "The sexual assault case."

"Like that, yeah. And then there's a general kind of…some of Alex's followers are real purists. Meditation as the way to change their life, to control breathing and heart rate and have optimal cognitive health. But then it turns out he's, you know…*enhancing*."

"It sounds like you're worried about how this will affect his public image," she said. "You and Chet – it seems to be all that you're…" She shook it off, not wanting to offend Drew, and also knowing it wasn't true. The world could be unforgiving. Banishment and boycott were often preferred over understanding and forgiveness when it came to private matters made public. Sometimes with good cause. Other times…maybe overreaction. Scapegoating.

"That's why I asked about Angie," Drew said. "Wondering what she said to you. Because if there's a scandal, publishers can be skittish. Especially these days, you don't want to be on the wrong side of a cultural issue."

"Angie would find him something else, if it came to that. Another place for the book to go."

"Yeah, she's good. She's good. But it's…I don't know. We'll have to see."

Corrine watched the onrushing road, the daylight already dimming, as she outgrew her initial sense of betrayal. Now she felt defensive, protective of her husband. "People appreciate Alex for researching the brain. Maybe they'll see this as part of that."

Drew nodded eagerly. "Sure, that could be. And you have the whole progressive crowd, people that think LSD should be legal and regulated, things like that. Sooner or later, this sort of mental enhancement, you know – we can't keep that in the closet forever. We're mentally enhancing ourselves all the time – our smartphones, the internet, GPS. I mean, they're using psilocybin on end-stage cancer patients to treat fear of death. Ayahuasca for addiction and depression. This is the next wave of psychopharmacology."

She almost told him about her dream – almost blurted it, really – because somehow it seemed absurdly relevant. Instead, she said, "But you still think this could hurt him. Is he up front about it in the book? The *Flow State* book? Is it part of it?"

"I don't know. That's the thing. I don't think so – I think *Flow State* is about natural things, creative states. Optimizing your workday. Deep focus. Things like that."

A moment later, he waved a hand in the air, as if waving away all the philosophizing, and sat back again. "I just wanted you to know, so you didn't find out some other way."

"Thank you," Corrine said. Emotions kept rising to the surface, but she tried to let it all go – nothing she could do about it. Not now, anyway. What was going to come out was going to come out. She needed to stay focused on her family, on what was right in front of her.

Drew drove them along, south toward Croton, wipers sluicing the wet snow.

She needed to focus on the kids, she decided. On stability. On keeping their lives from totally melting down.

That was enough.

20

L ayla blew out a cloud of vapor. Kenneth tried to watch the
kids out on the skating rink, but it was hard not to stare at
his cousin. Her hair was crazy – that was one thing – the kind you
saw in Manga, cut real sharp and angled to her chin. He didn't
know if she dyed it black or that's how it naturally was. And she
had boobs, pretty big ones; you could tell even with her teal
winter coat on. When he caught himself checking them out, he
quickly turned away and watched the rink some more. Really, it
was an oval, a running track that the town of Croton flooded in
the winter for public skating. Some jangly Christmas song was
crackling with distortion as it blared from a speaker attached to
the warming hut.

Layla jiggled the vape stick in front of him. "You ever try it?"

He glanced at the thing, sleek and black. "No."

"Good, don't." She blew out another cloud that took time to
disperse in the cold, humid air.

"Are we gonna, um…?"

"Yeah, we'll get back out there. Just gimme a minute. If they
see me with this out there, I'll get a lecture." She was quiet,
watching the oval. "These kids don't know how to skate. My

mom started me when I was four. You gotta start young or you just never get it. Not that I'm any good. Ice skating – I mean, figure skating – that's like the hardest sport, ever."

His toes were starting to sting. Standing on the skates was awkward. But Layla was captivating. She seemed older than seventeen, like a full-on grown-up. She said, "My mom started me because Gramma started *her* when she was little. Your mom, too. Did you know that?"

"That mom figure-skated?"

"Yeah."

"Yeah – there's pictures and stuff. But didn't Aunt Mara – didn't your mom…"

"She got sick, yeah. It took her out of skating for months. And that was pretty much it." Layla changed the subject abruptly. "I like your dad. It's crazy what happened."

"Yeah."

"My dad is a dick. Well, he's my stepdad, so I call him Stephen. He cheated on my mom. Did you know that?"

"No."

This time, when she looked at him, she seemed to look *into* him. He felt his face flush. Her eyes acquired a devious look. "Do you know what cheating is?"

"Yeah. Course I do."

"Yeah – you're smart. You're smart for twelve. Or are you thirteen?"

"Twelve. My birthday is next August."

"August, huh?" She took another puff. "You remember when we stayed with you?"

"Yeah. Kinda."

"You were younger then. But that was why. Mom was sorting it out. That's why I lost my shit after that, I think. She took him back, and I was just like…*fuuuuck* this."

"Where's your – uh – real dad?"

"California." She didn't elaborate. "I met a guy at rehab named Noel. Did I ever tell you this?"

Kenneth shook his head. He knew things about Layla, but bits and pieces. She'd done some drugs, got caught, tried to kill herself, and then her parents put her somewhere to get better. Once there, she'd made two attempts to run away. Then, finally, she seemed to submit.

"Noel was cool," she said. "I ended up telling him, you know, what happened between my parents. What Stephen did. And I told Noel what had happened with my first boyfriend – I won't even say his name, because fuck him. And Noel set me straight, man. He told me that people who make a big show and act tough don't have any real power. People with real power are always invisible. Because if you have *real* power, you don't draw attention. Which means you and I never really know who those people are."

Kenneth nodded, because he didn't know what she was talking about. Maybe a little. But he wanted to get going, get skating again, at least, so he could warm up. Mostly, he wanted to be home. Was his dad a dick, too? His parents had their issues. His dad was gone a lot, but he wasn't a dick. He told corny meditation jokes, but Kenneth loved him.

Kenneth was relieved when Layla put the vape stick in her pocket. She started walking on her skates back toward the oval. "I mean, my mom's got her shit together. You mind if I swear?"

"No."

"They say it's better to swear and release tension. Yeah, my mom is cool. I get that now. She made a decision to forgive Stephen. He's like a project for her. Like a big art project. And he's coming along, I guess. He found Jesus and everything."

Layla stepped out onto the ice and gracefully spun around so she was sliding backwards, watching him. He took a tentative step, testing himself, then another. He pushed with his left foot and skated.

Layla smiled. "You're doing great." Someone passed between them, and she frowned. "Not like these yokels." She laughed after that, showing straight white teeth.

They went around the oval, Layla circling him like a protector as he jerked his way along. He thought about his father, shot in the leg. You thought about getting shot in the leg as lucky, but it could be bad, affecting the way you walk for the rest of your life. And then there was all the stuff people were saying. He'd been sneaking looks at the internet when Aunt Mara wasn't watching – she had this big anti-screen policy going on, said it robbed young minds of their potential – but he'd seen a few tweets. Things about how people at that Arts Center should be grateful it wasn't worse, because that was what happened when you went against God.

The music got louder as they passed the warming hut – *White Christmas*, sung by one of those old-time crooner guys. He grew more confident, got a better rhythm going, Layla cheering him on. "Yeah, man! Yeah, Kenny-baby! You go, boy."

She drifted ahead, spinning in circles, floating her arms like a dancer. Colored lights hung along the edge of the ice, a few fat snowflakes twirled down from the dusky sky. Kenneth watched Layla. He'd always thought she had a good life. Her mother was an artist; her stepfather made lots of money. Their house was old – Layla said it was a 1900s antique farmhouse. A rocking chair sat on the front porch. But you never knew what was going on inside a place, he figured. People liked to make things look a certain way. Like Layla had just said.

He pushed off with his skates to catch up to his cousin, resolving never to be that way.

21

The district attorney for Essex County was Louise Cantrell. In her fifties, round-faced with voluminous brown hair highlighted blonde. She wore a black blazer, a powder-blue, low-cut blouse, and a silver beaded necklace. When she smiled, she looked like a politician, but when she was quietly listening, she had the intensity of a seasoned prosecutor. Alex had asked that they meet in the hospital waiting area, which was a massive clerestory room with several couches, potted ferns, and thick-padded chairs. They made introductions and sat – Louise Cantrell plus Harlan Banger, the senior investigator – and discussed Alex's health and recovery progress. Then they moved on to the situation at hand.

"We aren't taking anything for granted," Cantrell said, glancing at his crutches. "You're a victim here, and this is highly unusual."

"He must have said something compelling," Alex said.

She looked at Banger, a lanky man dressed in an oversized gray suit, crooked tie striped green and gold. Banger said, "At first I thought – this guy – he had that look. The Colorado shooter, the Baptist Church shooter – blank eyes, kind of vapid. We tried to interview him. Made him comfortable, you know, got him a cup of coffee. He didn't say a word. So we talked to the judge, went through the arraignment, and Sheffield was assigned a public defender."

Cantrell broke in. "As soon as he met with his lawyer, he told her he wanted to talk. But only to you. So she came to me with that, I spoke with Investigator Banger and Roth – you met Roth, briefly – to get their sense of it. We each felt this could be something. The suspect has this...well, let's just say he's not like anything I've seen."

"Guys like this," Banger said, picking up the thread, "if they've got some mission, some big purpose, lot of 'em can't wait to tell you about it. This guy seems driven, but he's not saying about what. Roth was the one who really thought he was working something up. That he wasn't finished."

Alex gave Chet a quick look – Chet was doing a good job of keeping quiet, kind of the way you kept quiet around the real estate agent when you loved the house – and said, "So you think this is about past crimes? Or something he's planning?"

Banger sat back and exchanged looks with Cantrell. Then he leaned forward again, putting his hands between his knees. "I don't know. But this guy – like I said, he looked vapid, out there, but that was just at first. Now he looks like the cat that swallowed the canary to me. He's got something he wants to spill."

"Could it be he just wants to spill to me what you're talking about? His motivation, his belief, whatever's driving him?"

"Maybe. But I think there's more."

"Otherwise, we wouldn't be entertaining this," the DA said.

Alex said, without looking at Chet, "If we do this, I'd like to keep it quiet."

Cantrell and Banger shared another look. "We feel the same way," Cantrell said. "Best to get you over there with as little fanfare as possible. Make it as comfortable and easy for you as we can. You meet with him once, that's it. And of course, it would be at the jail. Everything supervised and by the book."

They talked a little more, and Alex's leg started to hurt. He tried to hide the pain, wasn't sure why, but waited until the two of them walked away before he asked Chet to get him a wheelchair – he couldn't manage the crutches right now. Everything buzzing in his head, and the urge to rest, to sleep, was taking over.

But he had to call Corrine first.

———————

She picked up the call from Mara's front porch, wearing one of her sister's thick winter parkas and sneaking a cigarette. As soon as she saw the incoming number was Alex, she rolled the ember out of the cigarette, hid the filter under her chair, and answered.

"Honey? I was just going to call you."

"You at Mara's?"

"She insisted we stay for dinner. Stephen is still in the city, and honestly, I think she's just happy to have the company."

"She wants to be there for you."

"I know. Yeah, I know." Corrine gazed over the front yard; the box elders and line of juniper blocking the road just visible in the porch lighting. Compared to suburban Scarsdale, Croton was the countryside. "How are you feeling? You sound tired. Is Chet letting you sleep? How many people did you have to deal with today?"

"Yeah, I'm tired. A lot of people. But, ah…"

Sensing something – like maybe he was going to talk to her about the microdosing – she stood up. "What?"

He told her that Sheffield wanted to meet with him. In the midst of it, she stepped off the porch, walked across the snow-crusted yard. Her first instinct was to not believe it. "Don't the lawyers have to meet and make a deal? Doesn't he have to be arraigned first?"

"They did, and he was. All arraignments are local in New York, so it was pretty quick. His public defender made the formal request on his behalf. They're all taking it seriously. But, Cory, listen, no one can know right now. Not Mara, not even the kids."

"So you've already agreed to it?"

"No. I called you so we can decide together. You tell me not to do this, and I'll walk away."

She hesitated. "The police are sure this is legitimate?"

"Well, they can't know for sure. But people could be at risk."

"And a phone call won't do? You're not even supposed to be released from the hospital until the end of the week. God, Alex…"

"He was very explicit. Wants to meet me in person. That's the only way."

"And what do you think?"

"I feel like I have to do it. Like it's the right thing."

"You'd have to face this guy –"

"I know."

"– this guy who tried to kill you. This guy who *tried to kill you* –"

"I know."

She stood in the yard with her breath rising into the air, looked back at the house and saw Mara in the window. Mara moved out of sight. "Why does it have to be kept quiet?"

"Everyone wants to avoid a media circus."

"Except Chet. Is he there? Are you in your room?"

"He's gone off to dinner with the CNN crew."

"The CNN crew?"

Alex explained about Amy Cross coming, that he hadn't known about it; Chet had set it up. Corrine let that go for now.

"You think maybe they want to keep it quiet because they think it's bullshit? And they just don't want it to be public bullshit?"

"They're taping it, actually. Everyone wants transparency, including Sheffield."

"What's going to happen to the footage?"

"Nothing. The DA keeps it."

Corrine let out a long breath and walked through the snow some more, toward the driveway and the road beyond. Bring up the microdosing? Not now. But this was...God, what was this? Her husband meeting with the man who'd shot up his talk? Who'd almost killed a security guard; who'd put a bullet in Alex's leg? It was frightening. "What do they think he wants to talk about? Are there any missing persons cases right now?"

"There are some that this could relate to, yeah. Maybe."

"Unsolved murders?"

"There's always unsolved murders." Alex sounded exhausted, far away. "Listen, honey, let's think about it. They wouldn't take me until tomorrow. We can sleep on it."

She got to the road and, not paying attention, startled when a car rushed past, headlights stabbing the dark. She turned, feeling cold, heart thumping like it had the other night, awakening from her dream. The questions bullied her: Did this have something to do with Alex defending the sexual assault victim? Some sort of crazy payback? What about the strange phone calls from California? Irvine, that's where the study was which had Alex taking tiny amounts of these drugs. Or was all of that speculation wildly paranoid, and this shooter, like probably every other crazed gunman, just wanted attention?

"Sleep on it," she said. "How do you sleep on something like this?"

"I know. Listen. How's Freda?"

"I'm taking her tomorrow to see Dr. Sunjay. But she's okay. I think she's got it, strep. But we'll see."

"And Kenneth?"

"Fine. Went figure skating with Layla today. He misses you."

"Chet said Drew went with you. He told me about Howard."

They talked about that, too. When the cold was really sinking into her bones, and Alex sounded like he was struggling just to form sentences, at last they said goodnight. She put the phone away and went inside and felt the warmth against her skin, heard her children laughing upstairs, smelled the vegan dumplings Mara was cooking. Drew must have heard her; he walked slowly out of the kitchen, a beer in his hand, which he set on the small table topped with keys and mail and helped her remove her coat. It was the weight of everything, the gravity of it...she turned into him, and he put his arms around her and held her.

22

MONDAY, DECEMBER 7

In the morning, she stared out the window overlooking the same yard, snow melting in a rising sun, revealing patches of grass.

"Corrine?"

"Yeah?" She turned her attention to her sister, seated across the maple-topped dining table.

Mara blew on her cup of coffee. "I asked how you're doing."

"Oh." At first she glanced at the ceiling, thinking a bit about the still-sleeping kids, and about Drew, who'd been up before she was, working on his laptop in the guest room. "I don't know. Good."

"Dad didn't call you, did he?"

"No. He didn't call."

Their father lived in Vermont, way up near the Canadian border.

"I haven't heard from him either," Mara said. "I don't think he even...well, I *know* he doesn't have a TV, but I don't think he has internet, either."

Still feeling dazed, Corrine considered a change of topic. Discussion of their wayward father invariably led to an argument.

Their parents had divorced when Mara was ten and Corrine twelve. Mara, perhaps because she was younger, had tended to take their father's side in the split. Even though she'd stayed behind with Corrine and their mother in Mt. Vernon, Mara would defend him. She saw him as an artist, like she was. Misunderstood. Using symbols and myth to express himself. It was true, Kemper painted, and he'd had his moments of brilliance, but none of that artistic angst excused his faults.

"I had this dream the other night," Corrine said to Mara suddenly. "And it was the same thing I saw once in India." She described it, Mara's eyes getting wide, coffee forgotten.

"That's like Revelation," Mara said. "Like the End of Days. That's what you're seeing."

"I don't know." Corrine looked away, but checked her sister with furtive glances. This topic was no better. Stephen had reconnected to religion in recent years – he claimed it was what gave him the strength to ask Mara's forgiveness for his infidelity. Corrine thought it was mostly bullshit, and that her sister did, too – Mara was a skeptic, not a believer. But for whatever reason, she loved Stephen and wanted it to work. Apparently, whatever brand of religion Stephen had adopted didn't require church on Sundays, so maybe that was what made it tenable for Mara, an art school graduate and lifelong secular humanist.

Mara looked away for a moment. "You remember when Dad was really going strong with all of that? The rapture and everything?"

Corrine felt a twinge, a nerve plucked somewhere deep in her gut. "Of course I remember."

"'And I looked,'" Mara said, "'and behold a pale horse, and his name that sat on him was Death, and Hell followed with him.' I remember that. Word for word. I remember when he quoted that. My eighteenth birthday."

Corrine cleared her throat, fighting the urge to get up and walk away from the table. "I don't know. I was in India."

"You were, yeah," Mara said, their eyes connecting. "You never told me much about it."

"What? Sure I did."

"I don't remember. Tell me now."

Corrine drifted back in time to Varanasi, a busy, colorful city. She told Mara about the rickshaws and motorbikes jostling in throngs of traffic, the endless invitations to visit a silk shop or sit for a massage as you walked along the unimproved roads. At first, she said, she'd been nervous about the daily cremation ceremonies – "all those burning bodies." It took roughly three hours for a body to completely disintegrate in an open-air funeral pyre. After the fire burned itself out, the ashes were thrown in the Ganges to the sound of ceremonial bells tinkling along the shore.

"There could be two hundred funerals a *day*," she told Mara. But eventually, she said, the low smoke hanging over the city grew familiar, less ominous, and the only smell she noticed was burning sandalwood. You could get used to anything, any place. It was only a matter of time.

"And the dream was the same thing you saw while meditating," Mara confirmed.

"Yes. I can see it almost any time. I just close my eyes. And it's not a memory. It's not like that. It's right there."

She did close her eyes, and she waited, inviting it. The darkness lightened and began to move, to roil counterclockwise, turning into gray clouds brightening toward the center.

"Does it scare you?"

She opened her eyes and looked at her sister. "No. Not really. It doesn't feel like...it's not bad. It's just there. Like a fact. It kind of feels, a little bit, like those death and dying dreams."

"Oh, I hate those." Mara's mouth turned down and she shook her head. "I wake up from those and I'm just...depressed. I'll either lose Layla, or lose Stephen....Or it will just be my time. And it's so sad."

Corrine took a chance. "How is Stephen? How are things with you?"

"Good," Mara said quickly. "He's got a big new account and that's keeping him crazy busy, but it's going to be major. It's going to put Layla through school. Wherever she wants to go. We're looking at Sarah Lawrence right now....Listen to me. This isn't time to talk about me." She reached out and touched Corrine's hand. "I want you to know, I'm here for whatever you need. I can go down there with you. Obviously you need it. I mean, Cor, you're seeing things. And Layla will be fine here..."

But Corrine was shaking her head. "It's okay."

"You don't need Drew there the whole time. You guys have been there for me, and I'm there for you. Okay? Alex is healing up, and when he gets home, I'll be there to help."

Corrine sighed. "We'll see how it goes."

They shared a silence after that, until Mara said, "I know you're not watching any of this stuff, but I went online last night, saw this thing on CNN – that woman came to the hospital. Did you know that?"

"I did."

"She was very sweet. Very sincere, I thought. But of course, you have all the losers making comments about it, saying she's trying to get famous. That Halloran guy is going on that she's just angling for a book deal. Under his tweet, people saying that these were crisis actors."

"Oh, give me a break. Paul Halloran? Really?"

Mara nodded. "So sad, how people react."

"I know."

Mara got out her phone, started thumbing the screen. "Here, listen to this – 'This terrible tragedy has shined a light that we need healing in this nation. The diminishment of religion in the face of modernization is an issue we need to address – is it really where society should be headed?'"

Corrine started to ask who Mara was quoting, but Freda called from upstairs, sounding upset. She went up, took Freda's temperature, and dosed her with children's ibuprofen. By the time she was done and carrying Freda back downstairs, Kenneth and Layla were up, each of them looking like early-stage zombies. Layla drank coffee and stood against the counter, holding the mug in both hands, wearing tiny pink shorts and a tank top. Kenneth fumbled halfway through a bowl of cereal, then looked up and said, "Mom, what about school?"

"We'll see," she said.

"But I have practice tonight. Game on Wednesday."

Basketball was important to Kenneth not because he was particularly sports-inclined, but because most of the boys he'd grown up with were on the team.

"I can take him to practice," Drew said from the bottom stair. He came in with his short hair gelled Hollywood-style, his turquoise T-shirt matching his eyes. "If that's what you want to do."

"We'll talk about it," Corrine said. She set Freda at the table and ran a hand through her corn-silk hair. "You hungry, baby? Want some cereal?"

The girl nodded, her face flushed, eyes glassy.

"Let me get it," Mara said.

Layla shuffled to the side as Mara pulled a cereal bowl down from the cabinet. Everyone milled around for a few minutes, almost like a normal morning. When Freda was done (she'd eaten less than half a small bowl's worth), Corrine brought her to Mara's couch, gave her a blanket and some juice, put *Bluey* on the TV, kissed her, then went up into the bathroom and locked the door.

Alex was just waking up when she called him.

"Alex, I think this is bait. The guy wants attention, wants to spread his message, wants to be important."

"It could be. Listen, Cor, everything you're saying, I've thought about. I've been lying here in this room and thinking about it. Nonstop. But if there's a five percent chance, if there's a *one* percent chance that he's got something to confess –"

"That's what makes it the perfect bait." Her voice coarsened with emotion. "Alex, just don't leave behind everything, everyone you love…"

"Of course I'm not – babe, I'm not leaving *anyone*. This is the right thing to do."

She could barely get out the words. "I don't want to lose you."

"You're not going to lose me. What do you mean? You saying you'll lose me if I do this? It's our decision. You say no, and I pull out right now."

She stood and ran the tap, cupped some water, had a quick drink to steady herself. "That's an unfair position. You know what you want to do. *I* know what you want to do. You say it's up to us, but what that means is it's on me. If something actually happened, or if this guy….You're asking me how selfish I'm going to be."

"That's not it."

"If I'm going to choose you, my family, over someone else. Someone who could be in danger. People who might be…" She sat down again, on the toilet seat. "God, Alex…"

"I know."

"Just go. Just do what you have to."

23

He'd slept for almost eighteen hours, but intermittently, startling awake from bad dreams and sharp pains. After the difficult call from Corrine, physical therapy went late morning to early afternoon, agonizing and tedious. By evening, Chet was wheeling him to the hospital entrance and Alex swung the footrests aside. With Chet's support, he got to his feet. A few snowflakes drifted down, powder on the parking lot medians. But it smelled good outside; snow plus a whiff of exhaust. Marvelous. Like freedom.

A Burlington police car idled near the entryway, a police van behind it. Sergeant Tandy approached and flanked Alex. As the three men started toward the van in the waning daylight, a reporter made his way through the lot. He watched Alex like a hunter about to miss the shot at a prized buck. A cameraman trailed him and flipped on a light.

Chet to Tandy: "We're just saying he's been released earlier than expected."

"You don't have to say anything. I can keep them back."

"Alex Baines!" The reporter was maybe thirty years old, his

face reddened by the cold air. "Mr. Baines, how are you feeling after the shooting?"

"Like a pin cushion," Alex answered.

"Why have you been released so soon?"

Tandy put up a hand. "Let's give it some space. All right? Give it a little space."

The reporter glanced at the vehicles and back at Alex. "Why the police escort, Mr. Baines? Have there been threats of more violence?"

Tandy started to respond, but Chet sailed out in front and spread his hands. "Folks, we're just taking precautions. As you may know, Dr. Baines –" he pointedly used the honorific 'Dr.', where the reporter had casually said 'Mr.' – "has been talking to several papers, sharing his story –"

The reporter edged around Chet, and the cameraman jockeyed for a better shot. "How is your health? You've been let go ahead of schedule, is there –"

"We'll have some news for you soon," Chet said.

Tandy opened the sliding door and helped Alex into the van while Chet continued. "This story is just beginning, folks – I'm not at liberty to say anything else right now – but we'll be issuing a statement soon. In the meantime, I believe the police are giving an updated press briefing tonight in New York. Thank you." He nodded to the reporter and then to the cameraman, almost a bow. After that, he stepped up into the van with a grunt. Tandy slammed the door shut, dispelling Alex's brief sense of liberation.

"Phew." Chet ran a hand through his hair. "They came out of nowhere. I thought after the story broke yesterday, that would be it for the locals. But these guys are out there just to get a shot of the hospital and do a follow-up on you. That's this thing. That's the way it is now. Wait until we tell them the rest of it."

Alex watched as the reporter and cameraman were urged back by one of Tandy's cops until they were standing up on the median.

The cameraman framed a shot on the van as Tandy got in the passenger side. There was a metal grate separating the front and back; hard not to feel like a criminal. He'd have to describe it to the kids later – they'd be excited about a ride in a police van. Corrine already had firsthand experience; she'd once been arrested.

The van got moving, the camera panning as they drove away from the hospital. They weaved through downtown Burlington, then got on a route to the ferry. Back to New York.

24

"We're all set here," Libby said to Roth on the phone. "I've got four officers with me. We're waiting on Bomb Squad. As soon as the house is cleared, I'll send in the crime scene people."

"Okay – and, tomorrow, I'll be keeping you updated on what Sheffield tells us," Roth said.

"Yeah. We'll be here. I'll start processing everything, but we'll have our eyes and ears open."

"Thanks, Libby." Roth hung up and looked across her desk at Harlan – his desk faced hers. The wind whipped outside the station, lashing the evergreen trees in the dark. She was about to speak when the desk phone rang.

"Hey." It was Matt.

"Hi, honey." She checked her cell phone, looking for a missed call; he didn't normally ring her work line directly. "Everything okay?"

Harlan's eyes got a questioning look. Roth gave a subtle shake of her head: *It's nothing.*

"Yeah," Matt said. "It's, um…I'm going to bed."

"All right. Kids okay?"

"Yeah, the kids are good. How are you holding up?"

"Just trying to get this all in for tomorrow. Are you – what's up?"

"Nothing. Just checking in."

She wondered again why he hadn't called her mobile phone, but figured the answer was plain – he knew she was at the station in Lewis. She might ignore her cell phone but was sure to pick up at her desk.

"This will be over soon," she said.

"I know. I just – it's been all everybody's talking about, you know? So I keep thinking about you. And you were standing there at the press conference…looking pretty good, honey."

A pleasant heat rose in her face. "You got everybody's lunch packed for the morning?"

"Yeah. Just a reminder – I'll be in Keene. On the Walter Ranch. After the kids get on the bus. We'll try not to wake you."

"No, I'll be up – have to be here bright and early tomorrow. How are things going on the ranch?"

"They're good." He talked a little more about the construction project. Matt didn't require much, just a little attention here and there. He was a good husband, a good man. It had taken some time to find the right one. Roth had always thought she was easy-going, low maintenance, until a friend from high school pointed out her high standards.

"You're very specific," Michele had said.

"Am I?"

"Yes. Look at Matt – he's cut, I mean, he's got a good body, he's handsome. But he's not a player, he doesn't seem full of himself. He hunts and fishes, and he's a man's man but he's Mister Mom, too, cleaning up your messes."

"I don't leave messes."

"Please." Michele had rolled her eyes. "I lived with you for almost two years. You used to give your clothes the sniff test. The dog ate more food off the floor than in his dish. And remember that mystery splotch on the carpet?"

"All right, all right..."

Michele had been right about Matt – he was a catch. Roth met him just before the police academy, and he'd been supportive when BCI wanted to relocate her two and a half hours away from where she'd been a trooper. It wasn't easy; he'd had to start from scratch with his construction work. But he'd been loyal and committed.

Once you get the big wheel turning, he'd said, *you can't just jump off.*

"All right," Matt said, "I'll let you get back to it. Don't be up too late, huh?"

"Okay." She was ready to hang up.

"Smitty is always talking about how we're psychologically wired to be part of teams," Matt said. Smitty was an electrician.

"Teams," Roth said.

"People need a scenario where 'we' win and 'those other guys' lose. That's how humans are. That's what he says."

"Yeah?" She felt a smile curling the corner of her mouth. "Are you and Smitty cracking the case for me? Lack of nuance in the world is the bad guy's motive?"

Harlan's line rang and he answered.

Matt said to her, "No, I just mean...I was thinking about my coach. My old high school football coach. How he talked. He'd swear and everything. But you'd hear his voice in your head when you were out on the field. And you respected him. But you didn't always agree with him. And if you didn't agree with him, sometimes the other guys would keep you in line. And I think that...I don't know. It's like, that's how it works today. You can't go against your team. Your coach. Anyway, I don't know what I'm talking about."

"I think I know what you're saying."

Harlan finished his brief conversation and hung up the phone. He looked at her, waiting.

"Matt, honey, I gotta go."

"Okay. Be safe."

She set the phone in the cradle and raised her eyebrows at Harlan.

"They left Burlington fifteen minutes ago. You're up."

25

The shoreline was dark but for the bright lights at the ferry dock. Alex saw news vans. Apparently the Vermont reporter outside the hospital had told New York media.

The ferry cruised through choppy water, a column of moonlight riding the waves, and the police van rocked on its axles as the ferry came to rest against the pilings. The only vehicle aboard, they rolled off down a lane of orange cones and stopped. The door slid back.

"Alex! Alex Baines! Do you have any comments about Saturday's shooting?" "What are you doing back in New York?" "Are you going to speak to more of the other victims?" "Was the gunman someone you knew?" "Was he religious?" "Is this terrorism?"

A woman in plainclothes and two state troopers grabbed him. The troopers literally picked him up and put him in the back of a waiting police car like a child. The troopers piled in the front, the woman rode with him in the back, and they drove away with camera lights and shouted questions fading into the night. After a tiny little town, they were alone in the darkness. The few house lights were spread out over a rolling countryside amid crooked, leafless trees. The policewoman, he realized now, was Roth.

"I saw you," Alex said. "Right after it happened, I think. You were in the emergency room."

"Yes. I was."

"Thank you for how fast you worked on this."

"He didn't make it too difficult." Sheffield, she meant.

"Is everything all set?"

"My supervisor – you met him – he's working out the last-minute details with the jail."

"My, ah – Chet Warman – told me he's from Maine. Sheffield."

She gave a small nod. "Do you know anybody in Portland? Have any business in that area?"

"I gave a talk there about eighteen months ago. At the university."

She clicked on a lighted pen and started writing something. "Any way we can get a list of attendees? Just to check if he was there?"

"I'll ask Chet – um, Mr. Warman. But I told that to your supervisor. Mr. Banger."

He studied Roth as she made a note anyway. Young, maybe just thirty. The hair poking out of her winter hat was black, the eyes that had briefly alighted on him had been either blue or green. She was redolent of coffee, fresh air. "What do you think about Sheffield?"

Done writing, she sat looking toward the front of the trooper car, all the lights resembling an airplane cockpit. "He's never had a buccal swab before now – for DNA – and he's never even been fingerprinted until he processed into county. At first, all we knew was that he has parents, both in their mid-seventies, living in Florida, and a sister who lives abroad. His employment history's not exactly clear, but he was getting unemployment for a while after a paper mill closed down. A few odd jobs in California, including a short stint at BAX Global – a shipping company – then a gap where we don't know what he was doing. Then he moved back east and has been working as a delivery person for the past three years. Never married. No kids. No record of mental health issues that we've found. Oh – he's a runner; he's done a few marathons and –"

She broke from her spiel and looked out the window, up toward the sky. Alex heard the distinct chop of a helicopter.

"One of ours," Roth said.

"It's getting that big?"

"Big?"

Even in the semidarkness, he was keenly aware she was evaluating him, testing him for hubris.

"I just mean, as a case. Should I be worried?"

"No. Just being careful." She reached into her bag and set something on his lap. "This was one of the books you were selling at the talk. We took everything, but I pulled this one from evidence to have a look. Thought you might like it back."

"Thanks." He ran his hand over the cover, flipped a few pages, just a habit.

"It's dedicated to your mother," Roth said. "I'm sorry to hear she passed."

He smoothed his hands together, the skin feeling dry, cracked. "She grew up on a farm – not too far from around here, actually – they had horses. She played piano, became a school teacher, and then when she married my father, she stopped teaching school, but taught piano." He paused. "There were things that happened when she was young, things she never told anyone. Then one day she told me. That's when I started writing this book. In my head."

Roth was quiet, listening.

"I think when there's a trauma in a family, it often goes undigested," he said. "You don't know what it is, but sometimes it's there. I was doing a lot of research at the time – when she told me – I was looking at how the brain processes trauma. She said that she would have these dreams." Alex cleared his throat, feeling embarrassed. "It was breast cancer, spread through her lymphatic system. That's how she died."

"I'm sorry."

"My wife's mother passed away, too. Much longer ago. When I met Corrine, she called herself 'An American in India looking for answers.'" He smiled at the memory. "Now we're both motherless Americans looking for answers."

They rode in silence for a while, the radio occasionally crackling, a video screen between the troopers active with what looked like descriptions of incoming calls, dispatches, something like that. He found himself focusing on the gun Roth carried on her hip. The way she sat with her hands on the bench seat. Wondering why he'd just told her all of that.

"I can't find that this guy is connected to anything significant," she said. "We passed everything to the FBI, and they looked into him but haven't been able to pin him to any extremist groups. Depending on what he tells you, they may get further involved. He's not even on social media. He plays the stock market, but he's not wealthy. He really seems to be individually wrapped."

He waited for her to say, *He's a nobody – just another psycho seeking attention*, but she didn't. If Alex's intuition was on, Roth seemed fascinated. No, that wasn't the right word. She was hunting. Searching for what made Sheffield tick.

She tilted her head to scratch her neck. "We subpoenaed his cell service carrier today. Hopefully, we'll be able to track his movements for the past few weeks, see who he's been talking to. We can check that data against what he says to you. Portland police are searching his home, and we're working with them to process what was found, but so far, nothing that tells us what he might have done or is going to do."

"I'm having a hard time believing he's going to tell me anything incriminating."

She glanced at him. "Me too. But he might."

They lapsed into silence again. Alex checked his phone, saw a dozen missed calls, nothing from Corrine. He knew from her last texts that Drew was picking up Kenneth from basketball, and Freda had tested positive for strep. Her last words to him – that he'd been unfair to ask her to decide this with him, that she feared losing him – had bounced around in his mind all day. A few minutes into the ferry ride, he'd texted back to inquire how Freda was feeling, but Corrine hadn't responded.

The sudden distance from her opened up a dark hole inside. He questioned everything he'd done so far, and what he was doing now. His little girl was sick with a bacterial infection. His son was going to be confronted with all sorts of online gossip and speculation. And his wife was dealing with a major trauma in their lives. He missed her. He missed simpler times. Maybe when this was all over, he'd begin a process of disentangling from public life. Try to get back to the way things used to be.

Had there ever been a simpler time, though? Had there been true halcyon days or were those part of a fictive past? Had he been racing through life, even as he taught people to live in the now?

"So did you really think Sheffield was on the other side of that door?"

Roth's question was so out of the blue it took him a moment. That and the pain meds – he still felt like this could be some sort of drug-induced dream, or maybe he was still on the surgery table, under heavy anesthesia.

"I thought he was, but I didn't know. I thought he could be. I thought if he was out there, he'd try to come in, start shooting. I figured if I could knock him off balance, maybe I could get the gun."

"Really does make me think – someone who does what he did has a reason. Sometimes we can figure it out; other times we just don't know. But one thing that strikes me – you're getting lots of praise for how you handled it. You're alive. And you're a bit of a celebrity, so you're getting lots of extra attention…"

"That's what my wife thinks – that he's looking to gain something with this."

Roth looked at him. "Could he? Gain something?"

"I don't know."

Her eyes lingered for a moment before she looked out the window. "You're outspoken on a number of issues."

"I guess, yeah."

She looked at him. "You defended the woman who came forward with sexual allegations against the senator. When people said her memory was too hazy for her to be credible, you spoke up and talked about trauma."

"I did." He thought Roth was considering Sheffield's motives, not alluding to a conspiracy.

"And you're frank about your views on Islam," she said.

He took a moment. "I find it impossible not to see acts of militant extremism correlated to aspects of the Koran and the Hadith. Particularly the promise of paradise and seventy-two virgins."

"Sheffield is not Muslim, though. Not that we've seen. Do you condemn all religion?"

"It's not a matter of condemnation. It's about having an honest conversation about it."

"I watched one of your videos," she said. "The one from Melbourne. The part where you ask people to think of a movie. You really think people have no free will?"

He drew a sharp breath through his nose, let it out slowly. "It's a question."

"I admit I don't think about that stuff too much. I understand the basic idea, though, that one thing leads to another. Cause and effect. But we bear responsibility, at least. Don't you think so?"

There were lights collecting up ahead as they neared the county jail where Sheffield was sitting in his cell.

"Yes," Alex said. "I think we definitely do."

26

Corrine came down the stairs. Water sloshed in the kitchen sink as Drew did the dishes from their hasty dinner.

He looked up. "Everything good?"

"Her fever is still down. She's asleep."

"Good. Wow, I didn't realize antibiotics worked that fast."

"That's ibuprofen. That stuff is amazing. The antibiotics will kill the strep, but the ibuprofen is what keeps her fever down. Come on – you never take ibuprofen?"

"I got my degree in philosophy."

Drew had such a dry sense of humor it was tough to always know when he was joking. She watched as he placed a dish in the drying rack. "You don't have to do that."

"What I'm here for, ma'am."

"We have a dishwasher."

"I like doing them. It's therapeutic."

"You're a man among men." She moved past him to the fridge and opened it, unsure what she wanted. Maybe the St. Pauli Girl beers in the door. Six wine bottles sat in the rack in the corner, but right now, beer was better. She set two on the counter and rummaged in a drawer for a bottle opener. Alex dominated her thoughts. Among other things, how he'd been put up in a hotel when he needed to be in the hospital. Or home. With her.

She paused in her search for the bottle opener. Maybe drinking wasn't such a good idea. She was alone with Drew – well, functionally alone, the kids out of the way. There'd been a time, just one, when she'd been alone with Drew, the wine had flowed a little too freely and – one kiss. That was all.

Drew, oblivious to the turn her thoughts had taken, was speaking again: "Fevers were considered a gift among certain cultures. Still are, in some. You're brought closer to the other side."

"Mmm," she half agreed, still distracted. She and Drew had both agreed the kiss would never happen again, and it hadn't. But she was under such stress right now...

"That's what sweat lodges are all about," Drew went on. "Native American rituals and South American shaman – they're taking people to the edge of consciousness, pushing past it. The modern use of psilocybin too. And LSD."

That jarred her back to the present time, the unwelcome revelation of her husband's microdosing. The hell with it – she was having a drink. Except...

"Where *is* the bottle opener?" She closed the drawer with a little slap, harder than expected.

"Here. They just twist." Drew wiped his hands and popped the beer tops, set the bottles back on the counter. Their eyes connected and he seemed to be waiting for something – maybe for her to lose it.

She managed a smile. "Thanks."

"But it's all about set and setting," he said, going back. "Those drugs can be dangerous. You need a plan, and you need guidance."

She sipped the beer and leaned against the countertop, deciding to keep following along. Maybe it was better to be distracted from the anger lacing her thoughts. "You need guidance in case you freak out while you're tripping?"

"Well, you set goals. You know – so, for the people who have end-stage cancer, and they're taking psilocybin to have an experience, they set out that goal. To confront their fear of death."

"What do they...what happens? What do they get from it?"

"They have – you know – they detach from their identity. They sense much more to life. To existence. They get hope."

"But that's not what Alex is doing."

Drew pulled the plug in the drain and the water started to suck down. He toweled off his hands again and picked up the other beer, shook his head. "The idea is that it helps with focus. With mental agility."

"Alex has never had a problem with mental agility. Or focus." She took another drink and thought it through. "I think it could affect his judgment. Couldn't it? Right? What do we know? What do we know about it? He's acting this way, now he's running off to....You know what I'd like to do? I'd like to talk to Abendroth about this *study*."

Drew looked at his beer, then tasted it.

"It's three hours earlier in California," she said. "I'd like to talk about this with Jan. Can you help me out? His number is not in my phone."

He nodded. "Yeah. Sure. I mean, I know he won't say much. Not with an ongoing experiment like this."

The water made a slurping sound as the last suds were taken by the drain. A thought came streaking out of nowhere, knocking aside the desire to talk to Abendroth. "Wait a minute. You don't think there's any way..."

"What?"

"I couldn't have, like, caught anything? I know that sounds stupid. But, picked up something? You can take acid on your tongue, it can absorb through your skin..."

"No. Not this. This is a pill. They're little pills."

"Does he have some here?" She walked out of the kitchen, already going through the bathroom medicine cabinet in her mind, Alex's sock drawer, the desk in his study.

She stopped short of taking the stairs. And then what? So she finds his stash. Was she inadvertently taking them? No. Was he secretly dosing her? Ridiculous. Her vision was from deep meditation, dreams. Naturally altered states. Not drugs.

Drew stood behind her, waiting.

Corrine moved to the couch and sat down with her hands between her knees, feeling pulled in multiple directions. Best to just sit. Think. Alex had been keeping something from her, and while it wasn't earth-shattering, it was substantial. No, she wasn't privy to everything he did, everyone he talked to, but this was something he would have shared with her just a few years ago. Something he most definitely would have shared with her before they were married, when they'd walked the colorful and crowded streets of Varanasi, when she'd found him to be this genuine, open man, filled with compassion for the world, assured of his place in it and his mission.

It was sad, because it said something about a marriage, how time and children and the stress of modern life could so subtly separate a loving couple. It said something about *their* marriage, anyway. While she'd known there was distance, a loss of intimacy, there was a chance it had been only in her head.

Then someone had violently disrupted their lives, spilling secrets.

Drew followed her and took the easy chair beside the couch. His movements registered as careful, quiet, respecting her train of thought. The lights of neighboring houses shone through the large, otherwise dark windows.

She said, "It's not that I need some sort of fairy tale. Okay? I'm not my sister, with her farmhouse and artist life and her denial about her husband...I shouldn't say that. God, what am I saying? And anyway *my* husband has been out there doing things I don't know about. And now he's gonna talk to this guy, and I should be there for him, but I'm pissed. You know?"

"I understand."

"He's in the middle of a crisis, and I'm whining about all of this. I'm being selfish."

"I don't think so. I think you're legitimately affected."

"He's not sitting in sweat lodges or venturing into the Amazon for mind-altering ceremonies. I know that. But it still feels like a betrayal, you know?" She glanced up, afraid to look too long or closely at Drew because she'd feel guilty and stop talking. But she didn't want to. She needed to let this out. Drew had compassion in his eyes, and she continued, on a roll now.

"I know he's doing what he has to do. I'm proud of him. But afterward, he's going to be busier than ever. I wish he would just...we have plenty of money – he could take months to convalesce. A year. Work on his book – or another book. But he won't. That's not how he operates. He goes every year to the ashram. That's where he sits still." She shifted her legs, admitting, "I guess I signed on for this, though. I knew what I was getting into. I just...never thought it was going to get this big. This involved. Obviously he didn't plan for what happened. No one would. But I knew it. I knew it from the moment it happened. I felt such sadness for everyone this touched. Everyone it hurt. And then – and here comes the selfish part – I thought: Our lives are never going to be the same again. Alex is going to be taken away even more. I'm trying to have a *normal* life here."

"I know."

She looked at Drew, hopeful. "You think this will die down? When will it die down?"

He might've responded, but she rushed on: "Because the worst part, the scariest part, for me, for some reason, is how it crystallizes him. It pits him as the atheist hero. And I guess...I guess I never wanted that. I don't know why."

She settled back into the cushion. Her gaze fell on one of the showpieces in the room, a small ivory-colored Buddha made of bonded stone. Alex was always bringing things back from India. Wooden Padmasana statues in various devotional poses. Madhubani paintings and silk saris. Her favorite was the five-pound elephant sculpture upstairs in the bathroom. Ganesha.

Ironic statues given his commitment to atheism. Maybe it was his way of acknowledging *something* beyond him?

"Sometimes I wonder what I'm going to say to my kids," she told Drew. "Kenneth is at that age. He asked me the other day – because Christmas is coming up – he asked what we believe in. Alex and I have talked about how we want to raise them – we used to talk about it all the time. How people have expectations and desires, and they're almost always left unsatisfied. That's Buddhism. Right, but what else? Alex doesn't believe in reincarnation. He finds a physical correlation to any experience. He can point you to it, right in the brain. That's his career, his life. And it's like...it's like it's *infected* me. I know that's not fair, but that's what it feels like. I have this feeling; I have this *need* to believe something else. You're looking at me like I'm crazy."

"I don't think you're crazy."

"It's like in our little part of the world here, there's only room for Alex. What *Alex* thinks. What he talks about and writes in his books, and the people he leaves in *ruins* after a debate. Drew – he leaves them in ruins. He's just so smart, so good at debate – but does that mean he's right? Does it mean he's right because he's better at arguing, better at dismantling? Because to me, that's just – I mean, my God, maybe that's just..." She finally stopped, her words ringing in her ears, feeling like she'd blasphemed her own husband in front of his employee – or been about to.

Maybe that's just what? Evil? Evil was a word for things we

didn't understand or want to face – an angioblastoma pressing against someone's amygdala, making them violent. Abuse from childhood, a violent upbringing, desperate loneliness. Poverty. Shame.

There was no one essential answer – it just felt like Alex had some sort of intellectual boot over her all these years, and she'd finally realized it.

"Is that what you believe? Drew? Everything is determined; we're just an outcome of the universe? So we go around naming and categorizing everything, and then we die?"

Drew watched her in that cautious way; his knitted eyebrows and downturned mouth reflecting her grief and frustration. Then he looked into his beer bottle, took a drink, and set it down on the coffee table. "I find a little truth in everything, I guess. I think science…you know, science is sort of about photographing things. But religious people want to *feel* things."

She nodded, hesitant.

He said, "And…because I think that we can look into reality at its finest level, we can look at the smallest stuff that makes up existence, and we don't know what it is or what it's doing."

"Right! Yes, exactly." Relief, now.

"We just don't know."

She nodded more, perhaps a bit too eagerly. She felt wired. Was she dosed after all? Maybe just buzzed, but she'd only had one beer.

"We don't have a clue," she said at last. She got up and returned to the fridge. "All of these men – and they are all *men* – Newton, Descartes, Einstein – they conceived of something and then they build an instrument or theory to prove it. It all starts with their own beliefs and projections." She grabbed a fresh beer and walked back into the living room. Her sock feet swished over the hardwood floor, then the white shag rug beneath the living room furniture. A brass turtle about eight inches long shone beneath the lamp, lifting its head at her. "I just want to be open. I want to feel whatever it is and not judge it. Like you said – to feel it." She used her shirt to twist the cap. "And then I go around thinking that must make me stupid, or naïve, so I suppress it."

"That's tough."

"I think life is more mysterious than materialistic. Okay? That's how I feel. And I just...I don't want my children to grow up to believe there's nothing. Or that there's some cold absolute reality out there that doesn't feel, doesn't care about anything." She took a big drink, painfully aware she'd just unloaded on Drew everything she'd wanted to say to her husband for the past – how long? Days? Months? Years?

The sense of betrayal worsened, and some of the beer went down the wrong pipe, making her gag. She coughed and sputtered into her fist.

"You okay?"

She waved him off as she brought the cough under control. For God's sake – she'd had that dream *the morning he was attacked*. That had to count for something. That was more than coincidence. Could it be explained? Probably. She'd picked up on something – hell, maybe she'd been picking up on something for a long time: Alex living this secret, Alex being distant from her, her own suppressed conflict about their lives.

That was key, maybe. She was angry at him for withholding when she'd been hanging on to things – multiple things – for some time now.

She went to the kitchen again and poured the rest of the beer down the sink, took a handful of water and brought it to her lips, rinsed her mouth and spat. Then she slapped the faucet off and straightened her back.

Not answering Alex's latest texts – that was unfair; she was punishing him. He was about to face the man who'd tried to kill him, and she was being petty. It couldn't be this way.

Items from her trip still cluttered the kitchen; her phone was among them somewhere. She started pushing things aside. "Have you seen my phone?"

Drew walked in, checking his watch. "No, sorry. I'm sure he's just hanging out in the hotel room. Not much to do up there."

She kept looking, ignoring that Drew had practically read her mind. She dug through her purse until her hand closed around her phone. She dialed Alex, sifting through the possible things to say as the line rang. Things like how this was insane. That she was going to take the kids and go up there and check into the hotel – it wouldn't make any difference whether Freda was healing here or there. Alex was trying to do the right thing, but risking his health. He should have the support of his family. He should have his wife with him.

But his phone just rang.

27

TUESDAY, DECEMBER 8

A truck had run him over. That's how it felt. The pain branched up his leg, pulsing through his hip, stomach, and chest. He flopped back on the bed, teeth clenched, unable to stand. Fear of a heart attack streaked his thoughts. The nearby vibration of his phone barely registered.

The hotel was basically a big three-story house with uneven floors. They'd eaten a late dinner of pizza and wings from the one local place within fifty miles, watched the press conference online. After Chet spent half an hour trying to predict what the interview with Sheffield would entail, he'd gone to his room, and Alex dropped the brave, unaffected facade. Hot spikes dragged up and down his flesh. A deep, bone-level ache throbbed beneath the sharper sensations. Somehow it all burrowed in his hip, squeezed his spine, and punched at his brain. At this point, he'd already taken more than the recommended doses of painkillers, and he needed to have his wits about him for tomorrow's main event. He thought about calling Chet back to the room but decided against it. Chet couldn't do anything for him; only *he* could manage this. He had to.

He forced himself to stand, bent his head to keep from

passing out. After a moment, he sat on the bed, leg sticking out straight, and focused on his breathing. The phone quit vibrating. He would get it in a minute. Maybe it was Corrine. He hoped so.

In, out. Stay with the out-breath.

Getting in touch with the sensations in the body – that part was easy. Blaring pain, like a siren of nerves. He tried not to judge it. Not to think of it as bad, but mere sensation. To detach from it, like something happening, a weather event which was impersonal and acceptable.

Pain is weakness leaving the body.

Something his father had said once. Alex tried to push his father out of his mind, then stopped, let the thoughts come as they would. Didn't attach to them either.

Pain.

Many theories on pain. From Canadian psychologist Ronald Melzack and British neuroscientist Patrick Wall was the gate control theory: A person could endeavor to suppress pain, or at least control the degree of pain perceived, by training the mind.

Pain is in the brain.

Focus on the ventricular system. Imagine the periacqueductal gray matter surrounding the third ventricle. Imagine those opioid receptors opening up, like flowers drinking in the rain.

Rain; running from the car to the restaurant with Corrine. Young then, before the kids. Sitting beside each other at the table instead of across from one another – he'd read once that true lovers gazed out at the world together, side by side.

Pain. Freda was in pain – coughing and sore throat and fever. They'd named her for Freda Bedi, the first Western woman to take ordination in Tibetan Buddhism. Once, at four years old, their daughter had one of her high fevers and, for some reason, had started counting numbers. She'd gotten all the way up to twenty-six, her reedy voice climbing, before stopping. No idea why. Just decided to show off her preternatural counting skills while her little brain cooked away.

Breathe. Stop trying to control it. Stop slipping away. Stay in the present moment. Quit judging yourself for getting distracted –

Focus on the sensations, stay with consciousness and its contents. Come back to the baseline.

A hotel room, a car running outside, the murmur of voices.

Notice, then let go; move on.

That faint, wet smell in the room. The flush of a toilet and the hushed rumble of water through the pipes in the walls.

Rhythm. Breathing. Stay with the out-breath. Ride it. Stay in the moment. It is always now – the moment is eternal.

No, the moment was a lie. You were in the past. It took a millisecond for your brain to interpret the signals coming in, the sounds and smells, each at their own rate of processing, each lagging behind – so you were only ever experiencing what *just happened,* never what was *truly happening now –*

Stop. Flow. Stay with the out-breath. Notice what arises.

A door opened and closed. A clock in the room ticked off the seconds. The breath coming out of him was sour. The phone vibrated from his bag again.

He was suddenly a child, watching out the window of their house in Rockland as his father left for work. Always working, providing for the family. And what family? Just Howard and Muriel and Alex. He was an only child, like his mother. As if there was some genetic propensity in his bloodline for single-child families.

Of course, it wasn't that. If anything, it stemmed from a belief that parents could pour more knowledge into fewer children. One child was a super child. *Welcome to the Super Child podcast; I'm your host, Alex Baines.*

Let it go.

"Here and Now," with Alex Baines. How ironic.

Stop.

Nothing, just breathing. Remembering the snow falling out the hospital room window. That's okay to remember. Memories are in the moment. Let them pass like clouds. Watch them coalesce, begin to swirl, as if drawn up into the sky –

Breathe.

Thoughts of Sheffield tumbled in. Flashes of the event, moments suspended in time. Sheffield rose from his seat again and again. Standing, taking aim, the muzzle flash. Then, a realization: In order to stop it from repeating, Alex had to let the memory finish – he needed to see what he hadn't seen. He'd jumped away, but he needed to stay. Take the hit, let the poison round slam into his leg and become embedded in sinew and bone, rupturing blood vessels and shredding tissue. Stand there and take it. Don't flee.

He went through the memory like this, inspecting and reliving each moment, steadying himself amid the fear. He went down the stairs, his foot thumping over the treads as he dragged it behind him. He saw the top of the head in the doorway window, Amy Cross's frightened eyes as he pushed her into the dressing room.

A knock on the door. Alex opened his eyes, unable to ignore it.

"Alex? You okay in there? You're not answering, bro. I got Corrine on the phone out here."

The spell was broken. But it had worked – just a few minutes quieting the mind had built a little buffer against the pain. Either that or the extra meds were kicking in. He pushed off the bed, more or less fell toward the bureau and caught himself, grabbed the crutches and tucked them under his arms. He walked to the door, keeping the weight off his bad leg, unlocked it.

Chet had the phone to his ear. "Here he is," Chet said, and handed it over.

"Alex," she said. "I'm coming up there."

"Why?"

"I don't want you going through this alone."

"I have Chet."

"Come on…"

"Please talk to me, Corrine."

She did. She told him she'd been seeing things; a dream that'd passed the sleep boundary. She thought his surviving the attack was a sign for them – the bullet had been inches from his head. He could have been killed, but he hadn't been, not by the leg shot either, even though he'd been jumping all over the place and suffusing the Art Center with his blood as he acted 'heroically.' She didn't care if he believed it or not, but she felt that his survival was more than luck, that they'd been given a second chance. And there was something – she wasn't sure what, but something – which they had to set right.

The more she talked, the more emotional she became. She'd been withholding; now the dam had burst. He waited until she settled and said, "I hear everything you're saying. But I'm here now. They've got this set up for first thing in the morning. It's happening."

"I can be there in five hours."

"Drive up in the dark with the kids? I'll call you right after. And you don't have to worry – I'll be surrounded by law enforcement. The whole thing is happening inside a jail. Nothing is going to happen to –"

"That's not what it is."

"Okay….Hey, listen – the upside is I'll be home sooner."

"You're not going back to Fletcher Allen?"

"Not if I can help it. I hate that room. Smells like farts. I want to be home. To be with you and the kids. I can check in there and do the PT."

"Alex, I can hear the pain in your voice."

"I'm trying to deal with it. I'm managing it. It's better, talking to you. But I think you coming up here...I'd rather just get through this, okay?"

Reluctantly, "Okay."

"And, listen, what I'm concerned about is that you're seeing things."

She sighed. "I shouldn't have said anything about that."

"Of course you should have. What I'm saying is, go see Carrie Rice, get this thing checked out. Or I'll go with you." Carrie Rice was their friend and a neurologist. Alex was talking about an MRI scan.

After a pause, she said, "Alex, this thing just feels wrong."

"Listen, I want to tell you something. In Varanasi once, I saw something, too. Like you did. I found this building in the middle of the desert. Looked like a bunker, you know, dusty brick, sticking out of the ground. Glassless windows and a half-buried door. And I went down into it and into the dark."

"You never told me this."

He had her attention.

"And at the back of the bunker was this even darker space. I mean, impenetrably black. It just...emanated evil. It was like a living thing. A madness. It worked on my mind. And I just ran to it. I jumped into it. And then...it ended, and I was there in the ashram, and the nun was looking at me."

"Alex..."

He could barely hear her.

"I'm sorry," she said.

"You didn't do anything. I'm going to call you as soon as this is over. That way neither of us have any regrets. We know we did all we could."

They talked for another minute, mostly about the kids, and he told her he loved her, said goodbye. He gave Chet the phone back.

"You okay?"

"I'm okay. Just need some sleep."

"All right, buddy." Chet looked worried, but backed out and closed the door.

Chet gone, Alex sat back on the bed and closed his eyes, found his place from earlier: the memory of Amy Cross in the dressing room. Then it was Nyswaner coming down the stairs and falling, and the figure appearing outside the exit door. Just like his dream, he'd run toward it, crashed into it.

Just like he would now.

This was his truth: He never ran from anything.

28

TUESDAY, DECEMBER 8

W ater beading off his back, Alex balanced on one leg while trying to keep his wounded, bandaged leg out of the shower. He was already tired when he pulled on his pants and got a strong coffee from the hotel dining room, along with a breakfast he barely touched. When a state trooper showed up to escort them, the brisk chill in the air shrank his skin and tightened his throat. The drive was short; he mostly looked out the window at pine trees and farms.

They pulled in to the Department of Public Safety, comprised of the state police barracks, the sheriff's office, and the county jail, sectioned off by a high fence topped with cyclone wire.

The trooper's eyes shone in the rearview mirror. "Everything okay, sir?"

"I'm good."

Alex went for the door handle, but there was none. The trooper came around and popped it open, helped him to his feet. With Alex balanced on his crutches, the trooper let Chet out the other side. The rising sun tinged the clouded sky silver. Alex followed the state trooper toward the entrance, his hard-soled shoes slipping in the snow. Chet grabbed him when he almost fell, and then they followed the trooper in through the front doors.

Inside, Investigators Roth and Banger awaited. They stood up from a seating area and approached. "Thanks for coming," Roth said. The front door opened and Louise Cantrell came in next, followed by a man in a baggy suit and a young woman in black cargo pants holding a large camera bag.

"Good to see you again," Cantrell said to Alex over a quick handshake. The man was Todd Miggs, a forensic videographer, the woman his assistant. They went over it: Sheffield wasn't going to answer any questions about the shooting. He would only talk about crimes he knew about, had committed, or planned on – or some combination thereof. Nobody could be sure which. They would give it as long as it takes, but Cantrell advised that it run no longer than half an hour. "If he's not giving something up by then, I'll pull the plug."

She made a concession: Alex could, of course, end it any time he wanted.

"It's a bit of an elaborate process getting through security," Banger said when the briefing ended. "Follow me, please."

The seven of them turned out their pockets into plastic tubs. There were no cell phones allowed in the room. No pens or pencils. After a jail officer feathered a wand over each of them, Alex, Chet, and the video team were directed to sign some forms on a chest-high desk. Another officer guided them through a second metal detector, finally gathering everyone as a single group to go through the air lock.

They funneled into a room where, Alex was told, lawyers met with their clients. The camera operator started setting up. Even amid all the procedure was an atmosphere of nervous excitement.

After Cantrell and Banger left the room, Miggs looked Alex up and down. "Mr. Baines, can you take your seat, there?"

Alex eased himself into a chair at the large table. The U-bolts on the other side were presumably for linking to inmate restraints.

"That's good," Miggs said. The operator placed a camera on a tripod and pointed the lens at him and twisted some knobs to lock in the shot. A second camera was already set, presumably to cover Sheffield. Miggs: "And now, Investigator Roth, can you show me where – well, how – Mr. Sheffield will be seated?"

She sat on the heavy bench bolted to the floor opposite Alex and looked across at him, her face inscrutable. He focused on details, hoping to steady his mind: Her eyes were indeed blue, not green. Her hair dark brown. She wore it short, tucked around her ears, curling up along the back of her neck. The name Roth had multiple origins: 19th Century Ashkenazi Jews, from the Danish *roe* meant to signify a king, or the warrior class of ancient Germanic Deutsch soldiers. Maybe she was the child of an African and a Scot, or maybe –

"And is that right?" Miggs asked. "Sheffield will be sitting like that?"

Roth placed her hands on the table, enfolding her fingers, her wrists straddling the U-bolt. "This is where he'll be."

Breathe. Inhale, counting to four. Exhale to four.

"Boy, I'd love to be able to keep Kali in the room here, get a shot of him as he comes in the door and sits. Then we can get right out of your way."

"Just cameras," Roth said. "No operators. We need to limit the amount of people in here, bare minimum."

"That's a good idea," Chet said.

Miggs looked like he was biting his tongue. He stared at Kali as she set up the second shot, torqued everything down on the tripod so nothing would move.

"Okay," Roth said. "Thank you."

In and out, through the nose, jaw relaxed. Slow the heart rate. Clear the mind.

Chet held out his arms like a host gesturing for the guests to leave. The correctional officer in the room showed them out.

Roth turned to Chet. "You too, Mr. Warman."

Chet made a face, but left with Miggs and his operator. The door closed, leaving Chet to peer in through the small window until someone urged him on.

After the flurry of activity, the silence and stillness were profound. There was one window, high up, barred, and a single fluorescent light in the ceiling, bright and jittering. The seasoned public speaker in Alex mused that with no hair or make-up attention, he looked like crap – bags under his eyes, dry lips, his forehead likely shining with perspiration. Not that it mattered. The cameras were for transparency. For the DA, in case Sheffield opened up on other crimes.

Corrine's voice: *It's bait.*

"How are you doing?" Roth asked.

"Not my usual Tuesday morning."

"Do you have a usual Tuesday morning?"

"I do my podcast. Then I sit on it for the rest of the week, post it on Friday."

"*Here and Now with Alex Baines,*" she said.

"That's right. Have you ever, um…"

"I haven't listened to it. I've skimmed some articles, people talking about the content."

He had a hard time pulling his gaze away from the small, high window. For a moment, it appeared as though the wall around it was twisting counterclockwise. That kind of optical illusion could happen after a person spent time in motion and the fluid in their head was still unsettled. He wondered if Corrine was having some sort of inner ear problem, if that could explain her vision…

"It started with me talking about mindfulness meditation," he said.

"I'm sorry?"

"I have a book called the same thing – *Here and Now.* My first one. The podcast started as kind of an active rough draft. Then I just kept going."

"You're prolific."

Roth wasn't flattering him; it was just a statement of fact. He glanced at the camera trained on him, saw the red recording light. Alex had seen plenty of news cameras; these looked stripped to the bare essentials. "Has Sheffield been evaluated?"

"A mental health counselor was here yesterday. Found him calm, rational, no suicidal ideation. Not a harm to himself or others. Still, we're taking every precaution."

"I'm really curious about his mental acuity."

"There's no IQ test here. If and when he gets sentenced to state prison, that's when they do all that." She added, "In my opinion, he's exhibited an above-average intelligence. There's no question he has insight – he's aware of everything that's happening and seems to be making deliberate decisions."

Roth was direct in manner, so it suddenly felt like she was withholding judgment on something. Throughout his career, Alex had been on the other side of the table or stage from intellectuals and thought leaders, scientists and psychologists, priests and rabbis. He'd been in the company of presidents and CEOs of Fortune 500 companies. He'd had drinks with Elon Musk, Bill Gates, Desmond Tutu – it had been tea with the Dalai Lama. He'd spent years both training to overcome stage fright and diluting it down with real-time exposure therapy. He didn't slip; he didn't falter. Gary Sheffield was just a man, another broken human being, same as everyone else.

Except this man had gone nuts and shot up a theater. Tried to kill him. Maybe that was what he was picking up on – Roth's careful application of the phrase "deliberate decisions."

She looked at the door, as if catching a noise. The correctional officer moved to open up and Roth stepped away from the desk.

"Here we go."

Despite preparations, Alex's heart started beating harder.

Just take it as it comes.

They waited.

29

Chains rattled and clinked together, coming down the hall. The door opened and Sheffield shuffled into the room, an officer on each side of him. First impressions: He looked like a guy working in the Lawn & Tractor section of a hardware store. Youthful face broken by a few crinkles around the eyes. Average height and weight. Hard to tell in the orange inmate fatigues, but he could've had a slight gut. His arms were muscled enough to show he'd carried his share of packages for UPS.

"Stop here. Now raise your arms up, slowly, that's it."

The two officers unlinked the chain connecting his hands to his feet. The inmate was instructed to sit down and the officers ran his hand-chain through the table and reconnected it. There was a glint of the ironic in Sheffield's eyes, as if he hadn't expected to be here, despite his own actions.

His public defender came next, a woman with short hair and pale skin. Another correctional officer followed her in with a chair, placed it in the corner in proximity to the camera. The lawyer set a small sheaf of lined paper in front of Sheffield, scribbled with notes, then took her seat. Alex hadn't been told about the lawyer, but it didn't matter.

One officer stayed, the others left, shutting the door.

Alex met Sheffield's gaze. "I'd like to jump right into this. You claim you have knowledge of certain crimes, is that right?"

Sheffield glanced away. "First, I'd like to share a bit of scripture with you."

Alex opened his mouth, closed it. Not even ten seconds into this thing and Sheffield's agenda came through: he was a religious type after all. There was a certain relief to that, an end to speculation. "Mr. Sheffield, despite what you might think about me, you'll get no satisfaction engaging on this issue. I'm only here to —"

"It's from Timothy. You want to hear it, or you want me to leave?"

An ultimatum.

"All right. Go ahead."

"'All scripture is given by inspiration of God to instruct us in truth and to cause us to realize what is wrong in our lives.'"

"Timothy 3:16," Alex said.

"Would you say that applies to what you do? Spreading information, instructing in truth? Asking people to look at what's wrong in their lives?" His tone was soft, somewhat coy, but *their lives* came out *theyah lives.* It was a Maine accent; that sort of mid-Atlantic-meets-Bostonian tinge that evoked a working-class background.

Alex said, "My intention is to steer the public discourse toward openness and honesty. What I write isn't scripture."

"If we loosen the definition of scripture a little bit…"

"I'm not going to loosen it. It means the sacred writings of a religion. If a word doesn't fit, choose another one."

Easy, he thought. His adrenaline was up, unusual for him — he'd spent years debating. But this was a vastly different scene.

Sheffield dropped his gaze to the lined note paper he had with him. "The sacred writings of a religion? Isn't religion a

pursuit or interest to which a person ascribes supreme importance or meaning?" He pronounced it *impahtance*. Hard to take
the guy as an intellectual with that baby face and downeast
accent.

"Mr. Sheffield – this game – I'm familiar with it. We're not…
I'm not here for a semantic debate. I'm here because of the terms
you've set out, that you have something to share, or confess, and
you'll only do so to me."

Sheffield's eyes came up. "I *do* have information, and you're
gonna want to hear it. But first – I just need to lay some ground
rules."

Alex glanced at Roth, who was fixated on Sheffield.

"I'd like you to admit that what you do – your talks, your
books – these are a kind of scripture for your religion."

"That's not the definition of scripture."

"The objective of any religion is morality," Sheffield said.
"You believe science can show us a path to morality, same as any
other religion."

"Religion is based on belief, not proof. Science is based on
proof, not belief." His leg started to hurt as he spoke and he tried
not to squirm.

"On the contrary, all the great scientific discoveries *began*
with belief. And didn't Einstein say that science without religion
is lame?"

Who was this guy?

Alex said, "The rest of that quote is that 'religion without
science is blind.' Mr. Sheffield – is this what we're here to do?
You promise criminal revelations in order to control a religious
conversation? Equating science with religious fundamentalism is
just another game. I told you I don't want to play games."

Sheffield appeared thoughtful. That glint remained in his eyes,
a look of subtle bemusement, but there was also a jagged energy
pulsing beneath his veneer, an excitement. As though he consid-

ered this a real debate with an audience watching. He said, "You're really here to get criminal revelations?"

"Of course. That's the only reason. I'm on painkillers and steroids and would rather be anywhere else in the world. But if there's a chance I can help, that's why I'm here."

"So your interest is in, what – human well-being?"

"Yes."

He frowned. "I'm confused, though. How do you determine what well-being means? If you don't believe in God, I mean – how do you know?"

"I'd really like to get to it. Please tell me what you know, or what you'd like to disclose."

"You really don't like to talk about your atheism, do you?"

"Mr. Sheffield…"

The inmate tilted his head. There was definitely something rough about him, the type of guy who showered after work, as they said. But he was intelligent. The question was, Alex thought, did that intelligence mean he was the taskmaster? Or just a smart foot soldier, carrying out a task?

"I just want to understand," Sheffield said. "I've been following you for a long time, and I think you're afraid of really admitting your own philosophy."

"You've been following me?"

"Your work, I mean." Sheffield leaned back, as far as the chains binding him to the table would allow. He seemed to be getting more comfortable.

Alex's leg was a low drumbeat of pain, his ass already going numb in the hard chair. Too much time recently spent sitting and lying down, his muscles softening.

"I just want a straight answer from you," Sheffield said. "I want to know, right now, for the record, if you believe in God."

Alex sighed. "It's not a simple question to answer. Einstein said that, too."

"He was an agnostic. Not an atheist."

"Here's the problem, Mr. Sheffield – I don't know what you mean by 'believe' and I don't know what you mean by 'God.' There's an assumption that the question you're asking is the question I'm answering, and that's the wrong assumption. And that's why we get into trouble."

A smile tugged the corner of Sheffield's mouth. "Humor me."

"Humoring you is what I'm…" He broke off. "Fine; anything is possible. But a supernatural creator-God is incredibly unlikely."

Sheffield's forehead cleared and he nodded, as if satisfied. "Thank you. We'll call you an agnostic, then. So – would you say that humanity is what's most important – instead of focusing on eternal rewards, it's the here and now, like the title of your podcast?"

It was becoming clearer all the time that Sheffield had a different agenda – to interrogate Alex, get him to admit something – than the one he'd given police. If there was any chance of a confession, Alex needed to shift the conversation and take back control. "It's in my interest to care. To do what I can to help reduce suffering in the world. That's it."

Sheffield narrowed his gaze. "Do you really think by turning the world to atheism, or to your so-called science-based morality, you're going to reduce suffering?"

"I'm here today in case anyone has been hurt, or could be hurt. That's it. Now if we could –"

"You don't think you're hurting anyone with what you do?"

Another sigh escaped him. Even for the circumstances, this was ham-handed. Maybe Sheffield wasn't so much a religious type as he was a wannabe philosopher. This was his way of taking on Alex in a captive intellectual debate. The guy even had notes with him. What was he angling for?

Alex looked at Roth, who met his eyes this time, communicating silently: *Get to the details.* He opened his mouth, but

Sheffield beat him to it. "What's going to enhance well-being in the absence of spirituality?"

"Now you're talking about spirituality," Alex said. "Spirituality and religiosity are not the same things. If we could –"

"I thought we weren't playing word games."

"They're separate things."

"Will science save us? Science which gave us the atom bomb and weapons in the hands of our children? Science which gave us these machines and devices we've become addicted to?" Sheffield smiled when Alex didn't respond, and then looked down at his notes. "Science is going to stop evil, stop human impulse – how?" He glanced up and raised his eyebrows. "By controlling our minds? By gathering groups of people together in a big room, getting them to close their eyes, so you can fill their heads with your thoughts?"

A tendril of sweat tracked from Alex's hairline down toward his temple. He'd been here before, and with much more capable opponents, but he'd never had his personal life pulled into the debate, and it was throwing him off. This wasn't about confessing to or sharing information on any crimes. This was an ambush. "Who are you, Mr. Sheffield? You're somebody that feels disenfranchised? You're worried about a machine replacing your job at UPS? So you attack –"

"We don't need religion to help us? We don't need God or religion?"

"– You attack innocent people, you shoot me, then you lure me here to –"

"I needed to get your attention." Sheffield's face reddened as he leaned closer. "I needed to get everybody's attention. That's hard to do today. You've gotta be loud. All this praise of science, and – what? Science says we're headed for four degrees Celsius above average by the end of this century. To expect coastal erosion, mass migration, food shortage. But it was science that gave us all the problems in the first place. The cars, the planes, the factories....We're sheep who need a shepherd."

"Mr. Sheffield, please talk to me about these crimes you've committed. Or that you know about. If, in fact, you've got anything to confess." The psychological tug-of-war was taking a physical toll on Alex: His body was trembling, the pain now radiating up from his leg into his abdomen and chest.

"Because I have to tell you," Alex went on, "I'm really starting to think there aren't any other crimes besides the one we know about. And I think you're failing to see the irony here – that your situation is so desperate, your cause so out of whack, you need to terrorize people, hurt them, try to kill them – and when you fail, bait them into a debate."

The chains rattled as Sheffield gestured. "These are desperate times. People like you are destroying the world. I'll go to any lengths to try and stop it."

"Stop it? Stop *what*? I'm not going to make a good pariah. Most people in this country don't even know who I am."

Sheffield leaned back. "Well, that's false modesty. Of course people know you – you're the new preacher. You have the ear of millions. How else would you spread your ideas? How else would you solve all our big problems?"

"I never said I was going to solve anything. I'm hoping to steer the conversation toward –"

"'Toward openness and honesty.' Bullshit." Sheffield quickly consulted his notes before saying, "You're the newest version of a long line of materialists. And you know what? Your kind actually started back in Christianity, so you're a hypocrite, too."

"Where did you get that from?" Alex reached forward. "Let me see your notes, please."

Sheffield pinned the pages with his fingers. "Back then, your kind marveled at the glory of God. But then you kicked God out

T.J. BREARTON

and reduced everything to particles and forces and random interactions."

Alex focused on the lawyer. "Who did he call? Who is he in
contact with?"

When she didn't answer, knowing he was dangerously close
to appearing unhinged and not caring, Alex returned to Sheffield.
"This is a sideshow. If you actually have something to confess,
confess it. I'll be your counselor, priest, whatever you want."

Sheffield pulled an innocent, pitiable face. "I'm not like you,
Dr. Baines. I don't have all kinds of books and speaking tours and
big degrees. I'm just an average guy. Just have my crib sheets
with me."

Alex glanced at Roth next, wondering if she'd make a move.
She was eyeing the papers but said nothing. Cantrell, watching
from another room, had to be biting her fingernails, but she
wasn't about to call it quits either. He could, though.

Sheffield raised his eyebrows. "I may not be a genius, but I
call it like I see it. I know the devil's work when I see it. Telling
people God is a fairytale – that's exactly what the devil does."

Trying to rile him up now. To get him to say something, to
slip.

It was time to end it. But first: "Mr. Sheffield, there are people
in the hospital right now because of you. Whose work is that?
That's God's good work? People likely to spend the rest of their
lives afraid of public spaces. They're having nightmares about
you and what you've done. And you sit there with your Cliffs-
Notes, believing you're some soldier of God? You missed your
time, Mr. Sheffield. You were meant to live during the Crusades.
You would have fit right in, murdering and pillaging." Alex was
sweating harder, breathing fast. He needed to stop but couldn't.
"You're so bad at this, you're so *inept,* that you tried to kill me
and failed."

The silence was like a living thing in the room. Sheffield

smiled, really smiled for the first time. It touched his eyes, which shone like hard jewels, and then it disappeared. "You think I tried to kill you? You think I tried to kill you and missed by accident?"

Alex opened his mouth, but the words were stuck in his throat.

Sheffield pointed a finger. "I know how to shoot. I don't miss. I put it right where I want to put it."

"I'm done here." Alex stripped away the microphone clipped to his shirt. He grabbed his crutches.

Roth leaned forward. "Mr. Sheffield, if you have anything to say about past crimes, or anything ongoing or in the planning, now is the time. After this, you'll get no special treatment. You'll have no chance at a plea bargain."

"All right," Sheffield's lawyer said, "I think we've –"

Roth barreled on: "You'll either plead guilty, or go to trial and you'll be convicted, no question, and get the maximum prison time. Now is the time, Mr. Sheffield."

On his feet, Alex shook with anger. The harder he tried to control it, the worse it got. He jammed a finger at Sheffield. "There are no crimes. There's nothing he's going to tell us. This has been a big show."

"Yeah, you'd better go," Sheffield said, turning to him. "Go on, mister 'openness and honesty.' There hasn't been an honest thing out of your mouth yet."

"Fuck you," Alex said.

Sheffield reared back, his eyes wide, a grin flickering. "Yeah – that's more like it."

Alex looked from Sheffield into the blank eye of the camera lens. He wanted to wrap his hands around Sheffield's neck, but he limped to the exit instead. As soon as the CO cracked the door, Sheffield said, "You can run, but this ain't over."

Alex stopped, spun around. "What? What did you say?"

Roth was leaning in, her mouth open, about to ask a question.

Blood rose in the lawyer's face as she stared at the table. "This isn't over," Sheffield said, shaking his head as if mournful. "This is just the beginning. The dark is always waiting."

It was the thought of Nyswaner bleeding out – and all those panicked faces and injured people – that did it. Alex dropped the crutches and went for Sheffield. He aimed for the eyes, thinking he'd push them into Sheffield's skull, but the correctional officer was fast, and built with a hard layer of fat around him like body armor. He slammed Alex against the wall at the same time Roth was up and shouting, "Get him out! Get Baines out of here!"

30

The local news van parked across the road, a reporter in the street. Watching from his bedroom, Kenneth wondered what she was saying into the camera. Probably something like, "Behind me is the home of Alex Baines…" and all of that. It was weird the way news people talked. Like they had their own language. Why did they do that? It was like a performance; actors reciting lines with careful pauses and voices curled into questions at the end of every sentence.

He wondered if the news people knew his dad had been shot in the leg. Probably. Were they allowed into the hospital, though? One group was – some CNN people – and Kenneth had sneaked online to watch a woman talk to his dad and cry a little bit and call him a hero for saving her. Mr. Warman was all over Twitter about it, saying that police had video showing it, video he was trying to get. In the meantime, there was the cell phone recording of Kenneth's dad trying to stop a security guard's bleeding and running for a door because he thought the bad guy was out there.

Kenneth wondered if he could do something like that. It scared him to think about, and then he felt ashamed for being afraid, but reasoned that – probably with enough adrenaline, yeah, he could. Because when adrenaline kicked in, you were almost like a superhero. People lifted cars off of trapped kids. And there were people who lived without feeling pain, too – he'd read about a family in Italy or somewhere and they lacked the gene for feeling pain. Scientists said it was the key to future medical treatment. But not everybody liked screwing around with genes.

He turned from the window to keep surfing the web on his computer. He scoured everything he could find on his dad and the shooting, and found at least twenty papers that had covered it, including The New York Times, and then found this piece by something called VICE which covered it, but from, like, a different angle. The VICE story headline was: "Microdosing a Factor in Baines's Quick Actions?"

Kenneth was just digging into the article when he heard his mother talking downstairs. He listened for a second. Her voice faded, then he heard it again. She sounded upset.

Corrine watched the reporter outside, knowing that Westchester's local news wasn't interested in Alex Baines's rich housewife; this was just background while they puzzled over why he'd left Burlington for New York and disappeared. There was no resentment in that; it didn't bother her that she went largely unmentioned in Alex's public life – it was preferable to retain privacy, to raise the kids in a more everyday setting. But now, she turned away from the window and wondered just how "everyday" this was.

High ceilings and light-filled rooms defined her house, a living room open plan to the white quartz countertop and marble backsplash of the kitchen, select four-inch oak flooring. It was more like an executive suite – all the traditional Indian showpieces in the world couldn't make up for that – than a home.

It had been Alex's choice.

Before going to law school, she'd studied psychology at Brooklyn College and thought she had a basic understanding of how relationships worked: Whether we knew it or not, we picked partners with traits similar to a parent whose love we truly wanted and did not receive. For her, that was her mother. Practical and driven.

Laura Wayland's ambitions had been for her daughters' success. Every day, in their cramped, two-bedroom apartment in Mt Vernon, she'd hammered it home: you need to go out into the world and make something of yourself. While she'd kept two jobs, supporting herself and her two daughters without help from their father, it was her restlessness, her perpetual dissatisfaction, which might have driven her to an early grave.

As if released, Corrine had taken a postgraduate year to travel and see the world after her mother's death. Albany was one of only a few law schools to offer a joint bioethics degree; the eventual goal had been to work in public policy for the government or as legal counsel to health care organizations. But India changed things. She'd met her future husband. And after returning to the States, she took a pregnancy test, saw a doctor, and Alex proposed.

She'd put law school on hold...and then it just never happened. Raising Kenneth was all-consuming. A "spirited" child, they said, boundlessly energetic, prone to tantrums. In the pre-housekeeper days, between caring for her son and often joining Alex to tour the country, every hour of the day was filled. For five years, having another child wasn't even on the table. And then Freda made her entrance. Freda, the little light of their lives. Impossible to imagine a world without her.

Corrine faced the window again and watched as the reporter handed her microphone to the camera operator, who bagged it and then the camera. She watched as they returned to the van and, when it drove away, felt heavy with loneliness.

When the phone vibrated on the bay window bench, she thought maybe it was Drew. He'd gone to his place in the city last night and might've been calling to check in. Instead, the incoming number had a 949 area code.

"Hello?"

There was nothing for a few seconds, just the soft white noise of a connected call.

"Corrine Baines?" The voice was male, somewhat muffled. Vaguely familiar.

"Who is this?"

"My name is John Creasy. I'm a private investigator."

Without thinking, she stood up from the bench and started pacing. "Okay. What can I do for you? You've been calling. You called my husband's phone the other day. Is everything okay?"

"Mrs. Baines, I need to ask you some questions. It's about your brother-in-law, Mr. Mayhew."

"Stephen? Why are you…?"

"Your sister, Mara, lived with you for a short time, is that right?"

"Why are you asking this? Does my husband know you're calling me?"

"I haven't been able to reach him."

"You called when we were at the hospital. Why are you –?"

"Mrs. Baines, please listen. You just really need to listen right now."

Her skin tingled. This was too strange. She thought she would call the police as soon as this was over – or at least call Alex.

Creasy said, "I've come across certain information pertaining to your sister and her husband. If you could just answer my questions, then I'll explain. If necessary."

Not knowing what else, she said, "Okay."

"Your sister lived with you for a time?"

"Yes. A month. A little less than a year ago. She and Stephen were –"

"That's fine. Was there money paid to her?"

"*Paid* to her? No one paid her anything. We offered…Alex offered to help set her up, financially. She was thinking of leaving her husband. Of leaving Stephen."

"And, to your knowledge, what does Mr. Mayhew – Stephen – know about this?"

"What does he know? I don't know."

"You don't know if your sister told him about it or not?"

"No. That's not something we discussed. It was a very simple offer. We were being supportive. Stephen seemed to…Mara had learned a few things. Things that he was doing."

"With other women."

"Two. There were two women who – why are you asking me this?" Afraid Kenneth might overhear, Corrine closed herself in the pantry. It held the stale reek of cigarettes, even though she'd been outside when she smoked hers half an hour ago. "Listen, Mr. Creasy, I don't know what you're inferring. Stephen admitted everything to her. He had a…he turned over a new leaf."

"He got religion."

She wasn't comfortable with this man, his gruffness, his knowledge of intimate things. Chet was going to hear from her about his unorthodox PI.

"I'm going to hang up now, Mr. –"

"No, you're not. Because you want to know. Because you want to make sense of this."

That stopped her. No more pacing the enclosure, no more clenching and unclenching her fist. For a shocking moment, it blazed around her, this sense that she was *right*, that there was some bigger, even cosmic meaning to recent events. "Excuse me?"

"What I'm telling you, Mrs. Baines, is that what happened to your husband, to those people at his talk, was not random."

She panicked. But she couldn't believe it. "I don't like what you're suggesting, or how you're talking about my family. And I don't know anything about you – who you are, how to take what you're saying." She came just short of adding: *For all I know, you're the one who's a part of this.*

"Take it up with your sister, if you want," Creasy said. "But I'd be careful if I were you. If you don't know what she's saying to her husband, you might want to watch what you say to her."

"Mr. Creasy – whatever you think you have on my sister and her husband, you're wrong. They're good people, and they wouldn't be involved in any of this."

She waited, and for a moment, thought he'd already ended the call.

But Creasy said with a softened tone, "I've been doing this for twenty-five years, Mrs. Baines, and there's something I've heard again and again: 'He always seemed like such a nice guy.' You just have to follow the money, Mrs. Baines. Ninety-nine percent of the time, that's what it is."

With that, he hung up.

31

The handcuffs bit into Alex's wrists. One CO kept a hand on his chest while the other moved Sheffield toward the door. The handcuffs made it hard to stand; the pain made it hard to think. Someone, maybe Roth, said, "This is for your own safety," but all he could do was watch Sheffield shamble away, rattling those chains.

"Hey!" Alex strained toward Sheffield, and the CO pressed him back. "Hey! Talk to me, man. You threaten me and walk out? Talk to me!"

But it was over. Sheffield never looked back, and then he was gone. His lawyer started for the door with an apologetic expression, as if representing Sheffield was a hazard of the job. "I'm sorry."

"What do you know? Tell me what you know, please."

"I'm very sorry, Dr. Baines." She showed him her back and hurried out.

The CO got in Alex's face. "You going to be cool?"

Alex lowered his head as a fresh wave of pain drove through him. It was like his leg wanted to detach from his body, to fire away like a missile. He gnashed his teeth and fought against blacking out.

The CO said, "Does this guy need medical attention or what? He doesn't look so good."

"Leave him with me," Roth answered.

"No can do."

"Just for a minute."

"Ma'am, I can't have someone in the holding area. If you want, you can talk to the undersheriff."

"I'm just asking for five minutes. While I speak to my supervisor and the district attorney."

Alex stared at the floor. The corrections officer hooked a hand to keep him from falling over. "Do what you got to do. I'll sit with him. Five minutes."

"We need to take those off him."

The CO muttered something but removed the cuffs, then the CO and Roth helped Alex sit down on the bench where Sheffield had just been – the metal still felt warm. Roth bent and got eye-to-eye with him. "Dr. Baines? You okay?"

"I need my phone. I have to call my family."

"You need to just sit tight. I've got your wife's number – I can check and make sure everyone is all right."

The pain burned through his thoughts, worse every minute, making focus impossible. He tried to remember exactly what Sheffield said. About it not being over.

"I'll be right back," Roth said.

Harlan and Cantrell were in a nearby room, watching the monitor as Roth came in.

Cantrell looked at her. "My God, what was that?"

Roth felt the gray walls closing in. This whole place smelled like urine not quite masked with bleach. She promised herself a half-hour shower when she got home. "I don't know." Her thoughts ran in multiple directions.

"This guy's just crazy, and we fell for it," Harlan said.

"If he's crazy, he got past the evaluation," Roth said.

Cantrell: "This is an absolute mess. I brought a victim here to meet with a violent offender, and the guy just seems to want to play games. And then Baines turns into a cage fighter on us. What is Sheffield saying, 'This isn't over'? What has he got?" She leaned on the table and glared at them.

"He might still talk," Roth said. "He might get specific."

"I don't think so." Cantrell straightened up and ticked off the items on her fingers. "Nothing about any bodies, nothing about knowledge of any other crimes, and I can't do a damn thing with 'this isn't over.' He wanted to torture Baines, to rub his nose in it, to set him off, and it worked. And *I* let it happen. Hell, I *facilitated* it. This is terrible." The DA shook her head after a moment. "I don't know; maybe Sheffield will want to make a deal and give up what he knows after he's been at state prison a little while. If he really knows anything."

Harlan started for the door, but Roth didn't move. He held the handle and looked at her. "What?"

"I'd like to go down to Sheffield's residence myself," Roth said.

Cantrell's eyebrows climbed higher. "You think they missed something? They've been there all night and all this morning."

"I would like to personally get a look at this guy's life." Her eyes sought Harlan's permission, but Cantrell interrupted.

"And what's this thing I read this morning about Baines taking designer drugs?"

"I don't know," Harlan said. "We're waiting on blood test results, but apparently someone out there already knows, or is making claims, that Baines was in some kind of study that involved microdosing."

"It's usually small – ten to twenty micrograms," Roth chipped in.

"Well, some of the substances are schedule one narcotics. When do we get the blood?"

"Soon," Harlan said, his gaze drifting to Roth. She read what was there: *Cantrell is doing damage control.*

If Baines was on some sort of wild substances, this meet with Sheffield would be construed as a bigger screw up than it already was.

Roth said, "Baines tried to do the right thing here."

"I agree," Harlan said.

They all watched the monitor, Alex Baines sitting there with his leg stuck out at an angle, head down. "I told him I'd call his wife," Roth said.

"Let him go," Cantrell said at last. "He's been through enough. No way we're going to arrest him. If the jail puts up a fight, I'll call the AG. Let him go. Let him call his wife. This Sheffield is full of shit." Then she put her hands on her hips and looked into a corner and said, "*Fuck.*"

32

Chet caught up to him in the parking lot, limping and slipping in the wet snow, holding the phone to his ear. "Hey – you're gonna break your neck. Where are you going? We don't even have a car."

The pain threatened to swamp him. He was light-headed, vision spotting, but he kept moving, waiting for Corrine to answer.

"Alex?"

"Hey."

"Alex, I got another call from that number."

It took him a second. "What number? You mean when we were –"

"From 949. He said his name was John Creasy. Alex, he knew things about me, personal things…"

"Babe, slow down. Where are the kids?"

"They're here with me – why? Alex? What's going on?"

Her voice was rising; she already sounded close to panic. But he needed everyone safe. "What about Drew?"

"Went home."

"Call him. Get him back there to the house."

"This guy acted like we were in danger."

"Why? What did he say?"

"Hang on…" She spoke to someone else, probably Kenneth.

Chet stood beside Alex. They were in the center of the parking lot, state trooper cars all around.

Corrine came back over the line, her voice thick with emotion. "That was Kenneth. Freda is awake. I've got to go."

"What did Creasy say?"

"He knew things about Mara, when she was here. Well, he asked me. It was like he was confirming it." The words trembled, almost too soft to hear. "He asked about Stephen. He acted like Stephen and Mara could be involved. Which is nuts. But he acted like he had good reason."

"Involved? With what happened?"

"Yes. He…I don't know. I have to go. Should I call the police? What would I even say?"

Alex swallowed the bad taste in his mouth. He imagined Corrine standing in their house, a house he knew she pretended to like but never really felt at home in, her mascara probably streaked, face flushed. *My poor wife.* His love for her began to harden, to form a pit in his stomach. "Listen. I'm going to go tell the police here as soon as we're done talking."

"Oh God, Alex, what is happening?"

"Take it easy. It's okay. Can you give me the number?"

"I can, yeah, hang on…"

He made a writing gesture to Chet, who took out his phone. When Corrine read it, he relayed it to Chet, who typed it into his phone. Alex held up a finger, meaning, *Don't call yet. Wait for me.*

To Corrine: "But everyone's okay?"

"The kids are okay. Freda is getting better, but…"

He could hear Freda crying in the background, sort of mewling, the way she got when she was sick, and his heart sunk deeper.

"Cory…I'm so sorry. Honey, I'm just so sorry. I'm going to call Scarsdale police, too – I want someone checking the house. Just as a precaution. But get Drew there, too. And I'll get right back to you. Okay?"

He could hear her soothing Freda, then something – maybe water poured in a glass. Corrine said, "Wait – your meeting is over? What did he say to you?"

"We can talk about it after. Just do what you need to do." It was cold, the wind piercing his thin jacket.

"Alex. I know about the study you're in."

His brain felt squeezed. Either she'd seen the article, or Drew might've told her, anticipating it. Alex couldn't be mad at Drew; he should've told Corrine himself already.

"Is Creasy tied up with that? Alex – does this whole thing have to do with the microdosing?"

It came ripping out of the cloud-smudged sky: *blackmail*. Somehow Creasy was working with Stephen Mayhew? No. That was getting way too ahead of things. He needed to calm down, to put one foot in front of the other.

"I don't know, but I'm going to figure this out, okay? Hello? Cor? You there?"

She sounded close to tears again as she drew a shuddering breath. Corrine had always been sensible. She got it from her mother. Her father, not so much. Kemper McElhone was a drifter who'd never quite gotten it together, never had enough money, always had too much booze, blamed the devil while drowning his personal demons. Corrine had a little bit of her father in her, and those traits emerged under stress. Right now, she was fighting it – he could feel it even though they were three hundred miles apart.

He felt a deep tug of guilt and closed his eyes, suddenly

wondering how much of his own advice he really believed. He told people to view each challenge as an opportunity, each trouble as an instrument of growth – but that was hard to do when the chips were down. "I'll get right back to you, baby, okay? I'm going to get someone from the Scarsdale Police over there to check the house."

"Okay."

"I'll call you back." He hung up, unable to move, keeping the flood of grief at bay while Chet held the phone and watched him. "We need a car," Alex said to Chet. "I need to get home."

"I'm going to get one of these troopers to run me into the nearest – whatever constitutes civilization around here – and rent one right now. But – Alex you look bad, bro."

"I gotta get home."

"What happened in there? I tried to talk to Roth, but she acted all frosty."

Only Chet, a grown man living in Los Angeles, would actually say *frosty*. Alex directed the rising tide of anger at his personal manager: "Is that Creasy's number? The one I just gave you?"

"I don't know. It's 949, but…"

"What do you mean, you don't know?"

"I mean Creasy is like a real-life phantom. I always told you that about him. That's how he does his work – he lays low, stays off the radar. What happened? Was that who called Corrine? What did she say?"

"Come on, man. Fucking come on."

Chet looked struck. "What are you talking about? I'm sorry I went for this. They're gonna pay. We're gonna sue their asses. Okay? You've got that look on your face, but I don't know what happened in there because they wouldn't let me in, wouldn't even let me watch in the other room. You need to get back to the hospital. That's what's gotta happen."

"How did *VICE* know about it?" Alex squared his shoulders

with Chet – no easy feat, the way his body wanted to hunch forward. "What are you doing, Chet? Are you doing something?"

Chet stared back, his breath rising in a cloud, looking both angry and bewildered. "Am I *what*?"

"How did you get to the hospital so fast? You were supposed to be in LA."

"I told you – plans changed."

"You hired security. Really late in the game – didn't tell me about it until I met those guys in the morning. Why?"

He felt guilty for asking, but his mind was racing. There was a powerful movement behind microdosing, top players in Silicon Valley, even some unexpected champions like a high-powered lawyer from San Francisco, a developer from Los Angeles – the man who first had Chet's ear about the whole thing. Maybe Chet, being Chet, saw this as some absurd marketing opportunity right from the beginning. Maybe those guys were ready to take a product public and Alex was a way to introduce it. *Look at this man! Atheist Superhero Survives Shooting! And here's the new wonder drug he was benefitting from…*

No, that was ridiculous. He was grasping at straws. But his head was a carnival of conspiracy theories. Chet. John Creasy. Stephen Mayhew?

You think I missed you by accident?

"Sheffield wanted me here," Alex said. "He planned this from the beginning."

"How do you know that? What did he *say*, man?"

"He had things written down!" Alex snapped. "Like, he was quoting people. People I've debated…" He squeezed his eyes shut and pressed a palm to his temple in a lame attempt to relieve the mounting pressure.

Chet started to say something about getting Sheffield's notes as Roth emerged from the building, headed in their direction. Once she was standing with them, Alex told her about the call, and she led them toward the trooper barracks across the complex from the jail. Inside Roth's office, she gave Chet a studied look.

"Tell me about this private investigator."

"I had John Creasy on the payroll for a while," Chet said. "Used him to occasionally get background on people in Alex's orbit, sometimes to investigate social media users making particularly potent threats. In truth…he's a bit out there, and he's super hard to get a hold of. One of those, 'Don't find me; I'll find you' kind of guys."

"So he's not currently working for you."

"No."

"What was the last thing you had him do for you?"

Chet glanced at Alex, then looked at his hands, sighed. "I had him look into Stephen Mayhew."

It felt like Alex had the wind knocked out of him. "Stephen? What are you talking about? You did background on my *brother-in-law?*"

Chet's eyes came up, a lick of fire in them. "You and Corrine spent a month with Mara down at your place. I'm sorry, but it made a mess of everything – you were canceling gigs. I put Creasy on Mayhew to try to get to the bottom of it. Whether he was cheating. To fucking expedite it."

"He told Mara himself. He came home and admitted it to her."

"Well, yeah, eventually. And Creasy went back to the West Coast and you never knew about it. But obviously, he found out things that concerned him."

"Like what?" Roth asked.

"I don't know. I just mean, that's how it seems. That's why he's calling."

Alex shook his head. "So he calls *Corrine*? Why not call you? Or me?"

"He *did* try to call you, I thought. And he probably didn't call me because I told him to fuck off." Chet glanced at Roth and spread his hands. "Just in a message. I was frustrated with his lack of communication."

Alex ran a hand across his face. "Ah, Chet..."

Roth interrupted. "Do we know where Mr. Creasy is right now?"

"I'm sure he's on the west coast," Chet said, a bit eagerly. "No reason he'd be around here."

"Let's try him," Roth said.

Chet keyed the number and held the phone to his ear. After a few seconds, shook his head. "Nothing. But it's his number – he just disabled his voicemail or something."

"I'm calling Scarsdale." Roth put the phone on speaker so they could hear. When an officer answered, she asked for the sergeant.

"Sergeant Dukette here."

"Sergeant Dukette, this is Investigator Raquel Roth in Lewis. I'm with Alex Baines." She provided Alex's home address and briefly explained the situation.

"Oh, okay, right. I know Dr. Baines and everything that just happened up there. So his wife..."

"She received a disturbing phone call."

"Is she alone there at the house? They have a couple of children; is that right?"

"That's correct. Possible you could run a car over there, Sergeant? Have a look around the house?"

Dukette cleared his throat. "Ah, let me just check with my patrol – short answer is, yes, we'll have a look. You said the area code was what?"

"California. But it's a mobile phone."

"So you think maybe someone is...?"

"They made personal references. Private information."

"Uh-huh. Any direct threats made?"

"Sergeant, this is a situation that – it's really unfolding as we speak. Things are happening on our end. I would really appreciate it if you could drive over there."

"I understand that, I understand that."

"I could notify the state troopers, if you think that will help."

"Well – right, but – let me see where my patrol is at. There's an officer responding to a call – I'll do the best I can here. Is there a best number to reach you at?"

Roth recited one. Dukette said, "I'll get back with you shortly."

After, Roth looked at Alex and Chet. "All right. Try Creasy again."

Chet tapped in the number while Alex stared at him. They'd known each other for fifteen years. In that time, they'd not only been business associates, they'd become friends. Family, really. But there was something about Chet Warman that the man kept hidden. He didn't talk about his past, growing up in the outskirts of Los Angeles, his cigar-chomping movie producer father, his ingénue mother. Alex had always chalked it up to an East Coast/West Coast thing – like tribes, you just never fully understood the ways of the other. Alex said what was on his mind; Chet always seemed to be acting a little bit.

The sense of futility descended hard and fast. *Someone* had laid a trap – that was the only answer. None of this was random; it all went together, all designed to completely screw him up. His life, his marriage, his career. If you stopped assuming all people were rational and reasonable, when you knew they were motivated by emotions which could *supersede* rational or reasonable behavior, everything was on the table. Everyone was a suspect.

Chet shook his head at last and stared at the phone like it was defunct. "Yeah, nothing." He was silent a moment, breath whistling through his nostrils, and then he tapped the phone with his fingernail. "But listen, this is what I'm trying to say. Maybe Creasy found out something about Mayhew."

"What? That he's a shitty husband?"

"He turned to religion, right? Before Mara went back to him? He had a conversion, or whatever you call it, and came back to her begging, and she went home. That's what I thought happened."

"Something like that."

"Maybe he resents you. What you did with Mara, what you stand for…"

Roth was watching them, assessing the tension, Alex thought. He shook his head at Chet again. "If you're saying you think Stephen and Gary Sheffield are connected, I don't see that."

Chet pulled in a deep breath. "Or maybe you *can't*. Listen to me. Okay? We're in my territory now. You don't know the stuff that goes on out there. With all due respect, you're holed up in a lab or sitting on a stage. I'm the one wading through the filth, and this thing *stinks*. And yet you start making these accusatory remarks. Asking me how I got to the hospital so fast. Okay? That's where you want to take this?"

"Chet..."

"Listen to me. A guy with no record suddenly shoots up one of your talks? He was incited to do it. I don't know, someone might even have *asked* him to do it."

Alex put his hand up: *Enough.*

Chet said, "This is a hatchet job, buddy. This was all put in place to ruin you."

There was a moment of silence, then Roth: "Do you think that, Dr. Baines?"

"I don't know." The idea of that, of hundreds of people terrified by a gunman, dozens physically wounded, the rest emotionally traumatized, being all about him, about some sort of payback – that was too much. That was a nightmare.

"Dr. Baines," Roth said, "this might be above my paygrade. As far as the New York State Police are concerned, you're free to go. Though I'd respectfully request that you stay in the state. We may need you again, once the lawyers cut a deal."

"I'll do my best."

She seemed to hone in on his dilemma. "I'd advise you to talk to your attorney, Dr. Baines. Your best course of action might be a civil suit against Sheffield, and that may involve federal subject matter jurisdiction, since Sheffield resides in Maine. And if you can prove a particular motive, it may lead to punitive damages. With a civil case, it's either an intentional tort or it's negligence – in this case, reckless endangerment."

Chet looked bewildered. "Reckless endangerment?"

She cut her eyes to him. "Sheffield is on record – on video – saying that he missed Dr. Baines on purpose. I'm just advising that –"

"This guy is a country fucking bumpkin from Maine. He's working with somebody. What about finding out if –"

Roth's desk phone rang, cutting Chet off – and her, too, since she looked like she'd been about to give Chet an earful or throw him out of the room. She answered, said a few words, and hung up, looked at Alex. "Sergeant Dukette has a patrolman en route to your house as we speak. He's spoken to your wife to let her know."

"Thank you."

Chet said, "Can we at least talk about who Sheffield has been in contact with? He had notes with him. He could have called someone. The jail records those calls."

Roth addressed Chet's question, staying measured, Alex thought. She was addressing his question, too, albeit unspoken. "Mr. Sheffield never made a phone call. He had a bag in his motel room. It came in as his personal effects. There were papers in it that he requested for his meeting with you. Nothing on those papers but the notes you saw, and they appear to be in his own handwriting. Listen, if there's any truth to the theory that

Sheffield was influenced by someone else, that's a matter that may need to be brought before the Supreme Court of New York or to a court of special jurisdiction in Maine. Your lawyer can advise you and speak with a prosecutor about how and where to file the complaint." She stood and stretched her hand toward him. "Good luck, Dr. Baines."

33

From her window, she watched the men leave and then picked up the phone, dialed Portland PD.

"Things have changed up here," Roth said to Libby. "Our guy has made some loose threats that this thing may not be over. He's not saying what, but we need to take it seriously."

"Things are status quo here. You've got what we already sent up?"

"Yes – Investigator Banger and I have the file. Let's just go over it?"

"Absolutely. So, as you've probably seen, then, this guy lives like Mr. Rogers. No porn, no drugs, not a Metallica poster on the wall. He's got the stockpile in his basement; there's that. Years worth of supplies. Rice and flour and everything else stuffed in Mylar bags and sealed in buckets. There's a freezer full of steaks, chops, whole chickens – but no body parts or human heads."

Libby paused, as if waiting for Roth to laugh. She didn't.

Libby resumed: "Ah, he's got the three backup generators, two rifles, but nothing fancy; a .30-30 and a .22. Talked to his neighbors, who say he's hardly ever home, always working, but when he's around he's polite and friendly. Supervisor at UPS says he's never been a problem. Shows up on time; never calls in sick."

Almost like a guy who goes out of his way to be nobody, she thought. But why? Was there a long game? What and why?

Libby was still talking. "... all the stuff we sent up to you and your supervisor. So – what? The feds have nothing to say? With all his provisions, this guy's not on a watch list somewhere? Doomsday-prepper list?"

She wasn't sure if Libby was serious about the watch list, so she said, "They've got nothing on him but basic information. Born in Cousins, Maine, parents live in Boca Raton, Florida, one brother who died in a car wreck – a drunk driving thing – eight years ago."

"That's when he bought his place," Libby said. "All the house paperwork goes back eight years."

"Prior to UPS, he worked for BAX Global."

"What's that?"

"International shipping company, based in California. Have you seen anything there that relates to Irvine? Irvine, California?"

"My forensic guy is still going through the hard drive. Sheffield uses a virtual private network. You know – paranoid of government spying. So we can't get any of his browsing history. He's got a spreadsheet inventory on all of his prepper supplies. Not much in the way of pictures. Couple of boats he was looking at with for sale signs on them, pictures of his house. Not even with construction going on, just pictures of the house. Who does that?"

"And there wasn't much with the emails?"

"Nah. Tons of ads, some work stuff, but nothing personal. My guy here says he was probably using the VPN and communicating through some sort of messenger. Maybe chat forums. Could be encrypted chats."

"I'm going to give you something, hang on." She relayed

Creasy's number. "I'll check it against his phone records, but do me a favor, see if you can't turn it up in his email, address book, any of his notes. John Creasy…" She spelled it. "Also looking for anything on a Stephen Mayhew." She spelled that, too.

"Will do. Yeah, we're working on it."

"Thanks." She was about to hang up, but he kept talking.

"So how you doing up there?"

"Ah…we're good. It's an unusual situation."

"They always are. You know what I mean? You think you know crazy, but crazy's always one step ahead of you." Libby fell silent, police radio chatter in the background.

"I'll keep feeding you stuff from my end as I get more information. Any other names, dates. And I'm going to make my way down there soon as I can."

"That would be good. Send whatever you got right to my tech guy. No – scratch that. Pass them through me. I gotta see how this thing unfolds."

She heard the smile in his voice but didn't feel the levity. She had another call to make, one to the FBI, but by the time she said goodbye to Libby, someone from the Bureau was already calling.

34

The mountains drifted past, withering to hills as they headed south on I-87, Chet driving fast.

"I want to be done," Alex said.

Chet lifted a hand from the wheel. "Alex, the *VICE* thing was my fault. I don't know where they got the information on Irvine –"

"I don't care about that."

"– unless maybe they got something from your brother-in-law."

"They didn't."

Chet returned his hand to the wheel. "What you need is a couple of days with the family, see your physician, then –"

"This doesn't go anywhere positive. This is about rebuilding after a tragedy. Not assessing blame and lashing out."

"I'm not talking about lashing out…"

"Why did you hire security for the gig? I'm not accusing you of anything. I'm asking."

Chet went from sounding slightly wounded to harshly defensive. "I didn't have any fucking reason other than your safety."

"All right, all right."

"Let me ask you – how long we been together?"

"Come on. Don't."

"This is our chance to make it rain, buddy."

"You didn't just use that phrase."

"I'm not talking about 'lashing out.' I'm talking about strategy. This guy, Sheffield, sat there and quoted from something. Who'd he quote from? What did he say?"

"One thing he said was I'm the latest in a long line of materialists."

"Exactly. And you know who said that?"

Alex did. After leaving the jail and Roth's office, his head had cleared a little. "Paul Halloran."

"Paul. Fucking. Halloran. That's exactly right."

"So what."

"So what? So *what*? Alex, you practically coined the term 'stochastic terrorism.' Violence incited by a prominent figure? But carried out later by the followers he or she riles up? Come on, man. Now you've got some hillbilly sitting across from you, *quoting* Paul Halloran. You know what else Halloran has said about you? I've memorized it. 'Self-indulgent intellectual totalitarianism.' That's one. 'Something needs to be done about men like Alex Baines.' That's another. Know what he's saying now?"

"There's no way to link Gary Sheffield to Paul Halloran. Or if there is, the police will find it. Like Roth said, then it's a legal matter."

Chet was getting more excited by the moment. "Whether or *not* doesn't matter. He still influenced Sheffield. He still wrote those tweets about you, the articles, tearing you down, saying *something needs to be done*. In black and white! And he's still doing it. He's saying you're an opportunist, and so is Amy Cross."

"Isn't that what you're doing? Talking about starting a war with Paul Halloran because you think it will make money?"

"Jesus Christ. Alex, I am seriously offended. It's not about the money. That's already going to come in. It's about meeting this thing head on. Someone went after you – whether this one guy, whether working with someone –"

"It's not Stephen."

"– whether *incited* by someone; this is about facing that. This guy was fucking *quoting* Paul Halloran in there. Halloran, the bastard offspring of Rush Limbaugh and Deepak Chopra. We're on the verge of history. This was the opening salvo. No, this wasn't fundamentalism; this wasn't even about the apologetics. This was worse. This was New Age."

Alex checked, but Chet seemed more serious than joking. "He was also quoting scripture," Alex said.

"That doesn't mean anything – or it's exactly the point. Everybody quotes scripture, especially these New Age types. Hey, a few lines are great. It's when you endorse the whole book that it falls apart. Listen, bro – this is everything wrong in the world, right here in a nutshell, embodied by a man who shot up your gig. He's in there talking about Einstein, you said. Isn't this what you've always warned? People smuggling religion into the conversation? Slipping it through the back doors of conspiracy theory, misinformation, bad science, denial? You – *you* represent the truth. The truth says, 'I don't know.' The truth says, 'moral order does not have to have a god attached to it.' 'Let's use science to figure it out.' And let me tell you, brother – this is suppression of free speech. Fascism right in front of our fucking faces. Someone that doesn't like what you have to say tries to shut you down? Ah man, it's happening all over the world – authoritarians blowing the dog whistle to minions who put bombs in the mail or shoot up a synagogue. This is already a war."

It was grandiose, typical for Chet, but maybe there was a kernel of truth. If this *was* some kind of domestic terrorism, if it was about the suppression of ideas, then that was a fight where he had some skin in the game. But his family weighed heavy on his mind. Corrine and the kids needed him home, stable.

Still: "What are you proposing?"

Chet was waiting for it. "We get you into a debate with Halloran. Right away."

"No."

"You've never shied from the truth; why start now?" He unfurled a finger at a time. "This grows your platform ten times the size. You've gone national. It's new book deals, movie deals – okay? I mean do you have any – you know who I've been talking to? David fucking Letterman's people. Jimmy fucking Fallon's people. Colbert. I've been talking to Roger Albee – you remember Roger? He's talking about a documentary, okay; a fucking story of your life. For Netflix. All right? Alex? This breaks you wide open. You and your buddies – now listen to me – you play coy like you're part of some intellectual dark web on purpose. Let's cut the shit. This is the moment, right now, to bring your brand into the mainstream, become a household name. Carl Sagan. Neil Degrasse Tyson. Fuckin' Bill Nye the Science Guy. And for the right reasons – to bring this *fight* into the mainstream. This fight, Alex."

He was quiet. "I want to know why Creasy called."

"I'm gonna find him. I'll beat it out of him if I have to." Chet gave Alex a sidelong look. "And listen – I can always talk to Howard."

"We're not bringing my father into this."

"He knows guys who –"

"No." It was loud, and it shut Chet up. For a few seconds.

"Fine. But whatever Creasy got into, I'll find out."

Alex turned his body toward Chet. "Are you already setting this up? With Halloran?"

"No….Well, I put the feelers out."

"The feelers. You're unreal."

"It's the exact right thing to do. He's already practically begging for it. We'll call it *The Future of Religion Summit* or something. You come out, you're on crutches, just got shot. And there you are ready to lock horns. 'Baines brings the pain!' It's brilliant, bro, I'm telling you."

"I folded with Sheffield. I fell apart."

Chet smacked the steering wheel. "*That's* your concern? That you're not up to par? It was a rigged *game*, man. It wasn't your fault."

They rode in silence for a while, vehicles appearing on the road the further south they drove. *The frog in the boiling water*, Alex thought. The frog doesn't know it's about to die because the heat comes on gradually. Like vehicles adding into the southbound lanes – for a while, it seemed no one else was out, then suddenly they were threading their way through thick traffic. By the time the frog realizes it's boiling to death, it's too late.

"I gotta get out in front of this microdosing thing," Alex said.

"That was a mistake. We'll never give an interview to *VICE* again."

"If they knew about it – maybe that was Creasy, too?"

"Of course it was Creasy." Chet set his jaw. For a guy as flamboyant as Chet, Alex wouldn't want to be in a room alone with him when he was pissed off. "Creasy turned on us, man. Somebody gave him top dollar."

"Then why call Corrine and warn her?"

"Because maybe he…I don't know. He might have a conscience? I'll ask him. I'm gonna find him, and I'll ask him."

Alex rested his head against the glass. Maybe he just didn't have the strength for this. Any of it. Not Halloran or whatever Creasy was after or even civil action against Sheffield. Not now. Corrine's words played on a loop in his mind, her fear of losing him, of everything falling apart. How could he put his family through anymore? He couldn't.

"Thirteen years," Chet said after a while. "That's how long we've been doing this together."

"Oh, come on."

"I took one look at you and saw this massive potential. I saw that you have a lot on your plate. I help you prioritize. I help you make a living at this. So don't sit there all slumped over with that pouty look on your face like things haven't gotten better since we started working together. Don't –"

"And how many other clients do you have? Right? You dropped 'em, one by one. So don't act like you don't benefit from this."

"Of course I do! Of course I do, you ninny. I benefit when *you* benefit. But I'm telling you, this is a righteous fight. This is a fight that…this has been going on since…I don't know. That's where you come in. How long have people like them been impeding human progress, causing damage?"

"Did you just call me a ninny?"

Chet stared ahead, ignoring the question. Instead: "You told me once, Alex, about a dream you had."

Alex felt his stomach clench. "What?"

"Yeah. You did. You saw something in the desert. The building in the desert. I remember. You said it had this really dark corner inside, blacker than black. And you said you felt the devil there."

"I didn't – I said that –"

"And you went right into it. You didn't hesitate." He gave Alex a long look before he faced the road again. "Okay? All we have to do is – shit, shit, shit, what is this guy doing?"

Alex tensed as the truck in front of them swerved between lanes. Chet hit the brakes and the rental slowed so fast Alex had to brace himself against the dashboard.

Horns blatted and tires screeched as everyone struggled to

avoid an accident. The truck then found a pocket and raced ahead. Everyone slowly resumed speed.

"Dammit," Chet whispered.

Neither of them said anything for a minute. An acrid odor of burning brakes sneaked through the vents and lingered.

Chet's color was returning to normal. "What was I saying?"

Breathe, Alex thought.

In.

Out.

Stay with the out-breath.

Breathe.

35

His sole bag rested beside his feet inside the door. Corrine's eyes shone with emotion. For a moment, no one moved. Then Freda rushed toward him, and Kenneth, and Corrine wrapped her arms around them all. "Group hug," Freda said, muffled under Alex's arm. She hadn't mentioned "group hug" in months, maybe a year. Alex didn't come from a hugging family – Corrine's side held the genetic load for emotions. He thought his parents had missed out. Maybe he had, too. But he was going to make up for it.

Freda squeezed harder around his midsection; Kenneth held Alex around his chest and lay his head on his father's shoulder. The kids knew their father had been shot in the leg. They knew the shooter had turned himself in and that Alex had met with him. They didn't know about the phone call or the idea that there were potentially still people out there gunning for their father in one way or another.

"So good to have you back," Corrine said. "We're here for whatever you need."

What he needed was – like an addict getting all the booze or drugs out of the house in order to properly abstain – to unplug.

They all did. To shut the world out. Nobody on the computer, phones, nothing. He told them this. "I'm asking for forty-eight hours, guys – okay?"

Everybody readily agreed, and an hour later, the boredom was as heavy as radon gas.

"All right, just a peek," Alex said.

"Fifteen minutes, tops," Corrine said.

Phones came out. Alex opened his computer. Nobody talked as they read from headlines and watched videos.

"Where's Chet?" Kenneth asked.

"Staying in the city. Setting up my schedule for the next five years."

Alex avoided Halloran, instead researching people wounded in the shooting. He took a pad from the desk and jotted names. Drew had everything, but this was better. Alex needed to internalize it.

Lenny Ames was a professor at SUNY Plattsburgh – his arm had been nicked by a bullet, but he was making a full recovery.

A pottery artist named Arianna Blakely had suffered a broken leg as people had fled the theater. There was a Facebook picture of her already balancing on crutches, a tentative grin on her face. Pretty, lots of hair. Twenty-five or thirty.

Nyswaner didn't have a Facebook page, but his wife did, loaded with thoughts and prayers. The retired-cop-turned-security-guard showed up in several photos, sitting up in a hospital bed, oxygen going in his nose, but smiling and giving the thumbs-up.

Alex recalled that a woman had been knocked unconscious in the rush to escape. It turned out she was an author with a website and a Twitter page with around 3,000 followers. Published by a small publisher in London, but she wasn't from there; she lived in Worcester, Mass. On Twitter was a picture of her sitting at a desk. Emily Granger. In her fifties, it looked, married to a restaurant owner named Max. Two kids. Took trips to Martha's Vineyard once a year. She was comatose.

"Oh no." Alex covered his mouth.

Corrine picked up on the tension and neared, closing out the kids. "What?"

"She – this woman – she was there."

Corrine read over his shoulder then leaned in and clicked the mouse. She read with a whispering voice. "'God be with you, Emily.'"

They read the reply tweets silently.

Hope science can save you

Come back to us and write about this!

Never should have been there Emily

Great writer ☹

Baines is dangerous #NoMoreBaines

Halloran was in there, too – at least, someone named @FerrignoFace had retweeted an article in *The Journal* pertaining to Granger: *Fallout from #BainesShooting Worsens as Baines Stays Silent.*

"What a dick," Corrine said under her breath.

Alex turned away to check on the kids. Kenneth was absorbed with his own iPad; Freda had moved on to coloring on the dining room table. Their father was responsible for people being in hospitals, in comas.

Corrine lowered her voice. "It says she was kicked in the head as she lay on the ground and people scrambled for safety. They're saying it's a traumatic brain injury, too much swelling…"

He reached out and shut the laptop. He rose too fast, knocking the coffee table askew and toppling the tall Christmas candles. "Sorry," he said, as he righted them. Then he walked away, but didn't know where to go and ended up looking down at the carpet, feeling his family watching.

Corrine took him by the arm. "Be right back, kids."

The pain was blaring in his thigh as they took the stairs. He gimped his way to the second floor, Corrine supporting him. She went into the bathroom and started the water in the tub. Then she sat on the lidded toilet and looked at him. "It's not your fault."

"Yes it is," he said, closing the door behind him.

She helped him get his shirt off over his head. The pants were a bigger challenge, and by the time they'd managed to remove them, the room had filled with steam. Corrine opened a package sitting on the hamper, containing the plastic to wrap his leg for bathing. She stopped when she saw the various bruises and scrapes on his chest and stomach. Gently, gingerly, she put her fingers on them. Then she pulled him close and kissed him.

His kiss back was hesitant at first. He gave in. The kiss deepened, his skin tingling as her tongue darted between his lips. Her hands went up his back, pressed into his shoulder blades, drawing him in as he tried to pull away.

She whispered in his ear. "You're a good man."

"I don't know what I am anymore."

"Yes you do."

"I don't know what to do now."

"That's okay. That's a good thing."

We'll start over. Either she said it, or he imagined she did. Maybe he read her mind.

He cupped her backside as her hand enclosed around him. Her breath still in his ear: "Tonight I'm going to give you more than a sponge bath, Mr. Baines…"

36

They lay in bed afterward, Corrine propped up on an arm, him on his back. "Is there still a lot of pain?"

"I'm okay."

"We need to talk about what Creasy said."

"I know." And he told her about Chet hiring Creasy to spy on Stephen in order to find proof of his infidelity. They agreed it wasn't enough to connect Stephen to Sheffield. Even if Stephen had found out, the punishment didn't fit the crime. You didn't learn that your brother-in-law had a private investigator do some snooping and answer it by aiding a lunatic gunman. Let alone hire him. Not if you were sane. Which Stephen was.

"Then why did Creasy call?" Corrine asked.

"I don't know. Chet says Creasy was in Iraq before doing investigations. He thinks he might have some real bad PTSD – he's paranoid. He's still not answering his phone. Sergeant Dukette said there's nothing we can really do at this point but wait to see if there's another call. There's not enough right now to subpoena the phone company or to have someone out there pick him up. Chet is handling it, though. In the meantime, the police went through our house, talked to the neighbors. Nobody has seen anything."

"Chet has such great taste in the people he hires."

"Usually he does. With Creasy, he just didn't see it."

They fell into a semi-comfortable quiet until Corrine started talking about the kids, how Freda was almost a hundred percent better, whether she and Kenneth were going to return to school anytime soon. "We need to decide – you know – what are we doing? Are we carrying on or hunkering down? Drew emailed me your schedule – you have doctors' appointments coming up, you're meeting with the lawyer, with Angie – are you going into the city for that?"

"No. We'll just…no."

He caressed her arm, stared up at the ceiling, his thoughts swinging back to Emily Granger. Wanting to know more about her – why she'd been at his show, how she'd discovered him. She seemed to have family surrounding her; that was good. Clinical practice required unambiguous criteria, and right now, Emily Granger was what you called unconscious. All philosophy aside, her network of consciousness, deep within the cingulate cortex and in the precuneus, was dark. She existed in nothingness, her internal voice lost.

Corrine watched him. "Babe?"

"I've agreed to an NPR interview tomorrow. It's not on the schedule."

"Why?"

"I gotta talk about this. And I don't want to do a press conference. I need to talk about the people who were injured."

"Are you up for it?"

"I mean – it's radio – I can look like shit anyway." He tried a smile, then sobered. "I also need to talk about this thing with the university study, set the record straight."

She wanted to say something, but he could see her holding it back. Then she swung her legs out of bed and started pulling on clothes.

"Where are you going?"

"Bathroom. Check on Freda."

Before he could say anything, the bathroom door clicked shut. The sudden isolation was unsettling. Since this thing happened, he seemed to have been surrounded by people at all times. Was that a terrible thing to have said just now? Terrible to be thinking about himself and his reputation when hundreds of lives had been affected, even shattered?

Like an answer, his phone buzzed. Alex rolled over on the bed and stretched for the table. It was Chet calling. At this hour, it couldn't be good news.

"Mr. Warman," Alex said, trying to be upbeat. "What can I do for you?"

"Hey, buddy. How you feeling?"

"I'm all right. Been better, been worse."

"I'm just going to come right out with this – Nyswaner is dead."

Alex pushed himself sitting. "What? I just saw a picture of him. Everything looked good."

"That was pre-op. If you mean the thumbs-up he was making in the Facebook photo. I mean, he'd already had the bullet removed, blood pumped in, all that. But he had to go back in for a second surgery."

"Why? Where did you find this out from?"

"I got someone at the hospital up there, keeping an eye out for me. Ah, they called it retro, something…"

"Retroperitoneal hematoma. Bleeding. Internal bleeding, ah, God…"

"He died at just after ten tonight."

Alex dropped back against the pillow. He heard Chet still talking and gradually brought the phone back to his ear.

"…up to a homicide," Chet was saying. "Capital murder. This is a whole new ballgame for Sheffield. New charges."

Corrine came out of the bathroom, glanced at him and said, "Gonna check on the kids now," and padded out of the room in her bare feet.

"Sorry to deliver bad news," Chet said. "Better you hear it from me than from Halloran."

"Man, you better not be using this to –"

"I'm giving you time, Alex. I'm giving you all the time in the world. But I gotta tell you, everything has come together. MIT is a ready-made audience. They love you over there. It's like the hometown stadium. Terry Deisart is in as the moderator. And he's great – I know you like Terry. Halloran's people…it took a minute. You could tell there was a little internal conflict going on over there. But they said yes. Eight p.m. tonight I got the call. I wasn't going to bother you until the morning, but then this thing with Nyswaner…"

"Chet," Alex said finally. "I'll talk to you tomorrow."

Alex rang off before Chet could protest and again lay back, letting his arms flop out at his sides. The elm tree between their house and the neighbor's lighted house cast long, shifting shadow patterns on the ceiling. He closed his eyes and Sheffield was there, seated in the middle section of the theater. The shooter stood up amid the seated crowd and aimed his weapon. It was as though his bullets shattered a stillness years in the making. Fragmented it into a million little pieces.

Alex remembered Nyswaner on the floor, the blood spreading. But in this reimagining, Alex put pressure on the wound, but the blood wouldn't stop, and Nyswaner's color turned yellow. He looked up at Alex and reached for him, eyes wet, mouth opening to speak. "Why did you do this?"

Alex opened his eyes. He'd fired a gun a few times in his life – it was louder than you'd expect, the recoil shocking, an explosion jettisoning a projectile through space at thousands of feet per second. Even on your darkest day, your lowest point, the vast majority of people could not bring themselves to turn a gun on another person and pull the trigger. What brought someone to that point? What motivated him? The police hadn't found any payments. But it could have been cash, under the table.

If not money, what else?

The shooting had terrified Corrine. Creasy's phone call drove the fear deeper. His family was at loose ends. One innocent person was in a coma, and now another was dead.

It ate at him. Crawled in his brain: What made it possible for a man to take such a final action – even if Sheffield's account were true, and the intention was harm, not death? Did that make it any easier? There was still jail to consider. Sheffield was sane. He had to know that, one way or the other, his life was never going to be the same. It had to be worth it to him.

Maybe someone who viewed Alex as the enemy had seduced Sheffield, giving him purpose and distinction. Motivation. Chet seemed sure of it. Even Roth had a look in her eye as she told him she'd come to the end of the road; she saw something in the Paul Halloran angle. At least, someone who was behind the shooter. A dark figure standing over Sheffield's shoulder, whispering in his ear.

Alex needed to know for sure. He had to look Halloran in the eyes.

37

T he court order had come through. Now they had Sheffield's list of phone calls going back the three years since he'd opened his account. Working backwards, Roth was able to eliminate work calls, his parents, takeout orders, a couple of telemarketers, and a guy who worked with Sheffield at UPS. The rest she couldn't readily assign. There were no 949 numbers.

"Libby's people are stuck against the VPN," she told Harlan. "What they *can* see is nothing revealing – there's a little bit of internet history that shows him ordering stuff for his doomsday pantry, but nothing that traces to Baines or to Paul Halloran or John Creasy. There's still a lot to go through that was accessible. Documents, photos."

"What's this on his call log?" Harlan pointed to a number that appeared six times in October.

"That's a burner. One of two; here's the other one."

"A 565 and a 386. So he's talking to two people who are using burners."

"Or one person," she said, "using two different phones. The 565 numbers come after the 386. Someone uses one phone for a while, maybe runs out of minutes or just wants to change it up. So now we've got to get into these numbers. Find the carrier; look at who's servicing them. That will narrow it down a little bit. Then we can look at retailers and maybe check store video."

"You're talking about a week of work. Maybe two. On top of everything else."

She was still following her train of thought. "It could be that the caller is in one place, buys a phone, uses and discards it, then later, the same thing." She went through the paperwork. "Here we go. First call originated in Philadelphia. Second one somewhere in the Five Boroughs." She looked up and sensed what he was thinking: This could be anyone, or two anyones, just ordinary people who used pay-per-use phones for whatever reason.

Harlan leaned back, his chair squawking. He ran his palms against the sides of his close-cropped hair and sighed.

Roth asked, "Doing okay?"

"Ah." He flicked his hand. "Didn't sleep last night. I was thinking about Peter Nyswaner. I actually know him a little bit – he was with Saranac Lake PD. Took his pension but couldn't sit still, so he picked up the security work. Good guy, nice family. He'd just become a grandfather. I sat up half the night thinking about it."

"Yeah." She thought about that, and then she imagined Harlan, who never married or had kids, sitting alone in the middle of the night. She'd been to his house once; he kept his boots and shoes by the door, lined up like soldiers in rank. Her supervisor had this naturally disheveled appearance, but it concealed a great attention to detail, reserved for the things that he valued. Like footwear. Like police work.

Harlan said, "I'm wondering who we got, if we got anyone at all. This Creasy guy is in the wind. What I could find on him – he was a Ranger, spent significant time downrange. Seems kind of like Sheffield to me, kind of keeps hidden…"

"But what's his motive?"

"Right. So, the other guy, Stephen Mayhew – I checked around on him, too. Investment banker. Also, a big religious guy. Born again. He's got that right on his social media stuff, in his profile bio, whatever you call it."

"Baines has more than a few people who have reason to dislike him. Strongly dislike him."

"Former Senator Blakely, for one," Harlan said. "Baines testified on behalf of the woman who accused him. People say it tipped things in her direction."

Roth nodded, still hung up on the burner phone idea. "That's true."

"What about the Halloran guy, though? Wasn't there some fraud case?"

The question redirected her. "There was. Halloran operated a religious charity for a little while but got caught directing some of that money into his own account. He's got some interesting things to say about Baines, about how he's part of 'the deep state,' he's a war hawk, he's anti-American. Things that edge right up against threats. Now he's saying, 'Keep a watch on Baines's book sales.' It's like he sort of stirs the pot and then sits back to watch." Roth picked up her notebook. "I wrote some of the responses down – people chiming in, replying to his tweet. 'Baines profits from misery.' That's one. 'When you dance with the devil your bound to get burned.' They spelled 'you're' wrong. Lots of Bible quotes, references to the whole thing being a sign from God."

Harlan shook his head slowly back and forth, as if the whole thing pained or mystified him. Or both. "I don't know a lot about this stuff. What these guys like Baines do – I don't know – I don't really understand it. Or even the other one, Halloran." He leaned back and shrugged. There was a spot of mustard on his tie from lunch. "Mostly it looks like…I think you got mainly young guys tuning in, and that's your prime audience. White males, anyway. On both sides. Guys sitting in the dark, looking at their screens.

Getting agitated instead of getting laid." He flicked a look at her. "Sorry."

"Sheffield followed Baines on Twitter." Roth searched her loaded desk for a sheaf of paper, a recent printout, found it and dropped it on Harlan's desk across from her. "Moritz put this together." Moritz was the FBI agent monitoring the case. Moritz had done some assisting, too; her first call to Roth had included the background on Halloran. "Sheffield's replied to 114 of Baines's tweets over the past six years," Roth said.

Harlan looked at the paperwork, squinting. "What's that mean? That's a lot?"

"It's substantial."

"'Your kind has tried to destroy us before,'" Harlan read. He scratched his nose with a fingernail. "That's nice. Here he calls Baines a 'fundamentalist,' here he says 'technocrat' – whatever that is."

"Sheffield follows a lot of people like Baines," Roth said. "Follows Paul Halloran, Jordan Peterson, Ben Shapiro..."

"I don't know any of them." He tossed the sheaf onto his desk, scattering the pages.

"Harlan, you really okay?"

"Why didn't Baines's own people flag Sheffield?"

"Because there's a thousand more like him. Like you just said. Either that, or...I don't know."

Harlan continued to gaze at her, his eyes unfocused. He opened his desk drawer and pulled out some gum, offered her a piece. When she declined, he looked at the paperwork again. "Sheffield goes by '@GoodShepherd.' Has 341 followers. How about that – is that a lot?"

"No, it's not really a lot. A guy like Sheffield, it just shows he's had his account a little while, accumulated some people."

Harlan rocked a little in his chair, nodding, then tapped the paperwork. "The big guy with the scarves and the camel coat – he seemed hot to trot."

"Chet Warman?"

"You said he was convinced someone was behind this in one way or another. Especially this Mayhew guy, because of Baines's people uncovering his infidelity. Maybe I'll give Mr. Mayhew a closer look. And let's plumb a little on the Halloran thing. The charity. Because someone is using those burner phones, talking to Sheffield, getting him riled up."

She stood and gathered her badge, keys, and phone. Her gun was already holstered at her hip. "I'm hoping I'll get a better sense of things just by being there myself, in his house. And I'll look at everything Libby brought into evidence. See if there's anything that jumps out."

Harlan worked the piece of gum, watching. "Be careful, okay? Try not to step through any of this wacko's trap doors."

38

S he made the five-hour drive to Portland with the rain
drumming her roof like dimes. Less than a half hour from
the city, she tuned the radio to NPR and waited for *Fresh Air* with
Sherry Olsen.

"My guest today is Dr. Alex Baines, neuroscientist, author,
lecturer and – most recently – shooting survivor. Dr. Baines,
thank you for being here."

"Thank you, Sherry."

"Before we talk about these more current events in your life,
I'd like to introduce you to anyone unfamiliar with your work
prior to this past weekend."

"Sure."

Olsen consulted her notes. "You've written four books, each New
York Times best sellers. *Here and Now* brings attention to mindfulness meditation and delves into cutting-edge neuroscience on
matters of consciousness. In *Letter to a Religious Nation,* you
describe issues with an 'Iron Age' god influencing everything

from public discourse to public policy in the modern world. *Moral Animal* then tackles things like the importance of family, keeping marriages together, having two parents in the home, and calls attention to the danger of identity politics. Let me just stop there – politically speaking, you're a bit of a maverick. Is that by design?"

He smiled. "Good people often disagree on moral hazard. I guess any take on an issue is going to fall somewhere on the political spectrum. But I'm not starting with a position and working back from there to make my case."

She moved the large microphone an inch so she could make better eye contact. "Science is the arrow, going from A to B?"

"You got it. I'm describing what the research shows, what the data show. When *Religious Nation* came out, there was the expected pushback from the right. With *Moral Animal,* it came from the left."

"You're trying to thread a very small needle, it seems like."

"I'm just trying to call balls and strikes."

She chuckled, inviting more from him.

"We tend to have a lens that skews our perspective," he ventured. "We build these narrow channels of our preferred stimuli, so that we get the same messages over and over again. It just floods our brain."

"In fairness, would that apply to you?"

"As objective as I've tried to be, the public mechanisms for consumption and communication seem increasingly binary. Something either confirms your team slogan or it doesn't. So, yeah, I'm just as susceptible. I try not to be." He laughed, feeling easy. "But I'm the same as anyone else – I like what confirms my thinking."

She smiled at him, then quickly turned serious. "Your work on trauma has been enthusiastically embraced by the women's movement, by #MeToo advocates. You've laid out in clear, scientific terms why victims of assault deserve the benefit of the doubt, since selective or incomplete memory is a major feature of trauma. Which is a good place for us to segue into what recently happened to you. You've experienced your own trauma…are you finding, now that it's personal, that your research holds up? That the science holds up?"

He glanced away to the sound-baffled walls, the people in the control room watching from behind the large window. "I can remember some of it, but other stuff will probably take time. If at all."

"Can you talk about what you remember?"

His gaze came back to her. "Seeing the gunman. Then I remember the bullet going past my head – it sort of pulled at the air, tickled my hair – like the hairs stood on end for a second. I remember Amy Cross helping me backstage, to get down to the greenroom. Things get hazy after that."

"CNN recently aired a segment with your reunion with her at the hospital. Amy Cross was a stagehand at Alex's talk….She was very explicit that you saved her life. Can you remember those actions – getting her off the stage?"

"Yes."

"So what parts do you…what have you learned since the shooting, since the trauma, that you hadn't remembered?"

"I don't quite clearly recall rushing toward the door. I think I'd lost quite a bit of blood at that point."

They talked a little more about seeing himself on video. "It's a little surreal," he said. "We tend to think of ourselves – our consciousness – like a passenger riding around inside our heads, looking out through our eyes. Seeing yourself on video, it's kind of like seeing the car go on its own."

"Can you talk about your physical injuries? Is that okay? You left the hospital very quickly…"

"The bullet nicked an artery and struck a nerve in my leg. I had surgery to reattach the nerve. The doctors told me I could expect something called 'complex regional pain syndrome' – basically chronic pain – indefinitely. Blood circulation is an issue, and I need regular physical therapy to prevent muscle wasting because of the contractures."

She made a sympathetic face, then asked, "If the bullet had ruptured a vein or an artery, it could have been bad enough to lead to amputation – is that right?"

"Yes." He shifted to relieve some pressure on his leg. "But look, Sherry, I really want to emphasize this. I understand that I'm getting attention – it was my talk. But, as you know, there were multiple people injured and impacted by this. And tragically, Peter Nyswaner, a security guard, just passed away due to complications from his gunshot wound. So I would like to say that my heart goes out to his family. I'm so sorry for what happened. I'm so sorry that..." Alex found himself on the edge of tears and fought them back. He paused, then said, "I just want to really be clear about this – this was an attack on three hundred people. Including my own family. My wife, Corrine, my children. I'm just one of the people this happened to."

"It's very tragic. The whole thing. We've never had – I've never had a victim of this type of gun violence speak to it so soon, that I can recall. I don't mean to neglect anyone."

"No, please, not at all. I didn't mean that." He was still pulling himself back together after the unexpected jog toward emotion. Big emotion, like he might've started to cry and not been able to stop.

Olsen said, "And you've set up funding for a woman named Emily Granger to help her with her traumatic brain injury recovery...for those listening, you can find a link to that on our website."

"We're looking for ways to help in any way that we can," he said. "I just wish I could do more."

Olsen nodded somberly, then fixed her gaze. "Can we talk about this article in *VICE News*? About microdosing?"

It was an abrupt shift; he got the sense it was a perfunctory question for her. "Sure. So, I've been administered low doses of psychopharmacological substances as part of a neurological study. I've been involved for a little over six months."

"Okay. So how does that work? Your career has focused, in large part, on mindfulness meditation. Your PR people sent us something – you've received somewhere in the tens of thousands of emails and letters from people thanking you for helping to change their lives. You hold seminars on breathing techniques and champion meditation as the way we might evolve in collective consciousness. How does that wash with taking psychopharmacological substances?"

He took a quick sip of water, shifting gears, happy to be nearing comfortable territory again. Territory he knew how to better navigate anyway. "So here's the thing – neuroscience has a relationship with the East. No question. We've worked with Buddhist monks because we know that meditation can trigger alterations in the brain. And this isn't new – in the 1960s, doctors from UC Irvine and the Harvard Medical School conducted experiments to measure these effects. The study showed how meditation led to a lowering of blood lactate, indicating diminished stress and anxiety. The applications have been wide-ranging, including the use of meditation in the treatment of high blood pressure, chronic pain, insomnia, cardiac arrhythmias – you name it. It's even extended into AIDS therapy and treating the side effects of cancer."

He continued before she could ask the same question in another way; he could see in her eyes that she wanted to. "New research has focused on psychopharmacology. It includes microdosing. And that means subjects take regulated, very low doses of LSD. These subjects report a strength of focus, a greater ease of being. They're able to sustain attention on complex tasks longer than the control group. I was approached to participate in a second, longer-term study. I accepted. It was for one year and it was confidential."

Olsen studied him for a moment. "Let's get back to why you left the hospital early. There's been some speculation you met with the shooter, Gary Sheffield – that you were asked by the district attorney and investigating officers. Is that true?"

He'd anticipated this, too. His lawyer had laid out what best to say and not to say. "I can confirm that, yes."

Olsen looked momentarily flustered by his stark admission. There was a deep pause, even for radio. "Wow. So in addition to saving Amy Cross, trying to stop the shooter yourself, you went and met with him?"

"That's correct," Baines said on the radio.

Watching the GPS, Roth had made turns into a neighborhood on the outskirts of Portland and found Sheffield's street. She parked behind a patrolman in a Portland PD car and listened for another minute.

Olsen: "Okay, so, you're at the hospital, you're in the very early stages of recovery, you're in massive amounts of pain, yet you left. Why meet with Sheffield? As part of the investigation?"

Baines: "I wasn't allowed to talk about the shooting. That was Sheffield's stipulation. He claimed he'd only talk about other crimes."

"And did he?"

Baines paused, as if making sure he had the right words prepared. "In addition to the terrorizing of innocent people, I believe this act was designed to antagonize me specifically. I was lured to the meeting with promises of criminal revelations. There were none. Instead, Sheffield quoted me scripture. He suggested I was doing harm by the kind of work I do."

"So the man who shot you then claimed he had knowledge of other crimes – maybe his own, maybe someone else's – as a pretext to pulling you into a religious debate?"

"That seems to be the case."

"He pulled a gun and shot at hundreds of people, shot you, shot a security guard, put a woman in a coma, all to get to *you*?"

This had to be a calculated risk, Roth thought. Baines was smart; he'd know bringing up Sheffield's apparent motivation to debate him could trivialize the injured and terrorized people – including, now, a dead man – as just collateral damage. But Baines had to figure it would come out anyway. This way, he was in front of it, leading the story.

"Sherry, this is the work of someone who wanted not only to hurt me, but anyone who puts science ahead of superstition, anyone who believes that the best way forward is with openness and honesty about our issues. This was someone who wants to shut down what we stand for. That's not just everyone who was at that talk, it's all of us. Everyone who believes in consensus, data, peer review, hard reality."

Olsen said, "There's been a lot of back and forth on social media about this. If you've managed to mostly stay off the radar of the larger religious community before, you have their attention now."

"You could say that." He added, "And maybe that was Sheffield's purpose. I don't know. I shouldn't speculate, but it's hard not to. And I'm not a lawyer." He laughed.

Roth looked up at Sheffield's house, a small but stately Colonial hazed out by the rain. At the same time, the patrolman got out of his car, probably wondering what she was doing. He wore a bright yellow rain poncho and hat, clicked on a flashlight as he approached her car.

On the radio, Olsen said, "Do you think Sheffield was influenced to do this by another party?"

A bold question, Roth thought.

"I'd rather not answer that."

"But you yourself have said that people in positions of influence can be indirectly responsible for acts of violence by inciting it through rhetoric. It's been called 'stochastic terrorism.'"

"Well, stochastic actually means having a random probability distribution."

"Sure."

"We can analyze a pattern statistically. We can see where there's an uptick in right wing or left wing violence. But it's not about attributing a single act of violence to a single leader. It's like climate change. We can't say a single storm is caused by use of fossil fuels."

"But we can correlate them."

"Yes."

"And some leaders openly endorse acts of violence. Or, at least, they don't condemn it. Some people see this as implicitly giving them permission, even *calling* them to commit a violent act in the name of some ideology or belief. Bombs mailed to politicians. Mass shootings. That sounds to me like a kind of 'terrorism by proxy'..."

The patrolman knocked on the window. Roth clicked off the radio and showed him her ID. He stepped back as she opened the door. "Cats and dogs out here," he said in a thick accent. *Out heah.* "You got something for the rain?"

"Legs," she said. "Let's just run."

They moved quickly up the walkway, Roth jogging ahead. Thick clouds swelled in the dark sky, their low pressure making it unseasonably warm. On the porch, Roth sluiced the water off her coat as the patrolman pulled a binder from a plastic bag. Detective Libby's name was on the log-in sheet, along with several other

Portland cops, plus forensic people. She handed back the pen after printing her name and signing. The patrolman turned the binder around, checked his watch, and noted the time in. "You got your flashlight? Dark in there. Guy has like two or three lamps, and that's about it. Oh…here." He handed her a pair of blue plastic gloves.

"Thanks."

"Have fun."

She went inside.

39

Alex felt the heat creeping up from his leg, encircling his hip. Olsen's phrase 'terrorism by proxy' seemed to hang in the air. The whole room suddenly felt hotter.

Alex cleared his throat. "What I can say is that I take responsibility for what happened to me, to those other people. I take responsibility for the study I've participated in. I stand by what I've done."

Olsen waited, perhaps sensing more.

It was the moment, he decided, to say what he'd ultimately come here to say. "Throughout human history, we've been divided over one thing or another. There have always been people who are drivers of change, and people who fear change. But there's a new shape to it – I think we're all going a bit crazy. We retreat into tribal bubbles online. I never wanted to be on any one side. I just wanted the truth. You can change your life with something as simple as breathing – that's just the truth. Something you do every day, without thinking. Prayer, we can debate. Good thoughts, who knows. But breathe in to a count of four, breathe out to a count of four – do that ten times and your heart rate will go down, your mind will clear. And we don't necessarily need microdosing, but it was an experiment. That's how we learn. That's how we find things out. By being willing to try, to fail, to be wrong. We have to be able to admit when we're wrong – not just double down. But, now, someone has just made a very loud statement. They said, 'your way is not acceptable.' 'Science is not acceptable.' They took a firearm into a peaceful assembly and committed acts of violence. Terrifying people, injuring people, and now causing death. I'm not going to sit still for that. They've drawn a line in the sand, and I'm going to step over it."

Roth entered the first room, pulling on the gloves, stairs directly ahead with white risers and wooden treads. The place smelled stale, like it could stand an open window.

A living room to the right had a single lamp in the corner, dividing two couches. To the left, an antique table with six chairs in the dining room. She moved that way, noting a hutch with expensive-looking china behind the glass.

The rain made a muffled, background timpani as she flipped the kitchen light switch a couple of times. When the light fixture in the ceiling stayed dark, she pulled her flashlight. The beam revealed a farmhouse-style kitchen with yellow linoleum and dark wooden cabinets, a double sink. Sheffield was tidy; nothing on the countertop but a bowl of overripe bananas. She looked through the cabinets to find several boxes of crackers, some pancake mix, white rice labeled in two- and four-cup bags, and plenty of canned soup.

She paused to roll her neck, get out a kink – all that driving had made her stiff. A door from the kitchen led to the backyard, one to a tiny half bathroom with a toilet and sink; a third led down to the basement. Time to have a look at Sheffield's End of Days supplies. She found the light switch and flipped it – this one worked. Even though there was no one in the house, it still creeped her out to descend into the bunker-style basement. Down here were two large freezers against one concrete wall and a long workbench with tools hung neatly from a pegboard. It smelled of mildew and dust, with cobwebs quivering among the overhead floor joists. The shelves Libby had been talking about were stacked with enough canned and freeze-dried food to last the apocalypse. Copious batteries, large and small, bags of lye, and the brand-new generators Libby had mentioned completed the picture of a man ready for harsh times.

She found a box of toys. Old board games like *Clue* and *Monopoly*. No other telling memorabilia. No revealing manifesto. No signs of Sheffield's personality beyond his preparedness – not a box of fetish items such as women's clothes or animal skins – unless the lack of character was a sign in and of itself.

She went back upstairs, then took the stairs from the living room to the second floor. Three bedrooms and another bath. A big house for one man. After she checked through his bathroom medicine cabinet (toothpaste and brush, shaving cream and disposable razors, a half-drunk bottle of Pepto-Bismol, no prescriptions), she went into the first bedroom. The rain was louder and streaked the windows. Boxes filled the space along with a pile of outerwear clothing. The next room contained a double bed, dresser, end table. It looked like the guest room of a boarding house. She even found a Bible in the drawer – King James Version, well used. The closet offered a few hanging garments, folded sweaters on the high shelf. Sheffield was not necessarily a sharp dresser; there wasn't a single suit. The clothes were all off-the-rack, department store.

An assemble-it-yourself desk formed an office out of the final room. Three UPS uniforms were folded in a stack on a second chair. A faint square in the dust marked where Sheffield's laptop, taken into evidence by Libby, had rested. The Portland crime scene unit had been through the house soon after Sheffield hinted at "other crimes." They'd found no bodies, no victims, no fingerprints other than his own.

She sat down at the desk and went through the drawers. The bottom right contained files and she finger-walked her way past categories that included Sheffield's vehicle, his house – all the related expenses and renovations thereof – plus one for each of his utilities. She shoved the drawer closed and leaned back in the swivel chair. She pushed with the tip of her foot so she swung back and forth as she looked out the window. The lights of the city shone in the distance over the roofs and treetops. A nice little neighborhood. The other houses were like this one, two-story Colonials with porches. In front of one, in the street, was a parked car. The engine was running, because she could see a snake of tail pipe exhaust.

She stood and was moving closer to the window when her phone jittered against her hip. It was Matt.

"Hey – sorry to bother you –"

Roth knew there was a problem right away because of the way Alice was wailing in the background.

"– but do you know where the Fire Stick remote is? Because I can't find it. I checked under the couch…"

"Did you look in the junk drawer? Sometimes they leave it in the kitchen and I put it in there."

"No, I didn't check. Shit, I'm sorry. Let me – okay, hang on – sorry to bother you. She is just having a full on meltdown right now." He moved the phone away and his tone dropped in pitch. "Alice! That's enough. I'm talking to Mommy right now and – what? No, Michael did not take the remote and hide it on you."

Roth eyed the car outside another few seconds and moved away from the window. Her job could be tough on her family sometimes, but this last case had really taken her away, and it was in Matt's voice that he was wearing thin.

"Did you find it?"

"Got it! Awesome, babe. Thank you."

"Sorry about that. I always mean to put it by the TV."

"No problem. All right, it seems to be working…"

She went back downstairs and gave Sheffield's living room another look: not a throw pillow out of place nor a stray sock on the floor. It looked like the way the facade homes look when they tested nuclear bombs. As if Sheffield wasn't a real person with a real life, but fake. An empty vessel sitting in his grimly appointed home, awaiting the end. Awaiting something.

"Okay, everything's there," Matt said with breathy relief. He muffled the phone again and said, "Alice! Look – I've got the TV back." Alice's volume started to come down. She asked indiscernible questions. "Yup," Matt said to her. "Mommy put it in the kitchen. What? Yes – *Ally* – stop, go sit down on the couch." Speaking to Roth again, he said, "Sorry. I'll let you go. Everything going okay? You gonna be home real late?"

"Probably."

"Just that – you know this stuff is supposed to turn. Could get icy tonight – they're saying maybe five, six inches. So just be careful driving."

"Okay. Give them hugs for me." She was anxious to get outside and see about the car in the street. "I love you."

"Love you, too."

She ended the call and pushed outside where water came off the eaves in machine-gun drops. The Portland patrolman climbed out of the car and opened the gate of the white picket fence and jogged up the walkway. "You all set?" He held out the binder.

She looked past him; the car was gone.

"You see a vehicle sitting there about two, three minutes ago?"

"Sorry, I was texting my girlfriend." Hard to tell in the light, but it looked like the patrolman blushed. "We, ah, she thinks she might be pregnant, if you want the truth."

"Oh yeah? Congratulations."

"Thanks. Yeah, well, it would be a surprise."

"They always are. Hey, you know what? I'm going to run back inside for one more second. No need to get up."

The patrolman didn't have time to respond – she trotted back up the walkway, re-entered, and went upstairs, stood looking in on Sheffield's office, thinking about Baines on the radio. Sherry Olsen listing the books he'd written.

The one bookshelf in Sheffield's place was tall and narrow, stuck in a corner away from the windows.

His books were obvious – Libby had sent the information in the initial report: Sheffield had one of each of Baines's titles. She ran a gloved finger over the spines, then stopped on one – *Moral Animal* – and pulled it out. The copy was well-worn, either read with vigor or purchased used. She performed an automatic fanning of the pages with her thumb and replaced the book on the shelf. She pried another book free and flipped through it, put it away.

Hmm. Nothing interesting.

Not ready to give up, she went into Sheffield's bedroom, riffled through the bureau, and checked under the bed.

Libby had missed it. She stretched and grunted and managed to get a finger on the book and slide it out.

In Sight of God, written by Paul Halloran. The copy was in better shape than the Baines books, but full of scribbled notes. Sheffield – or someone – had dragged a highlighter across so many passages the pages were half black-and-white and half yellow. Also, as she discovered on another page, pink.

She used her flashlight and stood reading one of the pink passages:

As we have seen, the third and final level of morality is only made possible by God. What's created by man can be destroyed by man. But what's created by God is eternal.

She flipped to another, random highlighted passage.

Science came from religion; it began in the church, as a way to observe and exult in the many glories of God. Indeed, the first scientists were called 'naturalists.' Unfortunately, this naturalism became materialism, and man began to consider himself separate, an observer. Like the angel Lucifer, science soon thought too much of itself, craved too much for itself. It put man at the center of the universe.

It is only the Word of God which is at center; the Word which simultaneously encodes and undergirds the very foundation of civilized society. We deny this at our peril, for the dark is always waiting.

Roth turned the book sideways to read the notes written in the margin in blue ink. Hard to make out what was there, but she was either able to discern a couple of words, or saw them there because she wanted to, or thought they fit.

When the sign comes, we will be ready.

She took out her phone, took pictures. She continued staring at the handwritten notes, unsure what to do. But the thoughts were pulling together, forming an idea. She called Harlan and took a cleansing breath.

"Hey. What's up?"

"You at the house?" It was cop talk for police station.

"I'm at *my* house, darlin'. It's past closing time."

"Baines's schedule – we got that, right?"

"Ah, you mean his appointment book?"

"I mean his work schedule. His itinerary. Appearances and that. We had his guy, Warman, email it over. Or maybe it was his assistant."

"Yeah. Yeah, we got that. A spreadsheet thing."

"I'm wondering where Baines was for our two burner calls to Sheffield."

"Ah. Yeah. Okay…" She heard the creak of bedsprings. The old fart was already in bed, not even seven o'clock. "Why – what do you got? Something happen?"

"I'm holding in my hand a book by Paul Halloran."

"Okay. At Sheffield's place."

"Under his bed."

"Hmm. Can't pin anything on Halloran because his book's in the shooter's house, under the bed or not."

"I know that. I'm reading what Sheffield has written in the margins." She tilted it sideways again. "'When the sign comes, we will be ready.' 'I am your instrument.' And then you've got highlighted passages, including one talking about scientific materialism coming out of the church."

"You lost me."

"It was something Sheffield said to Baines when they met. There're other pages in here where the writing in the margins talks about poisons, floods, and massive fires. He's got a word here – looks like Botox? We need a handwriting person on this. Another scribble looks like the name Abby…I don't know…"

"Huh. Maybe I'll call Moritz."

She closed the book. "Hey listen, I was thinking I might just get a motel down here, bag out for the night, and see Libby in the morning, check with what he's got on cracking Sheffield's computer."

Harlan was quiet a moment. "A night away from home."

Roth felt herself smile. "It's not that."

"I'm just giving you shit. Yeah, I can sign off on that. And I'll send the whole file down to Portland. You can look at Baines's itinerary to bore yourself to sleep."

40

THURSDAY, DECEMBER 10

H is eyes closed in the meditation room, mind roaming:

The baby toddles into the bathroom and throws open the shower door to reveal Daddy and Mommy together in the steam and water. Daddy looks over his shoulder and Mommy looks from around Daddy, who's pressing her against the smooth tile wall, and they both start talking at once:

Him: "Be right out."

Her: "Go eat your cereal, honey."

"Just give us a minute."

"Just need a minute, Freda."

Busted.

Usually the shower was the safest place for a quickie, but not that day.

She hadn't really been a "baby," then, Freda – she'd been three and a half. But when you have more than one kid, as anybody knows, the last one stays a baby in some fundamental way, in some way you hope isn't detrimental to emotional development, but you can't prevent. You're barely aware of it in the first place.

They quickly rinse off and leave the shower. Corrine in her

towel, her long slender body. Once, he dreamt of her stalking like a horse, naked, through a party. She'd been ten feet tall.

His wife had an enduring vision, a dream of a nightmare sky.

He could see it, too. Or maybe imagine it. Hard to tell if he remembered it occurring before or after Corrine's confession, but there it was – clouds twisting toward a dark opening overhead as he stared upward, wondering if there was anything on the other side but tar-black silence.

It had to be a sympathetic vision. Something he conjured to relate to her. It wasn't real. Just a dream. The part of the brain that knows what's real is less active during sleep. Sleep that comes upon you like a frog in that boiling water. The line between consciousness and unconsciousness a blur.

He tried to remember what he'd been thinking last night just before falling asleep. He could feel the edge of it, nothing more. Like reaching beneath the couch for a lost item, only able to touch it with your fingernail. You can't get it out into the open.

These thoughts, like lights chased into shadow. Sheffield slides into view, floating overhead but below the slow violence of the churning sky. Sheffield, now sitting across from him at the jail, and when Sheffield looks at him, Alex sees someone else emanating from his eyes, but he's not sure who. *Do I know you?*

That eerily youthful face, that knuckle in the center of the bridge of his nose. The kind of diminutive way he had, almost vaporous; the belly protruding against the *Daytona Beach* T-shirt. What did they call the place where creatures had scrawny necks and massive bellies? The Realm of the Hungry Ghost.

Crack-thump!

Sheffield forms into a hard concentrate of matter, arrow-straight from a gun at high velocity.

The bullet breaks the sound barrier and then you hear the explosion.

Crazy – even then, even in the midst of a crisis like being shot at, people scrambling like mad to get away, the screams reverberating in the small theater, the acridly sweet smell of expended gunpowder, all senses heightened – and he's analyzing. He's breaking down reality into trivial components...

Why? Something to grasp, something to seize on. We need certainty. We need conviction.

The dark is always waiting.

Corrine found him in the middle of the meditation mat at six in the morning, wearing his flannel pajamas, in bare feet, his eyes lidded but twitching, breathing labored. His crutches rested against the wall near one of four potted ferns. In a corner was their treadmill, the belt still, the machine quiet, just the soft glow of the console. It was a beautiful space, but a loss leader of a room if there ever was one, with floor-to-ceiling windows through which vast amounts of heat escaped in winter.

Alex opened his eyes as she sat down beside him and folded her legs beneath her. Normally she wouldn't disturb him, but he'd left the door open, almost as an invitation.

He looked at her. "I'm like a record, skipping. Not just over one groove, but over the whole thing. Little of this, little of that."

She leaned back, stretched out. "I woke up and you weren't there. I couldn't get back to sleep."

"I screwed up," he said.

"No, you didn't."

"The publisher pulled out of *Flow State*."

She sat up straighter. "What?"

"Angie called last night. After the interview. She said they weren't very specific. 'At this time, we feel it would be best – yada yada.' She wants to meet with me."

Corrine didn't immediately respond. He'd lost a book deal. He had trouble meditating. Expressing himself. Handling his emotions. "I think you're pushing yourself too hard."

He didn't answer, only looked at his hands. Then with visible effort he got himself standing and hopped to the treadmill, climbed aboard. He pressed the button for the lowest speed but even that made him grunt in pain and grit his teeth. He stopped the machine and clambered off. "So much for that."

"Alex."

He looked at her.

"Talk to me," she said.

He lowered to the floor, stuck his leg out straight, started to massage around the bandaged area. "I was thinking about your dream."

"Okay."

He bent and stretched, everything working to protect his wounded leg, like water flowing around a rock. He was fit for a man his age, his white T-shirt showing the working muscles. She liked the stubble of his unshaven face. He needed a haircut, though; it was getting shaggy in the back.

"You going to explain it to me?" she asked, hearing the bite in her question.

"No. But I do think you should be looked at."

"I should be? And you? Nothing you want to talk about – what's happening to you – nothing to do with you coming off these experimental drugs?"

"What day is it?" he asked.

"Thursday."

"What year?"

"Very funny."

"There's no evidence for a drug-withdrawal issue. If I'm feeling fractured, it's from everything else."

"I'll get looked at if you get looked at."

"Deal."

She hesitated, then spoke anyway. "But even if...let's just say they find something. An MRI shows something..."

"I doubt they're going to find anything wrong with you, babe. It's just a precaution."

"Okay – I mean – let's just say they chalk it up to neurological activity."

"Well – it is."

"That's not the...you know what I mean. That's not the point." She turned her head away from him. "I just think, even *if they do* find something – so what? Why would that negate the experience? Or what it means?"

He blinked; she'd caught him off guard. "Well, it doesn't necessarily *negate* the experience, it just takes the spookiness out of it."

"The spookiness. Let's say someone has a near-death experience, okay? Hear me out; someone has a near-death experience. It's life changing for them. But someone else has to come along and say, Oh, look, we can replicate this. We can make you see a light at the end of a tunnel, all of it, we can make that happen..."

"It can happen in low-oxygen situations. It can happen to mountain climbers."

"See?"

"It's just something we know. We know that the brain is capable of organized electrical activity during the early stage of clinical death. It's been repeated in experiments. It's there."

"So what."

"So what?" He stopped stretching.

"Why? Why would it happen?"

He hesitated, gauging her with his bright eyes. "Well, we don't know."

"Exactly."

"But the point is being able to *say* we don't know. If we just start making claims to fill in the knowledge gaps, that's playing make-believe. A person keeps telling themselves the same story, and after a while, it starts to feel like evidence. You had a dream, honey. You weren't experiencing clinical death. People want to believe it's something magical or miraculous, okay, fine. But it's just the brain."

"Just the brain."

"This isn't like you."

"What's 'like me'? Agreeing with you on everything?" She stood up.

He tracked her with his gaze. "I didn't think you were always just agreeing with me. I thought we had come to some of the same understandings."

She helped him to his feet, retrieved his crutches. "Maybe I've changed."

"You've changed? Everybody's changed. Something like this does that."

"Maybe when your husband gets shot, yeah. Maybe when you feel like this is a profound moment, something is different." She tapped her temple. "Maybe I don't want to feel diagnosed and dismissed any more than you do."

She started for the door and he followed. "I'm not dismissing you."

Corrine turned and pointed at his chest. "Somewhere in you, Alex, is a person who can grasp that what he does has an effect on people."

"I don't…what I can't understand is…"

"I just want you to admit that there's a *possibility.* That there's more to it. Okay? Maybe it's selfish."

"You just feel like you need it. Is that it? You need to feel reassured. Well, join the club. Join the one billion Muslims or the two billion Christians."

She felt a sudden squeezing of her heart. They had two children together, years of marriage. A good life. Someone once said that a marriage endured when you learned how to argue with love. When you stayed on the same side, even if you disagreed. Did she feel that love now? Were they still on the same side or did this go deeper, down to the core? "I'm not talking about *me*. I'm talking about people. What *other people* need. From someone like you."

"What people? What are you talking about?"

She lowered her head. He leaned his crutches against the wall. They were both quiet a moment, just breathing, neither looking at the other. The wind picked up outside, sleet ticking against the windowpanes.

She resumed softly. "Any experience I have. Whether it's love, whether it's *awe* – you're going to cite me biology, Alex. You're going to talk about glands and hormones."

"But that doesn't diminish the subjective experience, Cor."

"That's exactly what it does," she said, raising her eyes to him. "To say that a chemical causes a feeling takes the whole thing and makes it abstract and rational, and that's what men do."

"Now you're mixing subjective and personal. They don't mean the same thing."

She pushed off from the wall. "Linear abstraction is a left-brain masculine trait and holistic visualization is feminine."

A smile played at the corners of his mouth. "Where'd you get that?"

"I can't think for myself? Men can only see the parts of things. They can't grasp the whole vision. And they've been dominating the conversation. You go out there and you debate people. Yes, you're a *PhD*, you're furthering the scientific *conversation*, but you're also alienating people who express themselves in different ways."

She watched the emotions work through his features, from smile to consternation. "So you're saying we don't have enough women's voices in the conversation? I agree."

"Forget it."

He reached for her. "Let's shift to the actual conversation. Okay? The one that's going on in your head. Can we do that? This isn't the conversation you really want to be having. This is about our marriage. How long have you been feeling this way? That you just can't stand me?"

"Stop it." She suddenly felt trapped.

"And don't tell me it's a dream you had – or anything else that's happened. I don't believe that."

"You're right." Her heart started to knock against her breast plate. "I'm freaked out. I'm completely freaked out, Alex. I feel like things are happening that I...you and Stephen never got along. And that was *before* his religious views."

"He cheated on Mara. What do you want me to say? I don't care what he thinks or believes, now or then."

"They worked through it. She forgave him, but you never did."

"It's got nothing to do with forgiveness. I don't have to forgive him. She lived with us for two months, Cor. She was devastated. And look what the whole thing did to Layla. But then Mara goes back to him?"

She could see it in his face – standing like this was hurting him. "Yeah, you weren't able to convince her."

"What does that have to do with anything?"

"Everything. Your need for people to see the world the way you do."

He took a step closer, wincing at the effort. "That's ridiculous."

"Is it ridiculous? Really? Why else would you be doing what you do? Why devote your whole life to –"

"It's not my whole life."

"Alex, how many appearances? How many debates? In the last year – can you even count? Plus weekly podcasts, plus books…you don't want people to see the world the way you do? That's all anyone wants."

"I don't know what you want me to say."

"These people – they just want you to admit that –"

"What *people*? Halloran?"

"No! Anyone." Something snapped in her. "Anyone you sit across from with your good looks and your degrees and books. They want to believe there could be something *else*. That's all any of them want. And you can't do it. You won't do it. Because you've got it all figured out."

He slammed his hand against the wall, making her jump. "I *don't* have it all figured out! That's the fucking point, Corrine! I don't have it figured out, but I'm not going to turn around and make claims I can't prove! I mean, are you kidding? I'm not saying I know for sure who did anything, only I know this was *some kind of terrorism*. I'm supposed to roll over and take that?"

So much flooding her mind, so much on the tip of her tongue, she tried to catch it all and couldn't.

He pushed past her, into the kitchen, limping hard.

"Stop – Alex – at least take these." She grabbed his crutches and chased after him.

He moved along by supporting himself on the kitchen island. He reached for the counter on the other side and kept going.

"Alex."

He stopped before leaving the kitchen, nearing the stairs, and he slowly turned.

"I'm sorry. I've always believed in you, the man I fell in love with. I just…I want you to use these gifts you have, Alex, but I think you have to look back. See what's in your own past, shaping you. You told me what your father did, what it was like to be raised in that house…"

She trailed off, seeing something never present in her husband's eyes before, at least not to her. He felt shamed by her.

He felt shamed by his father. His family past. Probably by things he'd never even told her.

She'd said almost everything she'd been holding back. There was just one last thing. "People need to believe. People need hope. No – listen to me. Sometimes it's more important than being right." She approached him slowly, still carrying the crutches. The kids were going to be up soon. She had the feeling that this was it; this was some fundamental moment, the kind that only came along once in a great while. A game changer for which the ramifications couldn't be seen, only felt in their potential, like all of fate rode on one single moment.

"Maybe it's time we get over that," he said. "Maybe it's time we all grow up. I've spent a third of my life talking about this, and you're asking me to throw it all away."

She gathered herself. "You're the better speaker. I don't know if I've said everything in the best way. I can't even say exactly why I think it's the right thing. But I know it is. I know – what I know is that every step you take from here on either brings us closer together or pushes us farther apart."

He finally relaxed and looked at her. There weren't many moments when Alex really let her see him. He'd always been guarded – not standoffish, which was different – but armed with his intellect.

The little boy in him shined through, just for a second. Then it was gone.

"I have to get ready," he said. "We can talk more about this when I get back from Boston." And he struggled up the stairs.

41

R oth walked into Libby's office at nine a.m. He was young, blue-eyed, with brush-cut hair and a blond mustache. "So there was something we missed? A book by this guy Halloran with some highlighted passages?"

"And some notes written into the margins."

"You had breakfast yet? Need anything? We're going to take a walk downstairs – I've got something for you to look at."

"I'm good," she said.

He rose from the desk and walked to her and they shook hands, Libby grinning ear to ear and blushing like he had a grade school crush. They went out into a corridor and took an elevator down to computer forensics where she was introduced to another guy, thin, shaggier black hair, sitting with a laptop. Sheffield's laptop. Libby pulled up two chairs and invited her to sit, the two of them flanking the computer guy, named Jordan. They both had that Maine accent.

"Got a couple things," Jordan said. "This first thing, we think this is a transcript from a chat room. Meaning, someone – probably Sheffield – copy-pasted this whole chat into a Word document."

"Really? Not encrypted?"

Libby glanced at Roth and said, "We think maybe for safe-keeping."

"Like an insurance policy," Jordan said.

"Okay." Roth wasn't sure what it all meant.

Jordan went on. "GoodShepherd here, this guy, we've seen this pop up in other places in Sheffield's stuff; it's a username he likes. You can see the time stamp, also included in the pasting."

She saw the dates; the whole thing was from November, over a year ago. Between eleven p.m. and midnight on the fourteenth.

Roth asked, "Do we know which chat forum? Like where this was online?"

"No, but we know it wasn't Facebook Messenger or Twitter," Jordan said. "Back in the day, before everybody was all lumped together in the same feed, people communicated in forums. Very specific groups. This is like that."

Libby said, "Our best guess is that this is some kind of anti-Baines group. Or, if it's not that specific, at least some kind of pro-religious group. You'll see. And it's like Socrates is trying to get GoodShepherd interested in something. He's fishing."

She leaned in for a closer look and read some of the lines.

Socrates03: You've got the right idea, but you need strategy.

GoodShepherd: What makes you an expert?

Socrates03: I've thought this through. Not saying you haven't. But I know things about him – I can help guide you.

Her nerves started jumping at that one.

GoodShepherd: I don't know what your talking about.

Socrates03: Come on. Yeah you do.

According to the time stamps, nearly ten minutes elapsed. "GoodShepherd," she said. "That's Sheffield's Twitter name."

"Yeah, maybe he uses the same handle," Jordan said.

"Could somebody find him? I mean, if they were looking for

Sheffield, wanted to talk to him online in this private room or whatever it is, how would they do that?"

"Well, like I said, we're probably looking at some pretty specific group. If you knew the guy, knew what he was into, it's not like there'd be a lot of places online to look for him. Would just take a little time. If you were patient, you'd get him. And like you said, it's his Twitter name, so if you knew who he was on Twitter, you'd have a pretty good guess this was him on here."

Socrates03: You still there?

Nothing from GoodShepherd.

Socrates03: I'm not FBI. This isn't entrapment. Anyway, you're on a secure connection.

GoodShepherd: Prove it. Let me see you.

Roth noted the two-minute gap in communication. "Is there some kind of video-call function from the chat room?" she asked Jordan.

"Can't say for sure, since this was pasted into a Word doc, and we can't see what online platform they were using. But a lot of platforms have both audio and video chat capacity."

Video. Roth thought about that. If Socrates had let GoodShepherd see his face, that was risky. There were other ways to convince GoodShepherd he wasn't law enforcement. To allow his face to be seen, it served some additional purpose, gave him some kind of credit.

Jordan spoke again. "It's odd, though, that they resume the chat. Why not just keep talking over video?"

After the two minute gap, Socrates wrote: *These people need to see their leader fall. They need to see him come apart at the seams. We need to get the world's attention.*

One word from GoodShepherd: *Yes.*

Libby asked, "Think we need to pass this to your FBI agent?"

"I think it wouldn't hurt."

"FBI are good at the online creeps, you know, chasing down

the pedophiles and everything. Maybe they can get a match for Socrates03."

She pulled out her phone and flipped through her contacts.

Jordan said, "But here's the other thing we wanted you to look at. This was pretty easy to find."

Roth returned her attention to Sheffield's laptop. The computer tech had brought up pictures of a gala event, people in tuxedos and gowns and wide grins. "What am I looking at?"

"This is in White Plains, about a year ago, a charity event put together by Paul Halloran." He started clicking through the pictures and stopped on a familiar face.

More than familiar. Halloran was a *famous* face. Well, semi-famous. If he'd been Socrates, was that why he'd needed video with GoodShepherd. It'd be one way to prove, flatly, that he wasn't an FBI agent trying to entrap Sheffield. It was, almost literally, unmasking.

Jordan was speaking again: "And here's Stephen Mayhew."

Roth leaned close and studied the photo of Mayhew and Halloran, arm in arm. "No shit. And Sheffield just had this on his system?"

"In the cloud. Took some time to get into it, but not too hard. Like he wasn't trying too hard to hide it, if that makes sense."

"What about the transcript? How hard was he trying to hide that?"

"I'd say a little harder."

She stood upright with her phone out again. "Anything on there about Botox or the end of the world?"

Jordan and Libby exchanged looks as she made the call to Harlan. When he answered, she caught him up on the laptop findings. Then she put her phone away and looked at Libby. "I got a file I need to print out, look at a few things. Is there a room I could use?"

"Yeah, sure. As soon as we're done, I'll take you back up."

Jordan was waiting for her attention again. "Okay, and so here's the third thing, the last big thing. We found a video clip. Eighteen months ago, Baines is giving one of his talks. You'll see it when you watch, there's a little hubbub in the crowd, like a heckler talking smack. Baines has got some security on this one, and they're in there quick, single out this guy, talk to him."

She watched as Libby said, "Guess who it is? Gary frigging Sheffield."

The cell phone video was taken at a distance, but there were a good few frames where Sheffield showed up with clarity. He was escorted away from the crowd by two men and it ended.

"Why didn't this come up?" Roth asked Libby.

"I wondered the same thing. I figure Baines never really knew about it. You can see from the video he's aware of some commotion, but he kind of just smooths it over."

"Where's the video from? Portland?"

"Yeah."

Libby glanced at Jordan, then at her. He hadn't completely stopped mooning over her, but he was clearly captivated by the work. "This guy is like prime horseflesh."

"What?"

"Just something that…" Libby waved a hand, looking embarrassed. "I mean, this type of guy strikes me as a ready foot soldier. You know what I mean? Smart enough to be pissed off at the world, but not smart enough not to be taken advantage of."

"Thank you, gentlemen."

Libby put his hands on his hips, looking pleased. Then he remembered. "Yeah, let me show you back upstairs, get you a nice spot to work."

They headed up. He said, "You been on the job long?"

"Seven years as a trooper, three with BCI."

"Probably none of my business, but is there a Mr. Roth?"

"My husband kept his own name."

42

A familiar setting. A stage, an audience. Only now, Alex found himself watching the crowd, distracted by them, wondering if anyone was going to get to their feet and take aim. The young, hip MIT audience of students and faculty had been patted down and sent through a metal detector. Chet had hired four guys to augment school security, dipping into Howard Baines's supply of ex-military guys. Two of them were called Ashford and Clayburn – Alex had yet to meet the others, though he could see them at the back of the large auditorium, flanking the exits, white cords curling out of their ears. Plenty of security, but it didn't change the fear.

Chet stood by in the stage wing. The moderator, an MIT professor named Terrence Deisart, sat between his two guests – Alex and Paul Halloran. Halloran wore a white shirt and red tie, black pants. There was a Bible-salesman vibe to his appearance, but Alex knew the simple clothing was more about appearing workmanlike. A man of the people. His gray hair was short and bristling, the skin of his face rough and ruddy, a filigree of burst capillaries on the nib of his nose.

But Halloran was educated, smart; his book, *In Sight of God,* was actually quite elegant. The caustic shock-jock persona was just that – a persona. Meant to maximize attention in a world where, like Sheffield himself had said, you had to be loud for people to notice. In reality, Halloran had grown up in a nice family from Dobbs Ferry, something he tried to distance himself from, even though he'd remained in Westchester for most of his life. He was from the very "elite" background he derided.

He now sat five yards away on the stage, Deisart between him and Alex. Time for debate. Chet's idea – and not his worst – was to call it *The Future of Science and Religion.* And because it was just before semester's end, they had an audience on short notice. But the framing was really a pretext. Everyone knew, from Halloran to the physics and engineering majors in the audience, that they were there for another reason.

Deisart faced Alex once introductions had been made. "You were shot at by a gunman less than a week ago," he said. "As I'm sure everyone has noticed, we have some extra security here today. You've been busy since the shooting. It's been covered by major national newspapers, and you've given some interviews. And, a couple of days ago, you spoke with Sherry Olsen on NPR. But this is your first in-person appearance, and we just want to express our gratitude."

The audience broke into applause which steadily grew louder and filled with whistles and cheers. Halloran clapped, too, a few flat slaps.

"To just sort of address the elephant in the room up front," Deisart continued, "I wanted to ask: How are you?"

Alex paused, looking over the audience a moment. Normally he kept his personal life out of any debates like these. "I'm good. I mean, there's pain, and there's the expected upheaval of my life, but I'm good, all things considered. Meditation helps."

"Have there been any difficulties with that?"

"Sure. Absolutely: Meditation has been more challenging than ever. My mind is constantly pulled away from the moment. I find myself in the past. Reliving what happened."

"How about anger?" Deisart asked. "Is there any anger?"

"Yes. Anger toward the assailant. Anger that this could have happened. The whole 'Why me?' of it. Anger for what happened to Peter Nyswaner, Emily Granger, all the others. But it's also made me realize my many blessings – things I may have been overlooking. My wife, my children, my life."

The audience applauded again. When it all tapered off, Deisart said, "Okay, well, let's get started. Alex, I'm going to have you go first. Can you just give us an overview of your position on where things stand between science and religion?"

Alex cleared his throat and looked from Deisart to the audience, passing over Halloran with his gaze. "So....There was a gentleman, recently, a Swiss gentleman, who came back home after eighteen years at a monastery. Maybe you heard about this. This guy left everything behind for eighteen years. Almost two decades. And then he comes back, and everyone is clamoring to hear what he'd learned. What was eighteen years of sitting in a room all day, what was it like? What's the great big insight? And finally he grants an interview, and they ask him, after eighteen years, what did you learn? And he says, I learned not to trust everything that enters my mind."

The audience laughed.

Alex, feeling a little more comfortable, continued. "We're masters at deluding ourselves. We're really good at it. And in today's world, most of us can access nearly limitless information – but we can get tripped up distinguishing *information* from real knowledge. Knowledge is something that's tried and true. It's not just whatever's on the internet. It's time-tested; it's results you can repeat. Religion is kind of the internet, pre-internet. The Bible, the Koran – they're widely shared stories. But they're not testable hypotheses."

"Where does Buddhism fit into the picture for you?" Deisart asked.

"Some Buddhists believe in things I don't, like reincarnation. But Buddhism is also quite scientific, in that it's been systematically studying the effects of meditation for twenty-five hundred years. And today we have the instruments to really verify those effects. So that's something we know. That meditation can have observable results."

"All right, great. Thank you." Deisart turned to Halloran. "So, Paul, I'm a qualitative sociologist, which means I analyze data. From all over the world, it's clear that modernization leads to an increasingly secular society. A diminishment of religion. How do you see religion surviving, or thriving, in the future? Do you think a relationship between religion and science is really possible?"

Halloran sniffed and took a beat. "First, I'd like to thank you for having me here. But I'd like to stay away from big proclamations and keep it personal here for a moment." His eyes connected with Alex. "Because I'm interested – when Terry asked how you were doing, you said this experience has brought you closer to your family, your appreciation of them. Maybe it's shifted your values?"

"I wouldn't say values, no. But my attention, yes."

"I guess what I'm curious about is whether you had any sort of experience during your ordeal. If the incident – I don't know – if it promoted any sort of feelings in you that we everyday people might consider religious."

Alex felt a twist in his gut. The thought tiptoed across his mind – *That's why this thing happened? For me to have some kind of revelation?*

On the heels of that thought – *Corrine did, didn't she?*

He smiled, but it felt wooden. "Well, even if I had seen the light at the end of the tunnel..."

"I'm not asking if you saw a light, per se, but something –

anything – transcendent. Something that moved you, something that –"

"At no point did anything happen I could not explain."

"Nothing?" Halloran's eyebrow went up. "Then what caused you to change your attention to your family?"

"Being close to death. Realizing that time is short."

"And why can't we call that a spiritual experience?"

"You can call it spiritual, sure. That's a broad enough adjective."

"But not religious."

"I wouldn't use that word, no."

He was reminded of Sheffield and defining 'scripture.' "We can go through the entire spiritual cannon, across the years and across various cultures, and all these supposedly 'spiritual' experiences are now understood as the product of standard biology. Near death. Out of body. The sense of a god or a ghost or a demon or an angel in the room with you. All these can be induced by stimulating specific areas of the brain, which is what any drug is doing. So, if you have a vision, and that vision is the sky opening up to swallow you whole, that's the result of an area of your brain being stimulated through stress or by some other causal force."

Halloran nodded, unfolded his hands and smoothed them over his colorful tie. His shirt and pants were sober, businesslike colors, white and black respectively, but the tie was loud. "Okay. And what would you say is the ultimate causal force? If you have a problem calling it God, how do you answer that question?"

And so the debate had begun.

Sitting in a small, empty office at Portland PD, Roth took a call from Harlan. "Sheffield wants to talk again."

"Why? Because of Nyswaner?"

"That's what we think. The medical examiner ruled Nyswaner's death a homicide, and Sheffield's charges just jumped to capital murder. He's been real twitchy since he heard about it. The whole cool guy can't-touch-me act is gone. It's like he didn't expect it."

Roth said, "I've seen part of a chat between Sheffield and an unknown subject, and this is without a doubt someone grooming Sheffield – or maybe that's not the right word, he was kind of already groomed – but sort of getting in his corner, massaging his shoulders, whispering in his ear." She reached for the transcript and read a little bit to Harlan.

"Shit," Harlan said.

"But Sheffield hasn't given up a name?"

"Not yet."

Roth considered that. "He might be trying to preserve the idea that he doesn't know, but that's a tough sell. This transcript indicates that they were on a video chat together, so he's seen this 'Socrates03.' Unless the guy wore a damned Guy Fawkes mask, which wouldn't be out of character for guys like these. Theatrical."

"Sheffield's also talked to this person on two occasions, by phone…"

"Our two burner calls," Roth agreed.

"And what do we know about those?"

"Well, I went through Baines's itinerary. Baines was in each location where those burner calls originated. So he's in Philadelphia for the first one, talking to a bunch of doctors about brain stuff, and then he's in Brooklyn for the second one. He's right there. Whoever made the calls was within miles of Baines when they called Sheffield."

Harlan was silent a moment. "So is it Creasy? Maybe following?"

"It's possible." She thought about the car outside of Sheffield's home.

"Listen, you got that video of Sheffield at Baines's Portland University appearance?"

"Yeah. From eighteen months ago. Before either of those calls. Or the VPN chats."

"We never did get that list of attendees from Warman..."

"No," she agreed. "But I don't know if that means he's hiding anything."

"What's the video show?"

"It shows Sheffield acting up. Waving his arms. You can't hear him. So it starts with – the camera is on Baines on stage. Baines gets a little sidetracked by something, makes a joke, but then the camera changes angle and you see someone in the audience – half of them are standing, don't ask me if it was a sold-out event or they just don't bring in chairs for college students, I don't know – but the camera zooms in on Sheffield; he's yelling, he looks angry, and then security is there, removing him. I tried contacting those security guys, but no luck."

Harlan grunted. "Well, what does Warman say?"

"He's not been answering. Baines is at a debate right now with Paul Halloran. At MIT. I'm sure Warman's there, just not picking up."

"Okay," Harlan said. "Need you to send that video to Moritz. She wants it. She's got eyes for Sheffield as a terrorist. The FBI is not liking all these references to poisons and floods. This guy is starting to look like the next McVeigh or Kaczynski."

"You don't think we're jumping the gun here? Adding things up that don't belong?"

He hesitated. "I don't know. I'm of the mind that someone set out to make an example of Baines. Maybe they used Sheffield, influenced him, helped him, I don't know. I think they sent Sheffield in to do the dirty work, and they're still out there. The question to ask is, who gains something? Because I had my little look at Stephen Mayhew…"

"And?" Roth felt her heart rate cooling, the kind of calm that came over her just before she got out to check a motorist's license and registration, just before she'd gone into a house a few weeks on the job to lay eyes on her first dead body.

"When I spoke to Mayhew," Harlan said, "he admitted donating to Halloran's charity."

"I've seen pictures of them together at an event," Roth added quickly.

"There you go. Obviously, that's not a crime – even if the charity was a fraud, Mayhew's not liable for it. And if anything, he'd be upset about it, not hewing closer to Halloran or plotting with him. You'd think, anyway. But it does connect them. Between that and the pictures, it connects Baines's brother-in-law with his intellectual enemy, Paul Halloran."

"Yeah," Roth said. "It does."

43

"Let me ask you this," Alex pulled his gaze from the sea of faces and looked at Halloran. They were midway through the given hour. "How much responsibility do you feel you have to the public? To human well-being?"

"That's what I'm here for," Halloran said. "I think that would be obvious. My concern is that, with human progress, when we throw away God, we're taking one step forward and two steps back. And any more steps back – we're in hell."

Alex ignored the last remark. "Okay. Stem cell research has saved lives, prevented suffering, but it's been challenged at every turn, progress hindered, by people in your position – people you support, organizations you help to fund. So it's arguable you've increased human suffering because of a belief."

"I have beliefs; you have beliefs."

"I have data."

The audience ruffled and murmured. Halloran glanced into the crowd and then his eyes came back to Alex. "You want proof of the soul? Show me proof of consciousness. That's something you talk about all the time – you say, 'All we know is that we're conscious.' Consciousness and its contents, that's your line. So?" Halloran's eyes glinted across the stage. "Show me proof."

"I don't have it," Alex said. "We're talking about something that is most likely an emergent property of the brain. You're talking about something that's put into a living being by an outside force. You want me to believe something – that the outside force is God."

"What's the difference?"

"What's the difference? Ask Meister Eckhart, brought before Pope John to recant everything he ever taught. Because he said 'God and I are one.' That's not conventional monotheism. If anything, Eckhart was the first 'New Ager' on record. Memory, identity, is material. It takes a brain to store it, and a brain is physical. Everything is physical. Anything anyone in this audience, or on this planet, has ever experienced – whether being awake, meditating, fantasizing, or dreaming – is firmly rooted in, indeed crafted by, matter."

Halloran leaned in. "Here's the problem. You and your school of materialists are coming out of the Renaissance as a continuation of this false binary premise – that man is the subject and the universe is the object."

Alex felt a jolt. It was nearly the same thing Sheffield had said to him, reading from his notes.

Halloran faced the audience and raised his voice, the cadence turning holy preacher. "The men who precede Dr. Baines were first called 'natural philosophers or 'naturalists.' Their mission was to explore the glory of God, the glory of both the cosmos and the micro-world. Their preconception? That man is living *in* this world. That he is separate from it. But everything quantum physics has told us – a science that is more accurate in terms of its predictions than classical physics – is that the observer plays an integral role in the definition of 'stuff.' The subatomic world is different when observed, different when it is bombarded with light particles. Different when seen."

Alex shook his head. "Some of what you're saying does apply to the micro-world. But it doesn't scale; it doesn't apply to the macro-world. We know that the moon is there whether we're looking at it or not."

"Without a conscious observer, the moon is just a swirling mass of quantum possibilities."

Some of the audience booed this, a few others clapped. MIT students were notoriously skeptical and atheistic – Alex was surprised at even the smattering of applause.

Halloran quickly returned focus to the audience. "My point is this. This whole thing, putting science over here, and religion over here, is false. Dr. Baines, sitting here to my right, is actually coming out of the line from religion. That's where his type of thinker originated, and here he is now, perpetuating the same mistake, that man is separate from the natural world."

"That's absurd," Alex said.

"*I'm* the one," Halloran hurried on, "who represents the reality – man is *not* separate from nature, that this separation was the first step toward atheism, because once man had named and categorized and codified all that he perceived, he *threw away* God. No, man is not separate. It is precisely his inextricability from the natural world, from the universe, that is the godhead, the logos, the great and unlockable mystery of all things."

Some of the audience members laughed, some booed. Deisart raised a hand to call for respectful behavior.

"Let's try this," Deisart said. "Let me see if I can steer us back on course. Paul, you said that without an observer the moon was a swirling mass of quantum possibilities. So let me ask you – if all sentient life on the planet, everything we call living, everything with a chance at perception, were to suddenly die, just boom, gone – would consciousness still exist?"

"Yes."

Deisart's eyes shifted to Alex, who faced Halloran and countered quickly: "To me," Alex said to Halloran, "you're just smuggling the idea of God into the conversation. This transcendent, immaterial thing. This absolute thing."

Deisart interjected again. "Alex, so there's no evidence of primordial consciousness? What Jung called the collective conscious?"

"There's no evidence of primordial consciousness any more than there's evidence of a soul. Not with our tools, not with all of the collective brains that have worked on the problem since the beginning of science. What Paul is talking about is faith. I really need to make this point. He's taking terms – he's using scientific-sounding words to support this otherwise unsupportable idea of a soul. This is not the way to build the bridge between science and religion."

"It is not unsupportable. It is merely –"

"It is unsupportable from a modern scientific perspective. You can argue against the metrics, but these are the tools we have at our disposal, and with them, we've sent rockets into space, we've cured virulent diseases –"

"We've created weapons of mass destruction."

The mass destruction line was another one Sheffield had used. Alex shifted his weight in the chair, favoring his leg, feeling the heat. "We can use technology for ill or for good. And the people who are using technology for ill tend to be people with specific ideologies, religious-borne ideologies –"

"Like the man who shot you."

Alex felt the room go utterly silent and tense. Deisart broke through. "Let's leave that aside a moment and bring this back to the focus of the conversation – Alex makes a fair point. If the aim is to bring science and religion together, how can we do that? Paul? How do you see that happening?"

"Again," Halloran said, "by recognizing the false binary that science and religion are separate to begin with. They're not. Science was built out of religion in the first place and is fundamentally flawed because of this."

Alex said, "Paul, the difference is, science looks at what it has yet to fully understand – let's say consciousness – and says, 'I don't know.' It's a mystery. And we're okay with that. *Religion* takes what it doesn't know and makes –"

Halloran cut him off. "You don't say consciousness is a mystery – you *just said* it is an emergent property of the brain, it has physical roots. You just said that. And you claim that everything expressed or felt in consciousness has a specific physical correlate in the brain, or if you haven't found one yet, you will…"

"I say that *I don't know*," Alex interrupted. It echoed his earlier argument with Corrine. "You say we need to take the answers on faith. But when pressed, you turn to quantum physics, even though you're not a quantum physicist. It is precisely this doublespeak, this convenient application of misunderstood science when it suits you, and rejection of it when it doesn't, which perpetuates the separation between science and religion. And it's why the two will never be happily joined in some cosmic matrimony you're trying to officiate."

The room burst into applause and boisterous laughter. Alex kept his gaze locked on Halloran, who stayed relaxed in his chair as the reaction died down.

Deisart spoke up again. "Well, we knew this was going to get a little heated, didn't we? But these debates bear fruit, and that's why we're all here."

Alex took a drink of water, felt his heart beating. Halloran kept watching him, this calm look on his face that was getting under Alex's skin.

Deisart consulted his notes. "Okay, before we open this up to questions, there's one last topic I want to bring up. It's going to be touchy, but I think we need to address it. Alex started to bring it up – the role of our responsibility as public figures. During his talk on NPR, Alex says he accepts certain responsibility for what happened to him. Now looking at –"

Halloran was quick. "I know where this is headed, and I never encourage violence."

Deisart shot him a look and held up a piece of paper. "Not with the line, 'Something needs to be done about Alex Baines?'"

"I shouldn't have said that," Halloran said. "I should have said his *ideas*. Of course I'm not advocating for violence. I meant that the ideas Dr. Baines puts *out* – I don't think it's the right thing to leave them unchallenged. I know who our audience is. They're like a lot of people here today. They're young, they're impressionable. I worry about a world of people growing up to believe life is just some random occurrence. I worry about a world that doesn't see each individual as divinely sovereign. A world that devalues individual human life – just sees it all as 'stuff,' as physical, something to be manipulated for the collective good." Halloran looked at Alex again. "But I would never call for anything to happen to you, no matter what's happened to *me* because of exchanges we've had in the past."

Alex began to respond – it was on the tip of his tongue to remind Halloran that he'd done his own sabotaging. That, during their one previous debate, it was his assertion that religion did more good in the world than secular organizations, that his own charity was helping to reduce poverty and hunger, which led to the article that exposed his fraudulence. But Alex held back. He thought of Corrine again. He felt something shift inside, like a lock disengaged.

He listened as Halloran finished.

"All I'm trying to say," Halloran said, "is that nothing is permanent in this world. Not even a rock. Even a rock is constantly changing. It might've once been molten lava beneath the crust of the earth. It might've been sand, compressed over eons of time. In a hundred thousand years, it may be dust inhaled by living creatures to become part of their bloodstream. A physical object itself is an illusion of the mind."

Chuckles rippled through the audience but Halloran pushed on, unfazed. "If you want to tell me that producing altered states is possible by stimulating certain areas of the brain, fine. But you've done no better than explaining how a lack of food in the stomach signals hunger and creates visions and smells of a greasy cheeseburger. That cheeseburger was once a cow. That cow was once a fertilized egg inside a heifer's womb, nurtured by grass and rain and sunlight. These physical objects are *conventional realities*; they are temporary and illusory."

The audience was quiet as Halloran paused.

"You're asking me to accept a world in which the biased mind prides itself on everything which it has conceived of." He tapped the side of his head. "But the mind conceives, then verifies its preconceptions with tools it has *designed itself*. I cannot join you there, Dr. Baines. I cannot, in good conscience, join you."

Corrine's face floated in front of Alex, itself an illusion. Yet he could smell her, feel her hands on him, as if she was there. He could see the pain that had filled her eyes that morning when she had, in her own way, tried to express the same thing.

Alex shifted his stiff leg again and looked at Halloran. "You're saying the trouble is the foundation."

"Yes."

"If we don't know enough to understand the way in which the mind deceives itself in its explorations, we are blind to our biases."

Halloran nodded, surprise lighting his eyes. "Yes. Exactly."

"That things lack certainty until measurements are made, but some crucial measurements cannot even be made at all – and if we can't even determine the initial state of physical systems, then we must consider that the systems as a whole are indeterminate."

"Yes!" The man's color had become nearly as bright as his tie. Alex glanced at Deisart, who seemed curious as to where this was going. The audience remained still and silent.

Alex thought of mainstream news and social media, seemingly designed to split people into one team or the other. Or at least capitalize on their tribal tendencies. A world with no gray area, only for and against. The possibility that a man had shot him because of that very sense of righteousness, of team loyalty.

"As a scientist," he said, "I have to concede the role that the observer plays in measurement. I have to admit the possibility that the act of observation is intimately entwined with the subjectivity the scientist brings – and this includes his or her preexisting beliefs. And that this, in part, determines the outcomes. It determines what we see."

He ignored the audience reaction, booing now as if he'd suddenly switched sides on them.

Halloran couldn't contain himself any longer. "Precisely, yes. So if you take neuroscience – the most recent incarnation of materialism – and you seek this physical basis for the mind, for these mystical experiences, how can I be convinced?"

Alex looked at his hands, then outward to the crowd. "I understand your position. We are the mind trying to see itself. Even if we have all the brains to infinity working on a problem, the issue remains the same – the foundation is unstable – the mind acts as a potent, cooperative force in determining reality. The entity which decides questions such as 'What are we?' will always be the mind itself, no matter its origins, physical or otherwise."

As the audience grew ever more rankled, Chet caught his eye, talking to someone offstage. At the same time, the security guards in the back were talking to a small group of cops – four, to be exact – Boston Police. People were turning around to look, forgetting their rebellion.

The Boston police started down the aisles through the auditorium. One of Howard's security men was talking, touching his ear.

Deisart stood up, signaled by the person off stage standing with Chet. She had to be a cop, too, in plain clothes.

"Ladies and gentlemen," Deisart said as he moved offstage, "please excuse me for a moment."

The plainclothes cop in the wing was joined by another, a man. They stood talking with Deisart and Howard's security guards. Then the man came walking out on stage. He moved to Halloran and asked him to stand. Alex's pulse picked up. There was something about Halloran after all.

After he was escorted off, the woman came for Alex, accompanied by the guard called Ashford. "Mr. Baines," Ashford said, "this is Special Agent Moritz. She's with the FBI."

"What's going on?"

Moritz had potently red hair. Gray eyes. "Going to need you to come with me, Dr. Baines."

"Come with you?" He looked past her at what was happening. Halloran appeared upset, his arms in the air.

Alex got his crutches beneath him. The audience seemed to hold its breath as Deisart returned. "Ah – ladies and gentlemen – so sorry about this – but it seems we're going to have to end today's talk abruptly."

The crowd murmured and began to move. Moritz held her hand out to Alex. "Please, Dr. Baines. We need to go quickly."

He hopped along on the crutches, watching as Halloran was taken away. Now his heart rate was redlining. "Are you going to explain what's happening?"

"We have a car waiting," Moritz said as they headed to an exit door. "There's a problem."

44

Corrine's phone buzzed on the bedside table where it was charging, no one in the room to answer. She soaked in the tub, her knees forming islands in the sudsy water, her head tilted back on the pillow suction cupped to the tub wall. Her sister had given her the pillow on a recent birthday. First, she'd laughed at it. Then tried it. Now, she couldn't live without it.

The candles lit on the sink cast shifting light onto the ceiling. Keeping still in the hot water, her face tipped upward, Corrine stared into the dark morass of clouds twisting their way into the black hole of sky.

Lightning trembled without sound, thick wreaths of wet cotton clouds slowly spinning upward.

She could feel her phone vibrate as it rattled against the hard surface of the end table next door – her sense connection to the real world was still very much intact. But she didn't want to break this – whatever it was. It was the most sustained experience she'd had yet.

It frightened her.

Be here.

Stay.

Don't run away.

She remained in the water, fixed on the ceiling – she stared *into* it – and she asked the vision what it was.

There was no answer, only a slow, noiseless churning.

The longer she looked, the more vivid it became. Intricate, delicate webbing flashed within the cloud bodies, as if the whole sky pulsed with an internal storm. The outer clouds moved more slowly, the eye in the middle drew in the clouds along the inner rim. Their cotton texture sheared away in gossamer strands, winding faster and faster until these shreds disappeared into the bright void.

What is this?

The voice was distant and muffled and sent a bolt up her spine.

She heard movement downstairs – Drew – then his voice again. Alex had asked him to stay at the house while he was in Boston. Now, Drew was talking to someone. She blinked and looked away from the ceiling, but the image traveled with her for a second, imposing itself over the rest of the bathroom until it dissipated, leaving her staring at the five-pound Ganesha statue on the nearby shelves, the elephant staring back.

She slopped water onto the tile floor when she grabbed the edge of the tub and sat herself up. She crossed her other arm over her breasts and listened, unable to make out Drew's precise words. But whomever had tried to call her had probably then reached out to Drew instead. It could be Alex. God, if there'd been another incident...

She grabbed for her towel and got to her feet, water pattering into the tub. When she blinked, the image of the roiling sky flashed behind her lids. Standing in the water, she closed her eyes and saw it again, but in negative, like a photo. It slowly drained away as she stood dripping, holding the towel against herself.

She got moving, hastily dried the wet ends of her hair, then shrugged into her bathrobe and left. From the top of the stairs, she had a better ear on Drew down on the first floor.

"Okay," he was saying. "Okay, yeah, of course. No, I will tell her. Yes, I understand."

She called down softly, mindful of sleeping Freda and – hopefully, by now – Kenneth. "Drew?"

He didn't answer. It sounded like he was in the kitchen, moving further out of range, still talking. If it was a real emergency, he would have come upstairs or yelled for her. Whatever it was, he was handling it, and it could wait until she got dressed. She went into the master bedroom and closed the door.

She stared at herself in the dresser mirror.

"You're not losing it."

Meaning: *You don't have a brain tumor.*

But there was the sensation of some gravitational force, pulling her upwards.

"Stop it."

She slapped her own face, unexpectedly hard. It did the trick. And like some electromagnetic pulse suddenly killing the power across town, the slap had the effect of clearing her mind completely.

No more of this now. She needed to pull her shit together. The kids needed a sane, capable mother. Alex needed to hear the truth from her – it was never the right time, but she couldn't let that stop her anymore. And as much as Drew had been a huge help lately, she needed to stand on her own two feet. It was time for him to leave.

45

"Sheffield was born and raised in Cousins, Maine," Moritz said. They were in the back of the SUV, crossing the Charles River. Alex glanced out at the lights of downtown Boston. Moritz had yet to indicate where they were taking him. Chet was gone, put in the back of another black SUV now following behind them, Halloran in another after that. Alex was alone with Moritz, with one other agent driving.

"Sheffield's mother worked the Chebeague Island ferry, while his father was an odd jobs man who came and went from their lives," Moritz said. "Sheffield started following you online after seeing you on a YouTube video compiling some of your more scathing religious criticisms. A little after that, he started criticizing you. Replying to your tweets."

"I never saw anything from him," Alex said.

"A New York State Investigator – you know her, Roth – went to his house yesterday," Moritz said. "She found a book by your friend Halloran. We've studied it, and Sheffield makes several comments in the margins, alluding to committing acts of terrorism. A compounding concern is that Mr. Sheffield was previously employed by BAX Global."

"I don't know what that is."

Moritz nodded like she understood. "BAX Global is a major shipping company that specializes in handling high-risk substances. They're headquartered in Irvine, California. That's a 949 area code. Wait – before you ask – Sheffield was fired three years ago for comments he made while at BAX. About how a substance used in beauty products and cosmetic surgery could be weaponized."

It caught Alex off guard. "Botox?"

"It's a possibility. Botox is derived from a purified toxin – *clostridium botulinum* – botulism. It's on the top ten list of world's most deadly potential agents of bioterrorism. A single gram, in crystalized form, would possibly kill a million people by suffocating them, paralyzing their lungs."

"I don't follow. You think Sheffield has –"

"BAX is in the supply chain to major pharmaceutical corporations. AbbVie, for one."

He recoiled at the name, AbbVie. They were just rumors, but AbbVie was supposedly getting into the microdosing business. It all felt like an onslaught of coincidence. His head was spinning.

"BAX Global are doing a full inventory," Moritz said. "So far, they've told us they have no reason to believe there's been any security breach. I'm working with them on a list of employees, but it takes time – due to their type of work they keep everything classified, so if I'm going to start pulling down walls, I have to have good cause."

The SUV took a hard left after the bridge, pressing him against the seatbelt. He recognized Massachusetts General Hospital as they passed. Then they were in Charlestown, heading toward the Mystic River. "Where are we going?"

"Sheffield has been saying he wants to talk. But once again, he'll only talk to you. We're going to a secure location where you can talk to him by phone. If Sheffield, at any point, managed to smuggle out any sort of toxic materials, we need to act on that right away. You need to get him to open up."

46

orrine found him coming up the stairs as she descended. "Listen, Drew..."

But his eyes were wide. "Cor – something happened."

She glanced back toward the kids' rooms, just instinct, and then they both went down to the main floor. "What are you talking about?"

"They picked up Halloran. Arrested him, right in the middle of the talk with Alex."

She blinked. "Where's Alex?"

"With the FBI. I talked to Terry Deisart. He doesn't know where they were taking Alex and no one is saying. It could be to the FBI headquarters in Chelsea."

She had her phone in her hand and stood in the kitchen as she searched her recent missed calls. Two from Mara, one from a blocked number, nothing from Alex. She tried Alex first, but it went straight to voicemail. Tried him again, then Chet – also straight to voicemail. "What about Chet?"

"I don't know. With Alex, I assume."

Corrine felt dizzy with uncertainty. Where was her husband?

What was going on? She focused on Drew. "Did Deisart say what happened?"

"Just that right in the middle of the debate, Boston PD showed up, the FBI showed up, and they took all three of them, put them in separate cars, and drove away."

She sat down heavily on the stool. Drew just watched her for a moment. "Let me get you something. Let me get you some water."

For a moment, she could only stare at the floor. "Something stronger."

"Coming right up."

"What's happening, Drew?"

"I don't know. But – you want a beer? Glass of wine?"

"I don't care. No. Stronger."

He moved past the dining room table to a hutch in the corner, opened up its lower cabinet and pulled out the whiskey. He brought out two glasses and poured them each about three quarters full. They drank in silence, sitting adjacent at the island.

When the whiskey was gone, she picked up the bottle and poured another glass, then walked into the living room. She sat down in the easy chair next to the couch and tucked one leg up under the other, took a long sip, and stared. She just wanted this all to be over, for her husband to be home.

Right now, he was with the FBI. The FBI had Halloran, too – why? Because Halloran had paid someone to shoot at her husband? Was there some other threat? Did she need to be worried? Dear God, were her sister and brother-in-law somehow involved after all?

Drew came in with his phone, texting or emailing with it, looking worried.

"What?"

"I hate to say it…Jesus, that's just insane."

"*What?*"

"Alex has been disinvited from the ashram."

It wasn't what she expected. "He...what?"

Drew held up the phone with a pained face. "An email from this morning. I don't think Alex has seen it yet." He flipped the phone around and read, "'Dear Dr. Baines, in light of recent events surrounding your participation in the University at Irvine study...'"

She lost what Drew said after that. Everything was happening at once. And it was along the lines of what Drew had feared. She'd just thought any blowback would come from the public, not from the publisher Alex had been with for twelve years, not from the ashram where he'd been visiting for nearly two decades.

"God, they're callous," she heard herself say. "This makes no sense. People are ruthless. Just concerned with covering their own asses."

"I know." Drew continued nodding in a distracted fashion, eyes on his phone.

She stood up, feeling incensed. "What the fuck is wrong with the world? I mean, what the hell is going on?" Her volume kept rising. "Where is Alex, Drew? Where is he? What is this? Huh? Why do I feel like our lives are falling apart?" She threw the whiskey glass across the room where it hit the wall and shattered.

He dropped the phone and rose with his hands out, like she was a wild animal. "Hey, hey – it's okay. You've had one shock after another. It'll be okay."

"This just doesn't..." She didn't know where to take the thought. This was just *the end* of rationality? The beginning of overreaction to every misstep and indiscretion? Where was the forgiveness? The tolerance?

Or maybe that was too much. Alex was just one man; this was just one situation. And maybe it was for the best. Time to sell the house and move out of Scarsdale and find a place in the mountains somewhere. Raise goats and chickens and grow Swiss chard in the garden. Teach Kenneth how to hunt, let Freda run wild in the open air and chase butterflies, in a world where selfies and Twitter didn't exist.

But that was fantasy. Pure and simple. In today's world, you couldn't run, and you certainly couldn't hide. Drew was reaching for her, but she turned from him, trying to shed the sudden and cloying depression that had found her by cleaning up the broken glass.

"Here," Drew said, "Let me."

"I got it." She carefully placed the shards in her palm.

Drew backed off. She could sense his indecision. When she had collected all the glass and stood, she faced him. "I'm going to get the vacuum. Get all the rest of it."

"Okay."

"Drew..."

"Yeah?"

She didn't know if she should ask him to leave. What if he got offended? Or otherwise tried to persuade her he needed to stay? She couldn't bear any more drama for one night.

Alex, where are you?

47

The FBI had descended on Boston; Roth's work in Portland was done. She took her time on the snowy Vermont back-roads, then she was moving northwest on the interstate. The going was worse when a fresh snow squall came ripping in, whiting out the world.

She hit the brakes when the vehicles ahead suddenly slowed and stopped completely. Beyond them, a tractor-trailer had jack-knifed. Roth carefully pulled over and got out in the swirling snow to help. The tractor-trailer had wedged itself between the uprights of an overpass. Something was burning.

It was more than a phone call – they had Sheffield on screen. He'd been escorted from the jail to one of the interrogation rooms at the state police barracks in Ray Brook. Harlan Banger was there, the district attorney, Sheffield's attorney, and captain of the state police BCI, Wayne Newhouse, who had driven up from Albany. A real party. With Alex in Boston were Moritz and two more unnamed agents, both men. They still hadn't told him where, yet, but he assumed FBI headquarters.

It had been less than a week, but Sheffield looked different. There were circles under his eyes like he hadn't been sleeping. Though the jail offered shaving implements, he had grown the beginnings of a salt-and-pepper beard. When the two sheriff's deputies had sat him down and linked his chains to the table bolts, he'd seemed stiff.

"So," Alex said, watching the screen. "I'm here."

Sheffield looked dour. "How was your week?" The familiar accent: *How was yah week?*

"We can't play any more games. People are dead." His hands were shaking.

Breathe.

Sheffield flinched a little, as if stung by the remark. He shook his head woefully. "But I never meant for that to happen."

"You brought my family into this. You understand that? You brought all sorts of families into this. People who've been terrorized. I'm not going to start feeling sorry for you. You asked for me again – here I am. Spit it out. What's your plan, and who are you working with? Halloran? Creasy?"

"My part in this was done. *Your* thing went on…but no one was supposed to die."

Alex tightened his jaw as the pressure built in his head. He stared at the screen and into Sheffield's dirt-colored eyes, three hundred miles away. "Who are you *working with?*"

Sheffield looked away. "He called himself Socrates. Socrates03."

They already knew that. That wasn't helpful. Sheffield was dodging.

Alex decided to meet him head-on. Enough bullshit. "Halloran."

"I'm not saying that."

"Fine. Did you talk on the phone to Socrates03?"

His eyes came back. "A couple times."

"You must have known who he was, then. You didn't fire shots in a crowded room on some random troll's say-so."

Sheffield looked mutinous.

Moritz whispered, "He's shutting down. Change tack."

"Please talk to me, Gary. They think you have some kind of weapon. Did you smuggle something from BAX Global?"

"I don't have a weapon." Sheffield got a peculiar look, emotion coming into his digitized voice. "It's true, I thought about it. What they're saying. I thought about doing something. But who hasn't, right? I mean, look at this world. Look at what's happening to it. Look at what's happening to *you*. Your own people turning on you."

"You're not...you sat in your house listening to Paul Halloran on YouTube and reading his books, and you decided to go up there to one of my talks and start shooting..."

Sheffield was shaking his head. "I don't really know that guy. I only had his book in my house because Socrates03 told me to get it, to hide it there." Sheffield added, "He knows everything about you."

"Like what? What does he know about me?"

"Just...everything."

"You have my books in your house. Did Socrates tell you to put those there, too?"

"No. I read those on my own. You're one of the most popular atheist figures and I thought, *know thy enemy*. Even though I think there's hope for you. That someday you might see the light."

"Gary, it's time. Just tell me what's going on. Tell me what

Socrates wanted you to do. So they can hear it. So I can go home, so I can be with my family."

Sheffield closed his eyes. "*I am the good shepherd. I know my own and my own know me, just as the Father knows me and I know the Father, and I lay my life down for the sheep.*'"

"*Woe to those who go to great depths to hide their plans from the Lord, who do their work in darkness.*' Who do you know in Irvine, Gary? I want names, man. I want answers, right now."

Chet flashed in his mind. Scenarios involving Chet and John Creasy; Creasy looking into Stephen Mayhew. A blackmail scheme: *Steve, we know you're cheating on Mara. Take some of that investment banker money and wire it to us or we blow you open, and she gets half – or more – of everything you got.*

Stephen then reaching out to Halloran, coming up with a plan to hurt Alex? To cause a major crisis like this, killing people and spilling secrets?

It was too much. The truth was always simpler.

From Sheffield on screen: "Are you willing to lay down your life for the sheep?"

Alex didn't answer.

"A great flood," Sheffield said. He slowly arced his free hand through the air with the fingers splayed. Over the distance and digital connection, the movement was stuttered. "A great drought, a great fire. A purging of the land. That's what's needed for human well-being." The rest of his fingers curled in, leaving one to point. "You know it just like I do."

"Whatever you say."

Sheffield seemed unfazed. He'd gone somewhere else now, like some kind of entranced preacher. Alex said, "I don't care about your philosophy, Gary. I need specifics. I need your plan, names, dates. You have to tell me something or I'm done. You're going to rot in jail. For murder. And the FBI is looking at you now for domestic terrorism."

Sheffield dropped his head forward, then slowly lifted his eyes. "We're headed down the wrong path. And you know it. You have to take action in this world. You know what sacrifice is? When humans first started doing it, it was when they first understood about the future."

"Gary –"

"Lose something today for a better tomorrow." His voice was rising; he sounded unhinged. "We need to take a little pain with the medicine! Right? I understand that. That's how I was *raised*. Most people today are completely helpless and dependent on the system. Totally helpless. I was raised to be self-reliant. You've got to take the bitter with the better, my friend. You've got to sacrifice. I know this will all pay off for me in the end. I *know it*."

Alex felt a twinge, a nerve plucked somewhere deep in his gut. Maybe the suspicions were wrong – Sheffield wasn't just teeing up for an insanity defense; he was legitimately insane. "I don't think it's real," Alex said anyway. "I think you've got everyone dancing to your tune. You have from the beginning. But you're sick, Gary. You need help."

"It's not about *things*, not physical *things*, not bodies, not *people*. It's about *ideas*." Sheffield pointed at his temple with a shackled hand. "You take the head, the body will follow." He aimed the finger at Alex. "And you're the head."

Alex stood looking down at him. "The head of what?"

"Of your movement. Your liberal, godless, socialist movement."

"Why did Socrates tell you to put Halloran's book in your house? Is Halloran some kind of distraction? But how am I supposed to believe anything you say, Gary? All you've done is lie."

Alex sensed Moritz moving away, but stayed fixed on Sheffield.

Sheffield smiled a grim smile, his eyes dancing. "The guy

who found me, the guy who showed me this plan, Socrates, *he* is the one." The smiled faded. "I just wasn't supposed to get life in prison for murder. That security guard's death was an *accident*. The woman, too – Granger. None of them were supposed to die; it wasn't supposed to happen like this. So if you get the lawyers to back off the murder one charge, get them to agree to manslaughter, I'll tell you everything."

48

When she was finished cleaning up the broken glass, Drew moved toward her again. "Corrine, come here." His arms were open, but she didn't hug him.

"Drew, I'm sorry. I'm acting a little crazy. But this has all been very hard. I don't know what to...I just need to know where Alex is. And that he's okay."

Drew looked at her a moment, a kind of pity in his eyes, and then he turned his face away. "You know, this whole thing...I have to admit, it's been hard to witness."

"I know. I'm sorry."

"No, I mean – you deserve to be happy, Corrine." His eyes came back. More earnest and intense than she was used to. "And I know this is horrible of me to say, but you and the kids deserve someone who is here for you."

It took her aback. She had no response.

Drew gave another shake of his head and put his hand over his mouth. "I shouldn't talk like this. I'm sorry. Forgive me, okay?"

She took a step toward him, deciding. "It's okay, Drew. I appreciate you. I'm really so grateful for everything. You've been so helpful. But I think right now – this just isn't the time for this, okay? Let me just deal with this."

She was close to asking him to leave. It was having to go through it all in front of someone. Drew was a friend, but this was her family. Her husband.

It was also that Drew seemed to…well, maybe she was wrong, but he seemed to be taking advantage a little bit.

Her phone buzzed in her hand and she glanced at the screen. The unknown caller again. "This could be them, the FBI. I need to take this."

Drew reached, as if for the phone. "Why even bother at this point? You want more of this? It's just more pain for you. I know this is – God, this is so hard for me to say – I think you need to think about yourself now. What *you* want. Let me handle this. Okay?"

"It's okay." Something told her not to take the call in front of him. "I'll take it upstairs." She hurried away, thinking he was going to follow her, but a glance back and he was still downstairs in the living room, watching her with those sad eyes.

Upstairs, she closed herself in her room. The phone had stopped buzzing. She tried to return the call but got a busy signal. "Dammit."

She looked at the closed bedroom door. Drew had become close to the family, to her. She'd always liked him, but in truth, he was a little odd; a brainiac who worked as another man's assistant, even picked up his dry cleaning – and he'd been doing it for years, not as a quick internship, not as a stepping stone. Or, if it *was* a stepping stone, he'd been stepping on it for a long time. She realized she didn't even know how much Alex paid him. It had to be pretty good, though. Enough to keep him around when a guy as smart as Drew could be doing just about anything. He had his Master's, for God's sake. He could be teaching about the Indus Valley and Hinduism – his obsessions. From time to time, she even found herself encouraging him to do so.

Had her desire to help shape him, to show him kindness, been interpreted the wrong way?

A stair tread popped as he ascended to the second floor.

"Drew? You just need to give me a little space right now, okay?"

After a pause, his voice floated back. "Yeah. No, I understand that. I'm sorry. It's all good. Was that Alex? On the phone? I just want to know if he's okay."

"I didn't get it in time."

At least the fire was small, Roth thought. No one was hurt – the truck driver was out of the cab and had called 911. They were going to have a heck of a time getting through all the traffic piled up – the stopped cars probably went back a mile now on the interstate – but they were on their way.

She retreated to her vehicle and sat with the snow melting on her shoulders, wondering how long she was going to have to wait it out. There were ideas crackling through her mind. Things that just didn't want to let go.

This thing, this person behind Sheffield. It wasn't Halloran. Or Mayhew. She understood that now. They were a part of it but only incidentally. They were used by someone else as cover.

She kept going back to the idea that Socrates03 had wanted a video chat with Sheffield, early on. To demonstrate it wasn't entrapment, yes, but Roth thought that Socrates was proving a particular point: *I'm part of Baines's in-group. I'm close enough to know how to hurt him…*

Able to get two bars of a signal, she called Harlan. "I'm with the DA," Harlan whispered. "Sheffield is talking to Baines."

"I think there's a question we need to ask Chet Warman."

"What?"

"We need to ask him who he told about John Creasy's findings. When Creasy did background on Stephen Mayhew, when he found out about the affairs, and he found out about Mayhew donating to Halloran – ask Chet Warman who else knows about that besides himself and Creasy. Because whoever else knows could've used that."

"Used it how?"

"As smoke. As misdirection. Get everyone looking at Halloran and Mayhew and their connection. Thinking between the two of them they have it out for Baines and would put someone like Sheffield up to hurting him. Whoever knows that would have ready-made villains."

Harlan paused. "And who do you have in mind?"

"Who else do we know that's part of Baines's inner circle? Who's close enough to him to convince Sheffield he had the necessary access to make it all work?"

Harlan was silent for just a second. "God dammit," he said. "Okay." And he hung up.

Roth sat with the heat going, watching the snow build up. Distant yellow lights twirled as the first emergency vehicles approached through the storm.

And then, whether it was proper procedure or not, she sent someone a text.

Moritz turned the computer off and Sheffield's face disappeared. The gunman had just asked Alex to lobby for him to get reduced charges, but Moritz was holding a sheaf of papers.

"What's that?" Alex asked.

"First – do you think he has some plan for an attack?"

"I think it's a bluff. I think he's scared now and wants help not going to prison for life."

She set down the papers. "Okay. Well, before we give him that deal, I need you to take a look at this. This transcript compiles some of the online interactions between Sheffield and Socrates03. Sheffield said he saved it as a kind of insurance policy. I wanted you to talk to him first – we had to treat the terrorist possibility seriously…"

"I understand," Alex said with some haste. He leaned forward and read the top page.

Socrates03: I chose you. I saw you, and I understood what you're feeling because I feel it too.

GoodShepherd: My dad taught me about men like him. Since I was a kid.

Socrates03: You need to channel that. I've got something even better than what you're thinking.

GoodShepherd: What?

Socrates03: These people need to see their leader fall. They need to see him come apart at the seams. We destabilize him completely. Throw his life into chaos and watch him fall apart.

GoodShepherd: How do you know?

Socrates03: They'll turn on him. Blame him for this. The people who already understand how evil he is; the people who suppress their real feelings around him. And this is a little out of the way place in the middle of nowhere. A couple hundred people in the audience. No security. You'll buy a ticket, you'll get there early – there's no assigned seating – put yourself right in the middle of the room. You'll be five, ten meters away. You shoot wide. Then you run. But you let them catch you.

There was a gap in time – several minutes before GoodShepherd responded. Alex's skin crawled with amoeba shapes. He felt cold in the pit of his stomach. A picture was forming…

GoodShepherd: Catch me?

Socrates03: You'll demand a meeting. You'll say that you have information on other crimes. It doesn't matter what. Nothing. We'll be planting clues for him that there is someone else behind you. I know who he'll suspect and what it will do to him. He won't be able to let it go and it will ruin him.

Another gap in time, almost fifteen minutes. Alex's hand trembled as he turned the page. Moritz had stepped away to take a phone call.

Socrates03: You there?

GoodShepherd: I'm here. Thinking. How can I know it will work?

Socrates03: I'm close. You know I'm part of the inner circle. I've gotten to know him for three years now, and I want to stop him. If not us, then who? If not now, when? The world is at stake. Liberty is at stake. If we let this man continue the way he's going, what's left? Who is going to be left to fight?

Part of the inner circle.

Alex felt sick. Moritz was back beside him now. "I just spoke with Investigator Banger," Moritz said. "He talked to your PR person, Chet Warman, who had some interesting things to say, particularly about another man in your employ."

Alex stared at her and his mind blanked as pure survival instinct seized him. Corrine. Kenneth. Freda. He dug for his phone, then remembered that Moritz had taken it from him. "I need my phone. I have to call my wife."

"We've left messages."

"Well, try again!" Alex stood up. "What about local police? Have you called Scarsdale?"

"They're on their way to your house right now to do a check. It's just a matter of –"

An agent came in and whispered something to Moritz. Alex could sense things changing, people rearranging themselves in the room, a new life coming into place. At the same time, he felt fear – real fear for the first time. An invisible charge scrambled the molecules around his head, raising the hairs on the back of his neck. Moritz reached for him.

Alex pulled away, feeling wild, terrified, unhinged. "Why are we just standing here? I need my phone. I need to get home!"

Moritz came closer again, grabbed him by the arm. "Whatever else was arranged between Sheffield and any other party – we don't have that concretely yet. But we have everyone detained – Chet Warman, Paul Halloran. We still have to follow through with the bioterrorism threat. So until BAX completes their security review, you need to stay with us, too."

"Give me my phone!"

"I'll try your wife again right now."

But Alex knew: it was already too late.

49

Corrine's phone vibrated in her hand, once. A text from a number logged in her phone. Investigator Roth.

Stay away from Drew Horvath.

Too late. The bedroom door swung open.

The scream rose in her throat, but Drew was fast – he crossed the room in a second and tackled her onto the bed. With his hand over her mouth, his hand on her chest, he leaned to her ear and whispered, "Don't move. Don't scream. Please. I'll hurt the kids."

Her mind raced. She forced herself to relax beneath Drew's weight. If she played passive, she might get a chance to escape.

He stared into her eyes. "Are you going to be cool?"

She nodded, with his hand still pressed against her lips.

"We just need to talk, that's all. You're going to hear some things – I needed to talk to you first – that's it. All right? Okay?"

She nodded again, but he wasn't convinced and remained above her, crushing her lungs. She was going to run out of air.

A tear glimmered on his bottom eyelash, then fell. "I'm going to let go now. I'm going to get off you. I'm sorry, I'm sorry for this – but if you yell or anything I'm going to…you know? Do you understand?"

Another nod. Her vision was spotting. The air above his head seemed to come alive again, to blur in the shape of a tunnel, sucking toward the ceiling.

Death. It was always about death.

Your own end.

He lifted his hand and then shifted his weight. The pressure gone, Corrine gasped for breath. She rolled over, buried her face into the comforter and coughed until it subsided.

She realized he was rubbing her back. "Shhh," Drew whispered. "It's okay. It's okay."

She didn't want to turn over again. Didn't want to look at him. The kids were in their rooms on the other end of the upstairs hallway, stairs in between. Corrine mapped a possible route of escape – if she went for them, then by the time she sought to descend the stairs, Drew would be blocking her way.

"Mrs. Baines," he said. "You've been through a lot. *We've* been through a lot. All of us – you, the kids – me."

She tried to say yes, but the word caught in her throat.

"They're going to say things," Drew told her. "About me."

He fell silent, and she realized he was awaiting her response. Muffled, she asked, "Like what?"

"They won't understand. But that doesn't matter to me. It only matters to me that *you* understand. Does that make sense?"

She nodded her head. Her hands were up, over her face, like a child's idea of hiding.

He took her by the arm and pulled a hand away. "Can you look at me, please?"

No. If she looked at him, he would see the truth. Whatever this was, Drew was hoping for an impossible outcome. Some fantasy he'd cooked up in his mind, about her, about them. He was calling her Mrs. Baines again. Only now, it was less than charming.

"Come on. I'm not going to hurt you. Here – sit up – let me help you up."

She was slack in his grip, unable to do anything else but go limp as he worked to roll her over, pull her up by her shoulders into a seated position. The way she was on the bed, her legs stuck out like a child's. She looked at the wall, at the floor.

"Don't be scared. Please, stop that. Mrs. Baines – it's me. It's just me."

Something in his voice, maybe, softened her, just a little, just enough that she dared make eye contact. Drew's face was contorted with sadness, remorse, longing. "I know how hard it's been for you," he whispered.

She searched for signs of humanity in his face, hunted for deceit.

He said, "It's been hard for me, too. All these years, being in love with you – no, wait – being in love with you, Mrs. Baines. Corrine. In a way that – let me finish, please – in a way that I knew could never be reciprocated. Okay? I put it away. I put my job first. I figured if I stuck around, maybe longer than planned, and stayed with you and the kids that…but there was too much in the way. And it's killed me. Not just how I feel, that's just the selfish part, but what you've gone through. Because I see you." He took her hand in his. She almost recoiled, yanked her hand away, but forced herself to remain still, to keep looking at him. "I see you," he repeated, emphasizing the whisper. "I know who you really are, I watch how this – all of this – what it does to you. What it's been doing." He let go of her hand. More tears fell. "I know what I've done. I know it got out of hand. It was never meant to be like this."

After a pause in which she listened for the kids, she asked, "What did you do?"

He sniffed, wiped his eyes with his fingers, and pressed his lips together. A quick nod. "I've known things about Alex for a long time. I've seen things that...things I wouldn't even want you to know, because it would hurt you. I've protected you from your own husband. But I couldn't anymore. I can't. No – I didn't want to. I said, 'enough.' I said, 'she deserves better.'"

"What did you do?" It was a coarse whisper. "You thought if you...if you set this all up, I'd leave him? For you?"

Drew cut her a sharp look. It was just a flash, a moment buried by the next, but she'd seen something in his eyes that scared her in deep places. His face seemed to crumble after that; he became repentant again, nodding, as his chest jumped with a sob. "I didn't think that...it was never supposed to be..." He gave a quick shake of his head. "No matter what I say, it's going to seem like some kind of excuse. But I never meant for Alex to be hurt. You have to understand that. You really have to. I know it seems...dammit, no matter what I say it's not going to work. It's not going to work." He stood up from the bed, agitated. "This got all messed up."

"How? What happened?"

"This guy, he –"

"Sheffield?"

"Yes. *Him.* It all got fucked up. He just..." Drew took a few steps back. "I know what this is – you asking questions. You're waiting for the right time. You're going to tell me what I want to hear. You're going to say – 'no, no it didn't get messed up, honey. Let's leave together.' But look at this – look at where we are. This is your choice. *Your* choice. Where is Alex? Where is he right now? He's not here. He's never here."

"I understand."

"*I'm* here, though – I show up. He lies to you. He leaves you. He's...it's death by a thousand cuts. Little by little, you've turned your life into his life."

She nodded.

"You even told me so," Drew pointed toward the door, indicating their earlier talk downstairs. "You told me how you felt. Everyone serves him. Look at Chet – Chet would lay down and die for him. No, he really would. You're...I can see it. I can see it in your eyes. You think I'm dangerous. You think I'm crazy. This wasn't how it was supposed to go."

He took another step back, then forward again, like he didn't know what to do. His body swayed slightly on his feet. "Alex would be running around, just like he has been, and I'd be there for you and the kids. And when the time was right, I was going to tell you. Not like this. Not like this, Corrine. And I'm sorry that I..." He reached out but stopped himself, lowered his arms. "I'm so sorry if I hurt you. I didn't know what to do. I just needed this chance to explain."

"I understand," she said again.

He studied her carefully. Did she really understand? Was she just placating him?

In truth, she did. Inasmuch as she knew what it was like to be desperate for a moment with someone, free from distraction, to really and genuinely communicate. It was something that was often missing in a loud, fast world. Real connection. Something that had been missing in her own life, in her marriage and busy family, for a long time.

Carefully, so as not to alarm him, she worked herself to the edge of the bed so she could sit properly, bent at the knees. He watched her, exuding tension, but stayed where he was, halfway to the door. Outside, a car went past on the street, engine noise fading.

If she screamed, would anyone hear her?

If she ran, how far could she get?

If she attacked him, what were her chances?

"I'm not going to tell you I feel the same way," she said, looking up at him. "That would be a lie."

He absorbed this truth, working his lips against his teeth, nodding almost imperceptibly.

"But that's because I'm married. It's not because I don't care about you." *Watch it now; don't take it past a point of no return.* Rather than risk saying the wrong thing, she waited.

"You know me," he said softly. "And I know *you.* I know you're not perfect. I don't hold you on a pedestal. What I see is the good and the bad. Well, you don't really have much that's bad." He smiled grimly. "Except maybe what you do to yourself."

There were footsteps in the hall. One of the kids. Drew's jaw tightened and Corrine sucked in a breath. The bathroom door closed.

Drew relaxed, but the spell was broken; his vulnerability was gone, replaced by something harder. "This is your chance to choose, right now. I've got to face what I did. What it turned into. I've got to answer for that – I understand that. I accept it."

When he didn't specify her options, she assumed he meant between him and Alex.

The toilet flushed, the faucet turned on.

Drew had – what? Hired Sheffield to shoot at Alex? Or somehow or other convinced him it was morally right to do? All so Drew could get her alone, tell her he loved her, and see if she would willingly enfold herself – her life, her children's lives – into his? "We don't always understand what we're doing," she said. "Or where it's going to lead."

He trapped her with a look that said, *be careful.* "You say that, but I don't think you mean it. You think what I did was crazy. That I have a problem."

"Well, if that's true, then I'm crazy too." She took her hair down and raked her fingers through, shaped it into a ponytail, and snapped the hair tie back into place. "So now what?"

But Drew didn't respond. He had his head cocked, listening. She heard it, too. Another car engine. This time idling in proximity. Someone was here.

Her skin went cold. Drew jumped on her again, pinning her down, this time with his hands clamped around her throat. "Don't move. I think that's them."

She kicked with her legs, brought her knees up against his lower back.

"I think that's…fuck. We can't. We're just not going to be able to do this." His grip stayed tight. His face was expressionless, his eyes empty. A spray of spit fell from the corner of his mouth as he grunted with the effort of strangling her. "I'm sorry."

Bits of light collected on the edges of her vision. The world went black, then turned on again. No air coming in. No way to get out from under him. She was dying. The ceiling dissolved, and in its place, the sky revealed was dark and swirling. It began to pull at her body, to draw her up and in.

Death. Always about death.

Time seemed to stretch, elongating the seconds as her body used up the last of its available oxygen. Turning them into years, millennia. The sky swirled above her, the End of Days, the rapture, pulling her up and in.

And she saw her father. Maybe it wasn't about death, but him. She felt him all around her. Felt the cascade of him – of his whole lineage – showering down on her. Everyone in his family, traced back to time immemorial. To the single-celled prokaryotes in the endless ocean. To the raw universe springing from nothingness – from the collapse of the universe before it. All swirling together, each gyre of nebulae giving birth to a new time and space in an endless series of rebirth.

I love you, Dad.

She said a prayer for her children. That Drew would spare them.

Take me, just leave them alone.

My babies.

Breathe...

But there was no more breathing.

And then it stopped, and the ceiling enveloped the sky, the light rushing back.

She lay on the bed, his hands gone from her throat, Drew flopped down beside her, unmoving.

Kenneth stood next to the bed. The small, heavy elephant statue in his hands was covered in blood.

50

S itting on his red bicycle as a boy, watching the bus take people to the ferry dock. Even at a young age, the area north of Portland – Freeport, Yarmouth, Cousins, and especially the island of Chebeague – was a study in contrasts. Gary Sheffield grew up listening to the locals talk about the non-locals buying and building their big houses on the island and driving up the property taxes. People coming from Massachusetts and Connecticut and New Jersey to have their summer homes. While the locals endured brutal winters and survived minimum wage, the outsiders came in and either ignored them or considered them "the help." His mother knew, because his mother worked the ferry. "These people have no respect," she would say. "This is their playground. They use us and step on us and they don't blink an eye."

It was those types of people who were impressed with the bullshit of Alex Baines. Those people who thought they knew best for everyone else – they knew about the environment; they knew about what jobs people ought to have, how people ought to live their lives. They'd taken God out of the country and put themselves in charge. They didn't believe in God, they believed in the "multiverse." They sneered at the Bible and yet couldn't prove the Big Bang. Arrogance was the new state religion, and they were the priests and bishops of the technocracy.

It was Drew Horvath, Socrates03, who explained what a technocracy was. A society ruled by theorems and numbers and, eventually, machines. Machines that would replace the human at every turn. Machines that would eventually overtake the very stupid humans who developed them and installed them. Humans who called for government regulations at every other turn but developed artificial intelligence apace without oversight, rolling their eyes at the public concern.

A godless world run by the rich and their machines – that was the future. And people like Alex Baines were paving the way for it. People drank his Kool-Aid like a numbing drug. Yes, please, take my freedoms away. Yes, please, let an amoral scientific community with its clones and its vaccines and its mind-altering drugs take away the very things that make me human. Yes, please, here is my ticket, let me buy your book, listen to your debates, fall hypnotically in love with the sound of my own erasure from existence.

People don't know what's good for them, Horvath had said to Sheffield.

Sheffield knew Horvath had used him, but that was okay. Self-interest was meant to align with the greater good. Horvath had exposed Baines – and everything he represented – for what it was – children trying to take over and run the shop.

"Because there's a reason why God is enshrined in the Constitution, isn't there?" Horvath said. "There's a reason it is God who endows man with life, liberty, and the right to pursue happiness. If we say that man has bestowed these rights, then they are not inalienable – man can just take them away, any time he wants. And that's what we see destroying every great society since the beginning of time. You're a soldier of God, Gary Sheffield.

You're – as your name suggests – you're a good shepherd. And now I need you to help show your flock the truth about this wolf that's found his way in."

And Sheffield had agreed. And Sheffield had said he was willing, ready, and able.

But Horvath had lied. He didn't really believe any of that. It wasn't easy to get information in county lock-up, but one of the guards, Travis or Trevor – one of those – told Sheffield that Horvath was really just another fucked-up liberal, a tender snowflake, jealous of his boss's life, his boss's wife.

Sheffield had been screwed over by a whiny bitch millennial who didn't want to work for it – wanted to take it from someone else instead. The crowning part was Sheffield had been just about to give Horvath up, to cut a deal with the authorities, in his second interview with Baines – and then they'd figured it out on their end. Then Baines was just gone, and the prospect of a deal with it. *Thanks for playing, Gary. Enjoy your prison time.*

But he hadn't known then how it would play out. He'd thought Socrates was like him – convinced that something needed to be done to save society, to save a country. They'd gone over it, and over it again. Mostly through the private server. Twice by burner phone. They'd nailed down when Sheffield would shoot. How he would get out, where he would go, how long, roughly, it would take the police to find him. How long he would wait before telling his public defender he wanted to speak with Alex; how he would manage to convince the lawyer to convince the DA.

The plan had been to cause a panic, but not to kill. Itchy as his trigger finger was, it made sense to Sheffield – martyrdom was overrated. He didn't want to die, and he didn't want to spend his life in prison. Seven to ten, out for good behavior in five? He could handle that. Hit the gym, play some cards, get three hots and a cot.

But then that fat fucker Chet Warman had hired those rent-a-cop security guards.

And that one, Nyswaner, had to play fucking cowboy. Sheffield was a practiced shot; he could hit the bullseye ten times in a row from twenty yards, but moving targets proved more challenging. And paper targets didn't shoot back.

It had been his idea to send that first shot cutting through the air inches from Baines's head. *Maybe this will get your attention, asshole.* And it had been his idea to whiz one past the skinny chick standing off to one side. But then Baines played hero and ran in front of her, taking it in the leg. And finally, it had been his idea, too, to drop a few extra clues for the cops. Something so they'd lose their shit. Everything happened for a reason, after all – working for BAX had been boring and uneventful, but he'd heard things about AbbVie; he knew about Botox, and there were these perfect connections to Irvine, California, to get everyone wetting their pants.

Just a couple of words scribbled in a paperback book, and holy shit did the cops come out of the woodwork. Good. Maybe it would inspire others. People with the means to do what had to be done. To buy us all a little time before we destroyed ourselves completely.

In the end, he didn't think in terms of radicalism. He'd grown up with a father who, when he was home, railed against the evils of the government and society, leaving Sheffield never quite sure whom his father blamed more – the people in office or the people on the street. Only that he would cite a loss of moral character.

"We've lost our way, Gary," he would say, bottle of Miller High Life to his lips, staring off with reddened eyes. He liked to wear that ratty flannel like it was a statement – life was black or white, like the checkered pattern of the shirt. And he liked to grab little Gary by the back of the neck and squeeze.

51

First, they knocked. When they heard the screaming, the Scarsdale police pulled their weapons and kicked in the door. Sergeant Dukette entered the house ahead of his patrolman. The shouting came from the second floor. Dukette glanced at Richardson, who moved off to secure the main floor. Dukette called out as he climbed the stairs. "Mrs. Baines?"

"Up here – yes – we're up here!"

"Is Drew Horvath here with you?"

"Yes. He's....He might be dead."

"Is he armed?"

"No."

"Is anyone armed?"

"No."

Dukette cleared the landing and checked the hallway before moving to the left, the direction of their voices. Corrine Baines was sitting in a bed with her two children in her arms. The boy had blood on his hand, some drops on his face. All three were white as sheets.

"Where's Mr. Horvath?"

"My bedroom," Corrine said softly. She pointed. "Other end of the hallway."

The door was ajar. The first thing Dukette saw were the man's feet – trendy leather boots. Dukette pushed open the door with his gun out. Horvath was on the ground, unmoving. Blood soaked the bed, stained the carpet. Blood on Horvath's shoulders.

Keeping the gun ready, Dukette knelt beside the man and felt for a pulse. Weak, but there.

Dukette's gaze fell on a thick little statue of some kind. Blood on it, too.

Richardson's voice carried up from below. "All clear down here, Sarge!"

The sergeant rose to his feet with some effort. He stepped to the doorway. "Call for the bus," he shouted down to Richardson. "Tell them we've got a male, thirties, blunt force trauma to the head. Vital signs are weak."

"Copy that."

Dukette heard Richardson use his radio to notify emergency services. He stood looking at Horvath. Either the mother had clocked him good, or maybe the son had, the way he looked. The sergeant holstered his weapon, put his hands on his hips. Now, how to handle this…

He went back to the other bedroom, the girl's room, he assumed, and invited them to leave the bed.

The Baines woman didn't move. "Do you know where my husband is?"

"Boston, is my understanding. The FBI took him to their headquarters there."

"Why?"

"Something to do with a threat."

"From the man – from Sheffield?"

Dukette shook his head. "I don't know, Mrs. Baines." He

could hardly take his eyes off the boy. "Son? Kenneth? Can we talk about what happened?"

Kenneth Baines looked back with a sharp, present gaze. "Drew was hurting mom."

At last Corrine got up from the bed. The little girl clung to her. Corrine looked at Dukette. "Maybe you can talk to him, let me tend to her."

"Of course, yeah."

The Baines woman left, talking softly to the girl. He heard them go downstairs. He asked Kenneth to explain about things, and the boy, very matter-of-fact, described hearing a confrontation, listening outside his mother's bedroom, making a decision.

Dukette said, "I'm going to need you to give a statement to my officer downstairs. Okay?"

The boy nodded. Then he got up from the bed. He looked at the blood on his hands. "Is he dead?"

"No. He's not dead."

"Okay," the boy said. "Good."

52

FRIDAY, DECEMBER 11

Alex's second return home was not the same. The hugs were different, at once more emotional and more tentative. The house was a crime scene, master bedroom taped off. A dark patch stained the carpet.

He was taken to the Scarsdale police station where he filled out a report. The police wanted to know everything about Drew Horvath. How long he'd been with Alex; if Alex had ever seen any signs he was mentally ill; if they'd had any recent arguments. They wanted motive.

I take responsibility. It wasn't an answer. He'd never mistreated Drew. He paid him generously, treated him with respect. If there had been any malice in Drew, he'd been a master of hiding it. Or Alex had ignored the signs. If there'd been something small – a glance, a phrase, a vibe – he'd been too busy to appreciate it.

Drew wanted Corrine. He wanted what Alex had. But there was more. Had to be more. Jealousy could curdle the blood, but hate made monsters of men.

Alex pushed the completed report across Dukette's desk. He lowered his head and he cried.

The police brought him home. When Chet called, Alex was standing in the driveway, in the cold, watching Dukette drive off.

"Hey buddy," Chet said. "How you doing?"

"They let you out, huh?"

"Yeah. God, they got into it with me. They let Halloran go, too. Couldn't connect him to anything, I guess. And from what I hear, which isn't much, nothing concisely tying Drew to the big bioterrorism scare. I think Sheffield just had some of his own ideas, nothing he carried forward, just these sort of dark longings, and when the FBI poked in, they saw some possible connections, and that's what happened."

Alex flexed his hand, fingers getting numb in the cold. But he wasn't ready to go back inside. Not just yet.

"God," Chet said. "I mean…"

"I know."

"I mean, what the fuck? Drew?"

There was nothing more to say, each man contemplating it. Fathoming it. You took one step, Alex supposed, then another. Drew, dreaming up a way to use what he knew against Alex. Exposing the Irvine study. But that wouldn't be enough. People might forgive that, forget about it at the conclusion of one twelve-hour news cycle.

Drew wanted Alex to self-destruct. To go after Halloran full force, to become fully engulfed in a battle against religion, to obsess.

The way Drew himself had obsessed, coveting Alex's wife. His life. Secretly hating him for what he had.

"It's my fault," Chet said. "I talked to Drew. I told him what Creasy found on Mayhew and Halloran being connected. I never thought Drew would see it as some sort of opportunity. I'm sorry, Alex."

"I know."

After a moment, Chet said, "Drew told me this story once –

you know how Drew gets; like, two beers and he's a different person – he started rambling about how when he was just a kid, like seventeen, he was involved with this older woman. How she broke his heart and all of this stuff."

"I'm not sure I care."

"Yeah. I get that. Last thing – I talked to Creasy. I finally tracked him down and talked to him. I wanted you to know. He said he called because he was worried. I mean he's a fucking nutjob, really. But he was calling for the right reasons."

"Chet, I gotta go. Freezing my ass off out here."

"Hey. Okay. Is, ah…how's Corrine? How are the kids?"

"I don't know. Not good. But I'm going to spend the rest of my life making it up to them."

Chet was soft. "I know, buddy. Listen – take care. I'm here if you need me."

With the kids in the living room, Alex sat at the dining table across from Corrine, trying to thaw his hands around a warm cup of coffee. It was growing dark outside. Neither of them had slept the night before. It seemed neither wanted to, as if afraid to break the continuity; what surprises might be in store if they did. But they hadn't wanted to leave the house, either. Now, it was in the air.

"I think maybe I'll take them to Mara's for the weekend," Corrine said.

He nodded, choking back the emotion.

"Stephen will be there," she said.

Alex looked into her eyes. He couldn't take anything for granted. But was she mentioning Stephen because he was invited?

Not knowing what else, he said, "I, ah…I think that's a good idea."

"For you to come, too?"

"Is that what you're asking?"

"Why wouldn't I? We're a family."

It was like a release in his chest, the air rushing in, filling him back up with life. He stretched closer and took her hand. "Thank you."

Corrine was strong, just a quiver in her lower lip. She looked into the living room where the kids sat on the floor together, playing a card game. As if he heard, or sensed something, Kenneth glanced over. Then he turned away.

"Can we?" Corrine's voice was a whisper. "Go up there? Leave here?"

"Dukette says there's nothing to worry about. He's endorsing Kenneth's statement about what happened. It's all self-defense. He'd like us to stay close, but Mara isn't far."

"Will we have to go to court? To see him?"

Alex pictured Drew in the hospital, still unconscious. The doctors were confident he'd pull through, Dukette had said. Not that he had anything to look forward to but prison.

"You're not going to have to do anything you don't want to," Alex told her. "Nothing."

"I don't want Kenneth to have to spend one minute in a court-room." She pulled her coffee to her lips and looked out the window. "But I'll go. If it comes to that, I'll go." The bruises on her neck were showing, breaking his heart.

"It's not our fault," Alex said after a minute. "Drew played us. He wanted to split us up, Cory. He wanted us off-balance, jumping at everything. Questioning everything, everyone. Coming apart."

She nodded but avoided his eyes.

"I love you," he said. "And I'm so sorry."

Neither of them spoke for a while. Corrine's failure to respond weighed heavy, but he was okay with it. Had to be. Had to earn it back, all of it.

In the other room, Freda giggled. "Not like that," Kenneth said. "You've got to hold the cards like this."

"What are they doing?"

Corrine shook her head. "I don't know. He's teaching her pinochle or something."

Alex thought about it. His son saving Corrine. What that might mean for the rest of his life. A mark he would forever bear – *The Boy Who Saved His Mother.*

We wore brands. There was no escaping it.

Alex made a jerking inhalation, the beginning of more tears, but he contained them. "Is he going to be okay?"

"I think so." Her eyes were on Kenneth. "Time will tell. He's talking about it, anyway. He slept through the night last night, even if we didn't. Said to me, this morning, that he didn't even dream."

Alex rose from the table, Corrine watching. He ignored the crutches and limped into the living room. Masking the pain, he got down on the floor with the kids.

"Daddy," Freda said. "This is how you hold the cards."

"Yeah?"

"Yeah, like this." She had a hand fanned out, and then her small hands lost their grip and the cards scattered. She laughed about it and started picking them up.

Alex kissed the top of her head and looked at his son. "Deal me in?"

Kenneth's eyes were quick, a darting glance, a smile pulling his mouth. "Sure."

After a minute, Corrine entered the room and joined them.

About a month later, after visiting the doctor and getting scanned, Corrine received her results.

She'd had errands to run, and so stopped by the doctor's office in person to pick them up. Emerging into the afternoon sunlight, she only took a few steps away from the front door before tearing open the envelope. Her fingers shook a little, and her eyes scanned rapidly.

There was a printout of all the official data in old-school dot matrix print, and even a cloudy representation of the MRI itself. But everything she needed to know was in a simple typewritten paragraph, written in lay terms for the patient.

She blinked a little. The sunshine, which had seemed too bright a moment ago, now felt appropriately, pleasantly bright.

No tumor. Nothing abnormal. She was in good health. The doctor was unable to find any physical correlate to explain her dream, her vision.

Which was just as well, she figured, as she headed toward her car and the rest of her day. It did nothing to diminish the experience.

THE END

TJB
    October 24, 2022
    Elizabethtown, NY

THANK YOU FOR READING THE DARK IS ALWAYS WAITING!

We hope you enjoyed it as much as we enjoyed bringing it to you. We just wanted to take a moment to encourage you to review the book. Follow this link: **The Dark Is Always Waiting** to be directed to the book's Amazon product page to leave your review.

Every review helps further the author's reach and, ultimately, helps them continue writing fantastic books for us all to enjoy.

You can also join our non-spam mailing list by visiting www.subscribepage.com/AethonReadersGroup and never miss out on future releases. You'll also receive three full books completely Free as our thanks to you.

Facebook | Instagram | Twitter | Website

Looking for more great Thrillers?

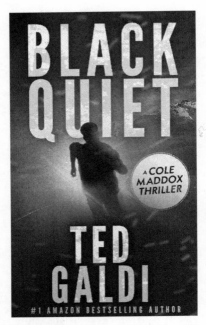

They thought they could run the town... Until they attacked the brother of an ex-Special Forces commando. Cole Maddox just moved back to his hometown in Montana after leaving the Army's most elite unit because his superiors lied to him. But his town has changed. A ruthless gang of bikers has flooded it with fentanyl, and when Cole's brother defies them, they put him in a coma. Big mistake. Cole unleashes his arsenal of Special Forces skills to take them down. However, he soon learns the gang is only the bottom layer of a criminal network much larger and deadlier than he imagined. **Can Cole get justice for his brother while keeping himself and those closest to him alive? Find out in this fast-paced, adrenaline-surging thrill ride from Ted Galdi.** *This gripping action packed thriller is perfect for fans of Lee Child, Jason Kasper, and David Archer.*

Get Black Quiet Now!

Sentenced to life in prison for a crime he didn't commit... Can he be exonerated? After ten years inside a jail cell, Andy Gibbons has abandoned all hope. Resigned himself to the fact that he will spend the rest of his life behind bars. But while Andy may have thrown in the towel, that doesn't mean his wife, Jamie, did. Disillusioned and worn out by the justice system, the Honorable Judge Regan St. Clair is just about to pack in too when a letter from Jamie Gibbons arrives on her desk. A letter that changes everything...

Digging deeper, she and a former Special Forces operator named Jake Westley stumble into a frightening underworld of deceit and menace. A world where nothing is as it seems, and no one can be trusted. All the answer these simple question: *Is Andy Gibbons really innocent? Is the price of his freedom worth paying?* **Don't miss this** crime suspense-thriller about a corrupt organization with a sinister agenda that exploits every weakness and every dark corner of the fallible justice system.

Get Unguilty Now!

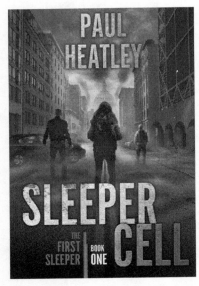

A deadly explosion rocks the nation's capital...
Three seemingly unconnected people – a British ex-
Special Forces operative, an ex-Navy Seal, and a
teenage girl – find themselves under suspicion for the
attack. Soon, they're in the middle of a conspiracy
that threatens to unsettle the entire United States. If
they have any hope to survive the dangerous situation
they've found themselves in, these strangers must
learn to rely on each other, all while the question
remains: Did one of *them* cause the explosion?
**Nefarious organizations arrange themselves
behind the political scenes. The players prepare
their moves. An entire Country hangs in the
balance. Can anyone stop them? Find out in this
adrenaline-pumping action-thriller from bestseller
Paul Heatley.**

Get Sleeper Cell Now!

For all our Thrillers, visit our website.

Made in the USA
Middletown, DE
13 February 2025